Eagle River

Isabelle Kane

Published by
Satin Romance
An Imprint of Melange Books, LLC
White Bear Lake, MN 55110
www.satinromance.com

978-1-68046-267-8

Published in the United States of America.

Cover Art by Caroline Andrus

To Andy, without whom Eagle River would not exist.

Acknowledgements

I feel very blessed to have friends who have supported me and helped me in my writing. Nancy Schumacher and Caroline Andrus, thank you for all of your kindness and your willingness to work with me to bring my stories to life. A special thanks to Jessica S., my proof reader par excellance, and to my writing friends. I know that my books would not exist without the talent, guidance and advice of many people.

Prologue

Sandra Odgers O'Halloran dragged the end table to the other side of the bed and studied the effect. She stood with her finger to her lip and debated. It wasn't right. She pushed the end table back into its previous location. As she pulled her hand away, her finger caught on a rough edge at the base of the table and a splinter plunged into the palm of her hand. Sandra examined her palm and, through pinching and squeezing, worked the long splinter to the surface. She squeezed the narrow wound between her thumb and forefinger. After a moment, she knelt down and, with her good hand felt along the base of the table. Her fingers encountered an edge. To get a better look, she tilted the end table up on its side. There was a thin piece of wood tacked to its base. Sandra went into the kitchen and grabbed the pliers from the tool chest beneath the sink. She popped the tacks out and the piece of wood dropped off, and with it, a narrow manila envelope.

She turned the envelope over in her hands. Nothing was written on it. To the best of her knowledge, no one had moved the end table since her mother's death six years before. Sandra had no way of knowing exactly how long the envelope had been tacked to the base of the end table. It was mysterious and exciting and Sandra savored the anticipation. Then, slowly, she bent the metal clips vertically and slid the contents of the envelope into her lap.

The first item was a high school picture of Jessica Odgers. *Mom's stuff. What was it doing here? Why had she hidden it?* A young Jessica was smiling what she must have believed was a mature, seductive, come hither half smile. Her mass of red blond hair hung long and loose about her shoulders, except for the tiny curls framing her face that Sandra knew sprung up whenever it was warm or humid. Next was a picture of Galen, Sandra's brother, posing with his prize winning 4H hog. In it, Galen was a tow headed, front toothless ten-year-old proudly holding up his prized blue ribbon. Sandra casually picked out a folded square of tissue paper and a spring of dried lilac spilled out onto the floor, perhaps a piece of a corsage from some long forgotten dance. She tried to scoop it back into the tissue envelope, but the flower had mostly disintegrated in the fall.

Next, there was a thin Kodak packet of pictures. Sandra slid the photos out then sank back on her thighs in disbelief. The first one was of her mother, young and completely naked. Jessica Odgers was on her knees crawling towards the camera wielder in a predatory manner. There was no question that it was Sandra's mother, her long lines, the half circle of her jutting hip bone, the full white breasts topped with large pink-brown nipples, Jessica's daughter took it all in.

The next picture was of a still naked Jessica lying on her back on a quilt with her arms tucked under her head, and the backdrop was cracked and faded red boards. The one after that showed Jessica turned sideways and coyly peering over her shoulder. Her rounded buttocks were in full view and by her legs were two stacked bales of hay. *The old barn. These pictures were taken in the old barn.* In the third picture, Jessica's head was tossed back and she was laughing. The final picture in the packet was of a naked man, from the neck down. The body was long, with heavily muscled quadriceps and only a slight thickening at the waist. It was clearly the body of an athlete. The shoulders were broad and powerful and the chest was dark with thick, springy hair that trailed down to a large, but relaxed penis.

It was most definitely not the body of Sandra's father.

Sandra sat, the pictures in her lap, a hollow, nauseous feeling forming in her stomach. After a moment, she rose, the pictures in her hand. She went back into the kitchen, and grabbed some matches out of the jar that stood on top of the fridge. Then, she headed back into the den. There, she knelt down, lit the match, and held it to the packet containing the nude shots. She held onto it until the flame grew unsafe. Then, she tossed the flaming envelope, pictures and all, into the fireplace. For a moment, she watched the flames consume it, then wiped her hands on her faded, dirty Wranglers, and went back to the task of rearranging furniture.

Chapter One

The Fair 1985

~ Ben ~

It was the kind of night when you held hands with your girl, rather than tossing an arm over her shoulders, because you were uncomfortably aware of the big sweat patches that extended all the way down to your belt. The evening breeze was heavy and sluggish with humidity, newly spun cotton candy, and buttered popcorn. Now and then, the heavy air would pick up a hot breath of animal smells emanating from the stock pens. And everything was sticky, especially the bodies of small, sun burned, black fingernailed children. The animals tied up in the fluorescently lit "Cow Palace," were drooping and soggy despite the flashing lights and the cacophony of sound that rudely interrupted the surrounding opaque silence of a fallow field in the Midwestern night.

Years later, Ben could still hear it, the manically cheerful music of the Ferris wheel, the melodic wailing of some local country band from the beer tent, the dull hum of voices speaking, the lowing and bleating of the discontented animals, and, occasionally, a mother's shrill cry for a child that had wandered off. He could still smell it and taste it, and it was right there when he closed his eyes. And then it would flood him and he would ache with the tight sunbaked skin feeling of childhood summers.

There was one such Saturday night that stood out as brilliantly lit among Ben's memories as the Vegas strip in the quiet, indigo emptiness of the desert night. He remembered being ticked because his mother had saddled him with Timmy Johansson for the evening, and that meant that Ben had to leave the fair by eleven to get the kid home on time. Timmy wasn't a bad kid. It's just that he tried way too hard. His mom knew the kid had problems. She was the one who made Timmy go out for football, the year that Eagle River made it to the State Championships. Galen's year.

That night, it turned out to be a good thing that Timmy came along. At least he was someone for Ben to talk to, someone easily impressed. Galen was in one of his moods. So, there they were, doing the fair thing: Ben, Galen the mute, and Timmy, shirt buttoned all the way up his neck, don't-look-over-at-the-beer-tent Johansson.

It must have been around ten o'clock and all three boys were about faired out. They had taken to wandering around the stock barns with no real purpose, blowing time, when they heard cheering and applause from over near the game booths. There was a pause and then the same again. A good sized crowd had formed around one of the booths. They walked over to check out what was going on. Ben couldn't see anything at first, but the three worked their way through the crowd. Ben was tall and so it wasn't long before he had a decent view.

The crowd had formed a semi-circle around one of those games where one throws a football through a ring. The size of the prize you win is determined by how many times consecutively a person can throw it through the ring. The area in front of the booth was all clear, except for one figure which was alternately illuminated and then shadowed by the rapidly changing Ferris wheel lights. The man stood a good thirty feet from his target. At first, Ben couldn't make out who it was. The guy was tall and strong. His shoulders were turned sideways. He stepped, reached back, and threw. The football sailed through the hole. The crowd went nuts. Their hero stood still, basking in their praise while some kid ran the ball back to him. Just then, a light from the Ferris wheel flashed across the man's face, illuminating him. But Ben already knew who it was; he had kept stats at too many football games throughout high school not to recognize that particular throwing style.

Timmy, who had followed Ben through the crowd, tugged at his arm.

"Hey, isn't that Cam Fawst?"

Ben spun, searching for Galen, but he had already lost him somewhere in the crowd.

"You know him, right?" Insisted Timmy. He pushed at Ben's shoulder. "Hey, Ben, what's up?"

"Yeah, that's Cam." *Where was Galen?*

"Could you introduce me to him? He's the Coyotes' quarterback! I watched him on TV. I can't believe that he's actually here!"

Ben watched again as Cam turned, stepped, and hurled the football. It spiraled tightly, powerfully through the hole in the board. The crowd cheered wildly again. Once more, the kid jogged the ball back to Cam.

"That's twelve, Cam," someone shouted.

"Don't miss this one, Cam."

The tall figure turned into the half-light cast by the carousel. "It's in the bag," that familiar deep, confident, sardonic voice announced over the manically cheerful tune shrieking out from the carousel.

"No one has ever gotten thirteen, the whole fair, Mom," Ben heard some little kid squeal. "Look how far back he is."

"Hush, Toby. You'll wreck his concentration," a feminine voice ordered.

Ben watched Cam critically. He turned and threw. The ball spiraled through the air once more. So controlled, so smooth. But Cam still threw with this arm, not his shoulder. Ben had wondered whether the coaching Cam received in Milwaukee would correct that technical flaw. But, no. It was still there. But, if you were really critical, if you examined his throwing style as a potential NFL player, then you would have to admit that he didn't use his shoulder the way the great ones did, the Johnny Unitases, the Dan Marinos. Still, Cam was impressive. And he remained Eagle River's favorite son.

Once again, Ben searched the crowd for Galen, but there was still no sign of him. *Is Kjersten here?* Ben's stomach twisted. God, he hoped not. It was way too soon for Galen.

Then, as he stared into the front rows of the crowd, the frenetic flash of the Ferris wheel lights reflected off moonlight bright long hair. He could just make out the familiar long, slender frame. *God no! She's here.*

Galen can't deal with her right now, too!

Desperately now, Ben searched for his friend. He moved away from the awestruck Timmy and began to shoulder his way back through the crowd.

"Hey, watch it, kid," a rather large farmer growled at him. In his haste, Ben had jostled the farmer's lady.

"Sorry," Ben shouted over his shoulder.

"That's Oscar Happe's boy, isn't it?" Ben heard the farmer's wife ask.

"Rude little bastard," the farmer responded.

Perfect. But Ben had no time. Later, he would go back and apologize, but after he got Galen out of there. As he pushed through, the crowd began to thin. There, at the very edge of the huddled masses, stood Galen. At six feet four inches, Galen easily observed the scene over the heads of most of those assembled. His hands were jammed into the pockets of the faded Wranglers that clung to his long, muscled legs. Idly, or was it with restrained hostility, he kicked the toes of his battered and scuffed Roper boots into the dirt.

"Galen."

He looked in Ben's direction, but he didn't notice Ben. Galen's eyes seemed focused inward rather than outward. His face nakedly revealed pain and shattered dreams.

"Galen? Kjersten's here."

"Yeah, Ben. I know, and I'm okay." Now Galen's face was emotionless.

"Let's get out of here, Galen. I've had enough of this hick fair." To be honest, Ben felt more comfortable seeing him this way. This was the face that most everyone else saw. Ben knew that he was probably the only one outside of Galen's family who ever saw him that other way. Galen had been through a lot with his mother dying last year and then the break up. No question. No one knew that better than Ben did. It was just that Galen hid it so well most of the time that Ben could forget or pretend, for a while at least. Then, he was the old Galen, the one he'd grown up with, not this new bitter and haunted person.

An "Aw," reverberated through the crowd. Clearly, Cam had finally missed.

"Galen Odgers, is that you out there?" Sal, the rotund bar owner's mellow baritone called out.

"Yeah, Sal. It's me." Galen answered as he raised his eyebrows at Ben.

What amazing timing. Ben tugged his friend's arm. "Let's get outta here."

"What you doin' out there, boy? Come on up here. You show Cam how a real football player throws."

Sal's great bulk parted the crowd like Moses did the seas, the round, glowing end of his thick cigar preceding him. He strode up to Galen, threw a great hairy forearm around Galen's neck and dragged him through the crowd.

"Galen," Sal chuckled, then cleared his throat of chunky cigar sputum. "You get up here and show Eagle River what you got."

"Sal, I'm not up for this."

"Hey Cam," Sal shouted out, ignoring Galen's protest. "I got a challenger here for you. Bet ya this high school string bean can out throw a college star. Galen here is a real ball player. You see that ring over there, Galen? Cam tossed that pigskin there through it thirteen times from where he's standing. I got a twenty that says you can make it to fourteen." Sal moved back towards the football toss, dragging Galen with him.

Suddenly, there was chaos. People shouted out to Galen and Sal's voice continued to boom out, taking odds.

Ben stood stock still. If you know a guy as well as Ben knew Galen, had grown up with a guy, you understood how he felt about things, about people, about Kjersten and Cam, in particular. Feeling anxious, he jostled his way back to the front of the crowd.

Meanwhile, Galen had taken Cam's place. He stood silently, facing the target. He had to be nervous, what with the whole town and Cam and Kjersten there. *Please God, don't let him screw up. Please.* Ben crossed his fingers. Galen drew his arm back and threw, quickly. Too quickly. *Yes! It went through. One*. The ball was run back to him. Again, he just drew back and blasted it. Two. Yes! Then, another. One more. On and on. The relief washed over Ben. Galen was keeping it together. He was sweet. Ben started to get excited, to get into it with the crowd.

Ben hadn't seen his best friend play ball for most of Galen's senior year. Ben had been away at college. He had heard that Galen was a real talent, but this self-composed, accurate quarterback was a far cry from the long limbed, loose cannon he remembered from a year before. Galen's weight was balanced delicately, dancer-like on the balls of his battered, old, laced up work boots. His facial features were relaxed while his eyes were focused on that white ring in the distance. He seemed not to hear the voices shouting his name all around him. He appeared equally oblivious to Cam, who stood just off to his right side, and to the din and the flashing lights of the surrounding fair. Effortlessly, Galen tossed that football through the hoop, pausing only long enough for the boy to run the football back to him. Unlike Cam, who had reveled in the adoration, working the crowd, Galen was lost in the job at hand and he was really, really good.

As one, the crowd shouted the number of the throw out loud, drowning out the sounds of men betting and the fair noises: "Ten… Eleven… Twelve."

The tension built with each successful throw. The crowd sucked in air as one, exhaled in relief as one.

"Thirteen." Galen had tied Cam.

Unable to resist, Ben searched for Kjersten again. In the shadows by Cam, Ben could just make out her profile. Maliciously, he wished that he could see her face as she watched her old boyfriend show up her new one.

"Fourteen…Fifteen…Sixteen."

Hysteria was building.

"Seventeen…Eighteen…Nineteen…Twenty… Oh," the crowd groaned as one. Galen had finally missed. The football had bounced just off the edge of the ring. Then, everyone went nuts. Galen stood still as the crowd swarmed around him. Ben saw Sal give him a few congratulatory smacks on the back. Then, Ben lost sight of Galen in the mass of people congratulating him. Gritting his teeth, Ben forced his way closer in. When he finally caught sight of Galen again, Cam had already cornered Galen.

Suddenly, Ben was fourteen-years-old and too chicken to help Galen out when Cam decided to make trouble for him. Cam wasn't really a bully. He had never really cared enough about other people to waste his time trying to dominate them. Besides, he'd always enjoyed the kind of hero worship that other boys give to superior athletes. But things were different between Cam and Galen. There'd always been something strange between those two, a heavy, dark feeling of which schoolboys should not have been capable.

Ben observed that Kjersten was on Cam's arm. Long-limbed and slender and fragile, she passed under the lights, completely visible for the first time. The high cheekbones, the full lips, and the elegant neck were the same. *Shouldn't people look different when everything changes so much?* But Kjersten was the same, albeit a thinner, more serious looking girl. She still wore her hair long and straight down her shoulders. She still moved with that particular step, seeming to dance forward, like the sprinter that she had once been. Her face was serene, still, and classically beautiful.

Ben watched as Cam held out his hand to Galen. "I'm glad that you're keeping the standard up at old Eagle River High. I was worried that the Warriors would slack off with me gone."

Galen stared at the proffered hand and then, slowly, hesitantly, reached out and took it. From his vantage point, Ben saw that both men were putting a good deal more than cordiality into their grips. Their hands remained interlocked, their eyes meeting, the smile thinning from Cam's lips, neither one giving in. Then, as if by mutual agreement, they released. A draw.

"Your name is Galen, right?" Cam continued, that bright "for the fans" smile accentuating the hungry lines of his jaw. "Galen Otter, or Oller?" Of course Cam knew Galen's name, but thankfully, Galen didn't take the bait.

"Odgers."

"I remember now. You were that weedy sophomore backup quarterback." Cam chuckled familiarly. "You always brought me towels and water all through my senior year." He punctuated his comment with a friendly nudge at Galen's shoulder. But Cam's eyes were sharp and focused on Galen. "I remember you had a big case of hero worship."

Unfazed by the clumsy jab, Galen stared straight back at him. "Too bad you didn't play much last year, Fawst."

Cam quit smiling. "Things are different in college. Players run faster and hit harder. It takes anyone a while to adjust. You'll see what it's like if you get that opportunity. Throwing a football through a hoop is a cute trick but it won't get you far in a college football game." Cam paused, regaining his composure. "You decided where you're gonna go next year? I'm sure that there are a lot of division three schools who would give you a shot."

Galen didn't take the bait.

"Well, see ya." Cam was tired of the games.

"Hi Galen," Kjersten's voice was soft but carried through the darkness like a knife.

Galen nodded his head curtly towards the girl, acknowledging her, but didn't turn to look at her. "Kjersten."

Cam assessed them, looking back and forth between them. "That's right, you two know each other." He tossed an arm possessively over Kjersten's shoulder and pulled her tightly to him, staring at Galen all the while. "Here's my good luck, Galen. You need to get yourself one of these," Cam chuckled at his own coarse joke. Kjersten's face remained determinedly impassive, her body, stiff.

"Hey Cam," Sal's cigar roughened voice cut through the weighted silence. The large bulk of the bartender appeared at Galen's side. "You gonna be around town for a couple of days?"

"I'd planned to stay through the weekend," Cam answered.

"Would you mind stoppin' by the bar during the Brewers and Twins game? You know what big Coyote fans we are. The guys would be thrilled if you would just come in and shoot the shit."

"Sure, Sal."

"Thanks, kid." Sal was pleased. With satisfaction, he twisted the cigar between his teeth. "Galen, you comin' by, too?"

"I don't know, Sal. There's a lot of work I gotta do at the farm. It's tough to get away."

No longer the center of attention, Cam turned away. "Come on, babe. Let's get out of here. I've had enough of this small town bullshit," Ben heard him mutter to Kjersten.

Suddenly, a hot, sweaty hand grasped Ben's forearm. "Hey Ben, I've been looking all over for you. I thought that you'd ditched me." It was Timmy. "Do you know how late it is already? My mom must be having a stroke. I haven't called her in over two hours and it's almost eleven. We've got to go soon or I'm gonna be late for curfew."

"Yeah, let's go." Galen broke abruptly away and strode off, his long legs eating up the ground, leaving Ben and Timmy in the dust. They followed and tried to keep up at first and then fell behind. A stalk of corn from last year's crop, suddenly jammed into the arch of Ben's foot.

"Shoot." Ben knelt down, pulled off his decrepit sneaker, and rubbed the abraded skin. He looked up as Galen swung open the door of his beat up, old pickup and hopped in. Ben cringed at the brutal clang of rusted metal on metal when he slammed the ancient door shut.

Timmy waited while Ben adjusted his shoe. "Is he okay? Galen's not pissed with me, is he? I didn't mean to act like a dorky little kid. It's just that my mom worried. Do you think he's pissed?"

"Don't worry about it, Timmy. Galen's not pissed with you or me. He's just dealing with some stuff."

As Ben straightened up, Galen started the engine. The ancient Ford was moving their way. It pulled abreast of them. "Come on, Ben. Let's go," Galen said impatiently.

Timmy hopped in and Ben followed a moment later. Galen shifted the truck into gear and swung it around. They spun off in a cloud of dust.

Chapter Two

Memories

~ Galen ~

After dropping off Ben and Timmy, Galen couldn't get home soon enough. He gave the old pick up gas, ignoring how it rattled like it was about to fall apart. It felt too tight, too close in the cab even with the windows rolled all the way down. He felt all twisted up, like he had something alive twisting around inside him.

Kjersten was still so beautiful. Still the same.

He slammed his knuckles into the dashboard. Then, he pounded them home again and again. The already dented blue plastic cracked, opening a knuckle. *Shit.* He pinched his eyes closed against the hurt. Tried to squeeze out the lines of her face.

Suddenly, he hit the big pothole at the end of the lane and Old Blue was air borne. When the pickup crashed back down to earth, it shook in every bolt. Galen's teeth were jarred. Then, he hit another pothole, went up and crashed down again and then the much abused vehicle popped out of gear as it slid into the grass on the side of the driveway.

Galen gripped the wheel and exhaled. The old truck didn't deserve this kind of treatment. He knew the driveway like the back of his hand, knew where every pothole and divot were and how to avoid them. *Get it together.*

It hurts so much seeing her with Cam and knowing that it's my own fault. Still, why did she have to hook up with that asshole? He leaned forward, resting his head against the steering wheel. *Kjersten.* He couldn't stop thinking about her. She was part of the best memories of his childhood. Memories, images of days gone past flowed through his mind, like autumn leaves in a river. *Kjersten.*

The moonlight shone brightly on the surface of the pond in the darkness. Both thirteen-year-old Ben and twelve-year-old Galen had known that trespassing could get them into big trouble. But, they weren't swimming alone, and the water in the pond was just deep enough to be safe to jump into. Besides, it was one of those humid summer nights in August when you're tired of the heat and just couldn't resist the cool darkness of well-fed pond. So, the boys had stripped down to their briefs and run as fast as they could to the small floating pier. Each one wanted to be the first one in, the first one to shatter the perfect stillness of the indigo water.

"Come on, Galen. You have a head start. That's not fair," Ben wailed. Both boys knew it was a load. Galen was just a lot faster. Still, he slowed down for his friend. He knew that he had to let Ben win sometimes or he'd quit trying. Ben shot past him and then off the wooden dock and into the air. Galen saw the surface of the pool erupt under Ben's cannonball and then he jumped, too, and lost all sight in the shock of the cold water.

The pond had been especially awesome that night. Maybe because it had been the last time before school. Maybe because they'd snuck out for one last dip. They'd heard that the property had finally been sold, and that a family was moving in. But the fact that it was now forbidden added to the allure, and that night lived in his memory as vividly fresh and late summer sweet with the thrill of getting away with something. They'd run, jumped, belly flopped, and swam until their fingers had pruned up and their lips had turned blue. When they got out of the water, the air was bitterly cold on their rail thin bodies.

It had all started when Ben was lining up for one last cannonball. He had stood stock still. "Don't move, Galen."

"What?"

"I just heard something. Like something back there," he'd gestured at the woods as he whispered the words to Galen, who had remained in the water, while he stood up on the pier.

"There's nothing there. You're hearing things." Galen had thought that Ben was being a chicken shit, to be honest. The kid had always been a little weird about going into dark rooms and hearing ghost stories and stuff. But Ben was Galen's best bud, and you don't tell your best bud that he is a wimp.

"One more cannonball, come on."

"I'm serious, Galen." His pale body was trembling hard now. "You hear that?"

"I don't hear a thing."

"I want to leave. Something or someone is out there. I know it." Ben sounded almost ready to cry.

"Don't be such a chicken."

"Please Galen. Let's go-o." His voice quivered.

"But there's nothing over there," Galen muttered as he doggy paddled his way over to the side of the pier where a ladder hung out over the water.

"Thanks, Galen." Ben turned and trembling with cold and fear walked towards the tree stump where the boys had stacked their clothes.

The shock of the night air coolness on his wet body started Galen shivering as soon as his shoulders left the water. The pond water felt nearly warm in comparison to the air. His teeth were chattering and the pine needle covered sand felt like shifting icicles under his bare feet. He hugged himself tightly and shivered his way over toward the clothes. Suddenly, he heard the sound of movement, of a body going through the underbrush from somewhere in the woods off to his left.

Both boys stopped, paralyzed. Suddenly, a huge dog burst out. The monster galloped towards them, open mouthed, barking ferociously. There was a bright white flash of the hair on its chest and its eyes were brilliant in the brightness of that summer's night.

Moving as one, they bolted. Galen jumped into the raspberry bushes that made up the undergrowth of the woods. The long branches smacked and stung on his bare skin. Blindly, he ran through the stinging pine branches. He didn't look back, but he could hear a big body crashing through the woods behind them, and the bark of that dog. It reverberated around them. Then, his foot hit a rise in the ground, perhaps a gopher hole. He sprawled out flat, the wind knocked out of him. Ben leaped over Galen's prone body and flew past. As Galen scrambled to get back to his feet, he watched Ben make the turn into onto forest path. Then, Ben was gone.

As for Galen, now the beast was upon him. Once he was on his feet, he backed slowly up, because he knew that you're never supposed to run from a dog. The monster dog had slowed to a muscle bound, hackles raised strut. Its bull neck was lowered, its body was sort of crouched, ready to leap, and tear out his throat, Galen imagined. A dull, shaky growl issued forth from the deep chest. He continued to back slowly.

"It's okay. You're a good dog. A very good dog."

"Heidi! Heidi, sit!" A girl's voice suddenly commanded from somewhere over by the pond.

The dog, a boxer, Galen now saw, whined and looked back towards the pond, but held her ground. She didn't obey the command. Galen began to back pedal even faster. Heidi, the boxer, clearly noticed his movement. For, she growled again and strutted the rest of the way up to him. There, she stood just inches from him, baring her teeth. Galen kept on staring down at the ground, not wanting to aggravate her by looking into her eyes. His mom had always warned him never to look a dog directly in the eye, or any other animal for that matter. "Heidi's a good girl. A very good girl," he breathed.

Heidi wasn't buying it. She continued to growl softly, menacingly.

He decided that moving probably wasn't the best plan. He was caught, well and truly caught, but he rationalized that getting into trouble was probably better than having Heidi take a hunk out of him.

"Heidi come!" A slight figure burst through the trees. A tall, skinny girl in blue jean shorts and a tank top rushed up and grabbed Heidi by the collar.

"Heidi! You're a bad dog! A bad dog!"

Heidi moaned and whimpered, with her cropped ears flat against her rounded skull. She pressed her hulking mass up against the girl and her entire body had wiggled with her rounded stump of a tail.

"I'm sorry about Heidi," the girl blurted out as she continued to hold the dog by her collar. Moonlight glanced off her long blond ponytail and it swished with her movement. She moved closer to Galen, with Heidi loyally wiggling her way between them. "Heidi doesn't bite. Well, except for mailmen and you're not a mailman. She loves kids, really."

"Maybe you should tell her that," he muttered since Heidi was continuing to eye him with serious interest.

"She's friendly. It's just that she worries whenever she sees anyone swimming. It freaks her out. We have to lock her in the house when my brother and I go swimming. She's friendly, honest."

As if to prove the girl's words, the dog made her way over to Galen. She sniffed at him, snorted, and then pressed her muscular side against him, gazing soulfully up. Galen reached down to touch her back gently. Her tail stump wiggled furiously in encouragement. The ugly cute boxer face grinned up at him in blissful encouragement.

He patted the dog with increasing enthusiasm. "Cool dog… Heidi's a pretty girl. Oh, yes she is." He went down on his knees. The dog licked his face, the broad abrasive surface of her tongue warming the chilled planes of his wet face.

"Wait here. I'll go get your clothes," the girl said.

In short order, she had returned with his T-shirt, shorts and tennis shoes.

"Thanks. Freezing, Galen nearly grabbed them from her.

Politely, she turned her back to him while he changed.

Galen's clothes were ice cold with the night air against his skin.

"I'm Kjersten."

"G-Galen," he shivered out as he thrust his sneakers onto his wet feet. He shoved his socks into his shorts' pockets.

"You live around here?"

"Yeah. Our farm's off County Y."

"How did you get here?"

"Biked. The bikes are over by the road. You're not from around here. How did you get here?"

"How did you know I'm not from around here?" the girl asked

suspiciously.

"I know everyone in Eagle River."

"We just, I mean, my family just moved here. You guys swim at the pond a lot?"

"Yeah. Everyone did 'till the place got sold. We used to skate here in the winter, too."

"Where do you live?"

She stared at him like he was some kind of moron. "Here."

"You mean here, like at the house?"

She nodded.

"You mean you're a Solheim?"

"Uh-huh."

"Shoot. I'm really sorry. I mean I'm not supposed to be here. I mean, we didn't figure you guys'd be moving in yet... Please don't tell on me. My mom'll kill me." The words tripped and stumbled their way out of his mouth.

Kjersten assessed him. "I won't tell anyone, don't worry."

Galen watched her. You never could trust a girl. They couldn't keep a secret. That was a known fact, one he'd learned from his sister, Sandra.

"Why won't you tell?"

"I won't tell under certain circumstances." She crossed her arms over her chest. "I'll make a deal with you. If you two go swimming again, you gotta take me with you."

He studied the girl. Kjersten Solheim was tall, taller than he was. She didn't look rich, that was for sure. Her denim shorts and T-shirt were faded with age and use. Her hair, except for the white blond ponytail, was covered with a Baltimore Orioles cap. There wasn't a frill, bow, or ribbon on her anywhere. She didn't look like a girly girl. Not that Galen wanted to have a girl around, but maybe he could cut some kind of deal with this one.

"You gotta swim with us and then you won't tell? No matter what?"

"I swear it." Kjersten held her hand out solemnly, like a grown up would.

Galen took her hand, wondering all the while how he was gonna explain it to Ben, who still thought girls were weird. "Swear by something important." His eyes fixed on the boxer. "Swear by Heidi's life."

"Okay. I'll swear by Heidi. Sorry girl." She reached down and patted the dog.

He took her hand and shook it. From that night on, they had been best friends, the three of them, Ben, Galen and Kjersten. Most of the time, it hadn't even seemed like she was a girl, she was just one of them. His mother had called them the "Three Musketeers." They had been inseparable, done everything together.

Galen shook his head, clearing away the memory of that first meeting with Kjersten five years ago. *I just have to forget her and move on.* But his mind was unruly and wouldn't obey his directives. Other memories drifted through him, like the day he'd taught her to ride horses.

"Riding is easy. Anyone can do it. I'm surprised that you never learned how at any of those fancy summer camps or schools."

"I just never did." A fourteen-year-old Kjersten spat the words out of tight, thin, frightened lips.

"How come? Riding's fun."

"Horses are... really big."

Her face was rigid as she sat absolutely frozen on the barrel-esque but somewhat swayed bare back of Jethro, the Odgers' old Belgian horse, in the farm yard. Kjersten's toes pointed straight to the ground and her hands were bound up in the thick, coarse mane. Jethro slowly swung his suitcase-sized head topped with fuzzy orange-yellow mane around. He rubbed the masticated, green slime on his mouth on Kjersten's denim clad lag, gently nuzzled her and then lifted his head high, rolled his eyes back, and raised his lip.

"He's laughing, isn't he?" Kjersten whispered.

"He's either laughin' at you or he thinks that you smell funny."

She began to giggle. Her laughter progressed to guffaws. Galen watched her, smiling himself. *She's so pretty.*

"You better pay attention up there. That's a wild animal you're sitting on."

Jethro gazed at him tolerantly with one enormous, soft caramel-colored eye and proceeded to yawn.

That struck Kjersten as even more hysterical. She leaned over the broad neck of the gentle giant and wrapped her arms around him. She buried her face in that thick, butter colored mess of mane. “He is friendly, isn’t he? And he smells good, too. Dusty, salty sweet, you know what I mean?”

“That’s how all horses smell.”

“He must be old. He’s so big.”

“Age doesn’t have anything to do with how big a horse is. Most horses are finished growing at two or three. Jethro’s a work horse, so big and strong. And he’s also kind of old. He doesn’t work hard anymore, except around Christmas time when Kyle hitches him and James up to a wagon and takes people for drives in the snow at the Christmas tree farm. Jethro loves that kind of stuff. He likes attention.” Galen patted the horse’s face with fond appreciation.

“He’ll let me ride him?”

“Well, to a point.” Galen enjoyed being the one in the know. “Jethro doesn’t like to go fast anywhere. But you can learn the basic stuff on him. All of us kids start on Jethro, just as soon as our legs were long enough so that we could sit up there.”

“How do I get him started?”

Galen saw that some of Kjersten’s fear had thawed. “Give him a kick with both legs, and you’re going to have to keep kicking him. He’s lazy and he’s not a motorcycle. Cluck a little, too.”

She brushed old Jethro with her heels. He swished at a fly with his stump of a tail. She kicked a little harder. Jethro swung his great head to one side, almost dragging Kjersten off with his movement, as she had a death grip on the rein, and began to industriously scratch at his shoulder. Kjersten looked perplexed but unafraid. This time, she belted Jethro one. His head cocked. Galen could see that canny old mind spinning. Jethro began to mosey along while Galen stood still watching, enjoying Kjersten’s excitement.

“I did it! He’s moving. This feels funny. But wait, how do I steer?”

“Pull on one rein or the other.”

Jethro’s head swung left and then right, but he moved inexorably in the same direction, towards the barn.

"How do I stop?" Kjersten's voice was shrill but not yet panicked.

"Act like you know what you are doing."

"He knows what he's doing."

Galen broke into a jog as the struggling Kjersten disappeared behind the wide opened barn door. He dashed into the barn, expecting the worst, only to find Jethro complacently standing in his stall chomping hay. Kjersten was still sitting on his back, patting the broad shoulders of the beast.

"I guess he's hungry."

"That doesn't make any difference. That was really bad of him." He walked into the stall and grabbed Jethro's reins. He struggled to drag the horse's nose out of the hay.

"He's tired and hungry." Kjersten awkwardly slid off of Jethro's back. The horse studied her with satisfaction. She rubbed the side of his head. Jethro eyed Galen uneasily and then rubbed his great head against Kjersten's side. Next, he rested his head on her shoulder and blew gently from his nostrils onto the side of her neck.

"He's telling me to take that thing…"

"The bridle," Galen supplied.

"Off. He's itchy. Isn't he cute?" Jethro was in hog heaven as Kjersten began to scratch him behind his fuzzy ears. "He likes me."

Galen watched, his irritation at Jethro giving way to enjoyment of the girl's happiness. *Kjersten was fun to hang out with, almost as good as a boy, and she sure was pretty.*

Even today, her beauty still made him ache. He didn't remember when exactly he'd become aware of her as a girl, but he'd gone along with them just being pals more or less successfully until the night of the homecoming dance her junior year. The memories of that night remained so vivid in his mind.

A sophomore, he had finally grown taller than Kjersten. He'd wanted to ask her to go with him to the dance, but hadn't felt he could. After all, they'd both agreed that they were "just friends," and she was a junior, besides. He had planned on going to the dance, but with Ben and a couple of the guys from football. He was surprised and more than a little shocked when Kjersten told him that she was going with Jeff Wilson.

"Jeff Wilson?"

"Oh, he's in my grade," she answered breezily. "He sits behind me in AP English."

"He's that preppy doctor's kid. I know who you mean." Jeff Wilson was pretty-boy cute and smart and rich, to boot. It frankly sucked that he was Kjersten's homecoming date. Then, it all got worse for Galen when he found that Jeff and Kjersten were elected to the homecoming court together.

That night, he saw her come into the gym. Wilson was with her, but Galen's eyes were on Kjersten. Frankly, he couldn't take them off of her. She was wearing a strapless silver dress with a short, silver, gum drop-like skirt. Her legs had appeared endlessly long, and her shoulders, back, and the tops of her white breasts had been so lovely and bare when her date took her wrap.

She looks amazing! She took his breath away.

He watched as she chatted with friends and wandered about oohing and ahing over people's dresses. Finally, when he didn't think he could stand waiting any longer, she stepped away from her date and approached the small round table where Galen and Ben sat with some other guys.

"Kjersten," Galen murmured as he rose to his feet.

"Wow, Kjersten," Ben remarked, also rising. He took her by the hand and turned her around. "You look really good. Don't you agree, Galen?" Ben, of course, knew how Galen felt about their childhood friend.

Kjersten smiled at him, and Galen hadn't been able to speak a word. *Wow.* Galen had thought he looked good, too. Galen was tall, nearly six two now and thin, and Kyle's dress up shirt, and trousers were loose on him, but Sandra had said he was handsome with his dimples and his sandy blond hair. He'd been happy with his appearance, until he'd seen Wilson in all his bow tied, plaid vested glory.

"Hi Galen," Kjersten leaned closer to him, her voice was faint over the song booming out over the sound system.

"Kjersten." He shuffled his feet, staring down at his shoes, then he raised his eyes and met her glance. For a moment, he could barely breathe. "You look nice," he said, but his eyes devoured her.

"You, too."

"Where's your date?" he asked.

"Oh," she waved her hand. "He's somewhere. Probably with his friends."

Then, they stood there staring at each other.

"You wanta dance?" Galen finally managed to ask.

"You mean us? Now?" She glanced over at the dance floor where couples were grinding against each other while Chris deBurgh crooned about a lady in red.

He nodded and took her hand, pulling her out onto the dance floor. Then, he turned her so that they faced each other. For a moment, he felt awkward, unsure of what to do or how to touch her. But then he gazed into her lovely eyes and indecision melted away. For once, he didn't hesitate. He simply reached out and drew her closer still. It felt right, natural. So, he linked his hands at the base of her back directly where it curved out into her firm, plump butt.

As she curved into him, her eyes fluttered shut, and she inhaled deeply. He became aware that she was wearing a flowery scent. She draped her arms up around his neck. Feeling her fully against him for the first time, Galen became aroused. Suddenly, there was nothing except the music and the girl in his arms.

"What about Jeff?" he whispered by her ear. The feel of the soft skin of her neck against his lips made his heart beat faster.

"Jeff?" she repeated blankly.

"Is he going to be pissed that we're dancing?"

"Shut up, Galen," she murmured. "Don't ruin it."

He felt rather than heard her chuckle.

Then, he lost himself in the moment, in the rise and fall of the song, in the rich sensory experience of holding a girl that he cared about for the very first time. He never wanted it to end, the moment or the song. But then it did, and still she didn't let go of him or raise her head. Instead, she'd burrowed closer.

"Hey," he said, finally stepping back. He reached out and tipped her chin up, gazing searchingly into her eyes.

"What?"

Then, he grinned at her, shattering the moment. "You like me."

"What?" She retreated from him.

"You do, you know you do. You didn't let go of me when the song ended." He grinned a cocky little smile at her.

She smoothed her dress and seemed to gather herself. "Don't flatter yourself, Galen. I just love that song. I'm going to go and find Jeff."

He watched her as she walked away. His eyes remained fixed on her ass, noticing for the first time the subtle sway of her hips.

"What was with you two?" Ben punched him in the arm. "You getting all hot and heavy out there?"

Galen didn't respond. Instead, he watched her progress across the floor. He saw Kjersten several more times that evening. Each time, he was aware that there was something different in her eyes when they met his and that she couldn't hold his gaze for long. Once or twice, he saw her blush and she seemed to laugh a little more loudly.

That was the night that things started to change between them. From that evening on, after that dance, everything was different between them.

Slowly but surely, they'd gotten together, become a couple. They'd dated for nearly two years, until even after she'd gone off to college. And, it had been good between them, very good. That is, until his mother got sick with breast cancer. *I just couldn't think straight. I just wanted to crawl into hole, so I wouldn't have to deal with things.*

Galen's thoughts bounced to that May day of his senior year when Kjersten had surprised him at school. Things had already started to go bad between them because, even though he didn't mean to, as his mom got weaker and sicker, he found himself shutting down. He just couldn't deal with anything more emotionally.

He was well aware that he was being cold and distant with Kjersten when they spoke on the phone. It was just hard to talk with her about college and her classes when he was watching his mom die. It wasn't like Kjersten wasn't sympathetic, she asked about his mom, but he didn't want to talk about her, about her physical decline. It just hurt too much.

More than once, he'd broken off a phone conversation with Kjersten with "I gotta go." Of course, Kjersten had known that Jessica Odgers was sick, and, in fact, dying. But on that particular day, she'd hoped that by surprising him at Eagle River High School, she could get past his guard and reconnect with him.

Galen walked out of the front door of the school. He paused for a moment, adjusting his backpack straps and took a deep breath. He was torn. He wanted to go home, but he dreaded what he would find. *Would Mom be worse?*

He was headed down the sidewalk toward his bus, when a car pulled up beside him. The passenger door popped open.

"Kjersten, what are you doing here?" The words burst out, unfiltered, because he was surprised, actually shocked to see her. Of course, he'd known that her semester was winding down. But it was only the third week in May and he totally hadn't expected her on this day. She hadn't told him that she was coming home yet. Clearly, she'd wanted to surprise him. He registered the instant hurt on her face.

"I just got back this morning, and I wanted to see you right away. Come on. Get in."

Thinking of his mother and all that awaited him at home, Galen hesitated. He knew that Sandra, Joe, and Kyle were likely to all be there. As for his father, he was likely drunk. The vigil had begun. It was clear that Jessica Odgers didn't have long to live. "I have to get home," he offered as he squinted through the rain at her.

Again, she looked wounded.

Galen felt horrible. *I don't want to hurt her. Why do I keep doing this? She's going to ask about Mom and I just can't stand to talk about it anymore. I can't think about more. I just can't handle... more.*

"They can wait a little while. Come on, get in, Galen. We haven't seen each other in months. You'll be home by four. I promise."

He closed his eyes for a moment. He wanted to spend time with Kjersten, but he also felt like he should be with his family, that he shouldn't take a break from the misery that was his life at the moment. Still, it was Kjersten. It was good to see her. After a moment, making his decision, he folded his long frame into her silver Camry. His heart was pounding.

"Hey." She smiled at him.

"Hey," he answered back with a soft, tentative smile that made him appear younger than his eighteen years.

She reached out and touched a rain drop on his nose, impulsively she touched it to her tongue. The car felt suddenly warm and close, and all of the silliness drained away from the two.

He leaned closer to her. His eyes held hers then, right there in the school parking lot, he leaned towards her, slowly. Then, they were kissing and touching, unable to get close enough.

Suddenly, the car's horn blared out. Kjersten was pressed up against it.

Outside, another student yelled, "Get a room, Odgers."

"Sorry, I didn't mean to." Galen sat back into his seat and brushed his hair back from his forehead with trembling hands.

"Let's go somewhere. Right now. Where we can be alone." Her cheeks were flushed, her color, high. Nervously, she licked her lips.

He couldn't take his eyes off the tip of her tongue. "Okay."

She turned the key, starting the engine. "I know just the place."

A few minutes later, they pulled into the parking lot at a heavily wooded county park.

"Come on." Kjersten climbed out of the car.

"Where are we going?" Galen was perplexed at the choice of destination.

"Just come see."

She took his hand and led him down the jogging trail through the woods and then off on a side trail. She stepped behind a large rock on the path and then they were in a grassy alcove with the rock on one side and thick brush on the two others. There was a flowery quilt spread out covering the ground and a few pillows tossed there as well.

"Did you set this up?" Galen asked.

"Um hmm." She wiggled her eyebrows suggestively. "For us. It's been so long, Galen. Too long. I love you. Always have."

Nothing more needed to be said. He reached out and gripped her hips with large, hungry hands pulling her closer. Then, they were tearing desperately at each other's clothes, unable to get them off quickly enough, ravenous with youth, desire, and the longed for taste of each other.

Afterwards, she lay on top of him naked, facing the sky. He stroked up and down her sides and cupped her breasts. "That was a rain drop."

She giggled, inhaling deeply the air that was rich and ripe with wet spring grass, sunshine, and young and nubile bodies.

"You feel so good," he said and groaned, pressing up with his hips and his cock against the silky firmness of her ass.

"Admit it," she teased, squirming against him. "You missed me."

"Of course, I did. I never said I didn't."

"You stopped calling me and you didn't write."

"It was just that there was so much going on with Mom…" His voice trailed off. *I'm not going to cry. Not now. Later. But not now. I am going to be happy now.*

Kjersten slid off of him and turned over so that her breasts were pressed against his chest, her long legs beside his. "Don't be sad."

"It's hard not to be. It just sucks."

"I know." Her blue eyes became suspiciously moist. "If you ever need to talk about it..."

"No." His answer was decisive. "Let's not talk anymore at all." He turned to his side as well and reached down to gently manipulate one of her nipples between his thumb and forefinger. Then, he shifted down and lowered his mouth to it. He licked his way around the edge of her nipple. Then, he oh-so-gently took it between his teeth.

Kjersten moaned, then reached down between their straining young bodies to grip the base of his cock. Then, she slid down his body and took the tip of his cock in her mouth, gently suckling it. Raising her mouth off of it, she lathed her tongue around the large, firm head as she continued to stroke her hand down the now wet shaft. Galen shut his eyes and bit his lip against the overwhelming sensation as she cupped his balls and gently gripped them. Then, she slid her tongue down and around the base of his balls.

Not able to take the sweet torture any more, he pulled her up and then set her down on the blanket beside him. "It's my turn," he murmured as he nuzzled the sensitive skin by her ear. First, he nibbled and nuzzled his way down her body. Then, he cupped her sex, feeling the moisture between the lips as she thrust up against his hand. He gently separated her lips, ran his tongue around her clitoris and then over it as he gripped her hips in his hands. Kjersten nearly came up off the blanket. He continued to go down on her while she gyrated about seeking satisfaction.

"Fuck me now, Galen." She gripped his muscled forearms, her eyes, hot and desperate.

"Ride me," he directed, lying back down and shifting her over him and down onto his aroused penis. Both groaned at the ecstasy of penetration.

She rode him, frantically, desperately. All the while, he stared up at her. He reached up and guided her hand down to her clit so that she masturbated as she rode him. Desperately, they thrust together.

"I can feel you so deep."

"I want to come. Fuck me," he directed, forcing her hips into a faster, harder rhythm. They strained together to ride a wave and then came together.

Afterwards, they lay together touching and chatting, avoiding discussing anything that might destroy the perfection of that stolen afternoon. They didn't return to their respective homes until near evening.

That very night, after Galen got home, Jessica lost her battle with cancer. So, there hadn't been any more time at all for Galen and Kjersten to be together.

Looking back now, Galen wished he'd handled things differently with Kjersten. But after his mother's death, life had been a pain filled blur for him. The visitation and the funeral hadn't seemed real. Afterwards, he'd gone through the motions of life, gone to school, worked out, but he had also closed himself off because he hurt so much inside.

Kjersten had called him almost every day at first. Then, it had gone to a few times a week, then weekly. For months, she sent him cards, letters, a care package, and even a playlist on a cassette tape.

A few weeks later, during dinner, the phone rang.

Galen and Kyle eyed each other, tired of the endless calls by well-wishers.

Finally, Kyle conceded and picked up the phone. "Odgers here." Then, he held it out to Galen. "It's for you."

"I don't want to talk to anyone."

"Come on," Kyle covered the receiver end of the phone. "It's Kjersten. Just talk to her."

"I just … I don't know."

"Take it," Kyle pressured.

"Fine," Galen muttered. "Hello?" he barked into the phone.

"Galen?"

"Yup."

"I can't believe I finally got you. I've been calling you, but you probably know that."

"I just didn't want to talk to anyone."

"I'm so sorry, Galen. I loved your mom, too."

He was silent.

"Are you still there?"

"Yeah."

"I'm coming home in a few weekends. I want to see you."

"No." The word burst out of him abruptly.

"Why not?"

"I just don't want to see anyone. Not now."

"You don't want to see me?" Her voice sounded hurt.

"I don't want to see anyone."

"Galen, please, what's wrong?"

Again, he was silent. "I just don't want to do this right now, Kjersten. I don't want to talk to you." It hurt him to say the words, for he knew they would devastate her, but he used them anyway. "Don't call here again." Then he'd hung up on her.

"Why did you do that?" Kyle demanded. "That girl cares about you. You're not thinking right."

But Galen's heart was broken with the loss of his mother. He wasn't ready or able to care about anyone else. He just didn't want to deal with any of it anymore. "Just leave me alone."

Looking back, Galen cringed at the cruelty of his words and actions. *I wasn't thinking right. I was truly crazy with pain and grief. I can't blame her for moving on. But with Cam? Why with that bastard?*

Chapter Three

Home

~ Galen ~

Galen cringed, pinched his eyes shut, against that final memory. *How could I be so awful, such a jerk? How could I be so messed up*? Looking back, it was like in those months after his mom died, a part of him had been dead as well. He had sort of locked down all of his emotions just to survive. He'd survived, but at what cost?

He still had his family, but he'd driven away a girl he thought he may have loved. *How can I fix things? Not sitting here, that's for sure.* He exhaled slowly and then turned the key. The pickup hesitated a moment, coughed, back fired and then turned over. He gave her a little gas and eased her the rest of the way up the driveway and parked at the house.

He got out of the truck. The moon was nearly full and bright and he paused, struck by how pretty the place still looked at night. *What a joke.* At night, an eye didn't get stuck on the work that still needed to be done or that had been done half-ass. It just looked so peaceful. And then, he could almost forget the real cost of this place, how much Kyle kept paying in blood and sweat. It had been a good place to grow up. Galen knew that he'd been lucky that way. That was probably why it all hurt so much now. He wasn't used to things sucking so badly, even though they had for some time now.

Still feeling all jumpy and wound up, Galen knew that there was no way that he would get any sleep. So, he turned away from the house and walked towards the hay barn that the moonlight had given a shadowy, silent sort of majesty.

During the day, the decrepit red wooden barn appeared to be nearly falling down and drafty with missing boards. But despite the fading red and brown wood and the pieces of metal tacked on here and there, the place was sturdy. It stayed up winter after winter, under big time snow loads. It was more than adequate for hay and equipment storage, and a great place for a couple of football crazy kids to play.

Kyle was the one who'd hung a tire from a chain from the roof at the far end of the long aisle. The hay was stacked high on both sides and a couple of bulbs cast a vague light down from where they hung high in the rafters. In the summer, they left the doors open at both ends. That way, there was plenty of light.

For part of one football preseason back when he was in sixth or seventh grade, Kyle had wanted to play quarterback. He'd had a strong arm, but had been weak on accuracy. Coach Murray had told him to rig up the tire and practice. But, unlike Galen, Kyle had gotten bored with it. He'd also gotten big in middle school. So, Kyle had been put on the line. It had probably worked out for the best anyway. Kyle liked to hit people.

Galen and Kyle had cleared all of the hay out of one corner and put a weight bench back there and an old radio. They'd covered the cracked, faded, and cobweb covered walls with a collage of sports posters, magazine pages, and newspaper clippings. The green and yellow of the Green Bay Packers, though faded and dust covered, were the dominant shades. There was a poster of Fuzzy Thurston on one wall and one of Paul Hornung on the other, as well as a vanity parking sign that read "Reserved for Packer Fans." There was also a cheesehead hat that Kyle had gotten when he and some buddies had tailgated at a Packer game at Lambeau field.

Below the Fuzzy Thurston poster there was a stack of Old *Sports Illustrated* magazines. Galen remembered when his face had appeared in "Faces in the Crowd," just last year. As a kid, he had fantasized about just that happening. But then when it finally had, it hadn't mattered all that much. His mother had just died, and there was no one to put the clipping in his memory book. That's how it was, whenever he started feeling okay, something always came up that reminded him that his mom was gone. *And now Kjersten was gone, too, and it was his fault.*

Shakily, he took a deep breath. He tried to let go of all of the self-pity and the misery that was eating him up. But, it stuck there, lodged high in his throat, like that home fry that he'd choked on at a Perkins once. His eyes caught on the blue and white of the jump rope that hung from a nail on the wall. He grabbed it and went to work.

Twenty minutes later, when he was dripping sweat and his calves ached with a satisfying burn, Kyle walked in.

"I saw the light on out here. You got quite a lather going there, Galen."

"Early night for you?"

"Slow night. The talent pool of ladies was weak."

"That usually doesn't bother you," Galen sniped as he tossed the rope down and picked up the football. He walked down to the furthest end of the barn and sent the ball sailing towards the tire. It bounced off the rim. Muttering under his breath, he walked the length of the barn, picked it up, walked back again, and then threw.

It bounced off the rim again.

"That's true," Kyle remarked laconically. "You having a rough night," he said as he sat down on bale of hay, took out his tin of Copenhagen, and put a chew in.

Galen's third throw made it through the tire, as did the next one and the handful of throws after that.

"I'd quit while I was ahead, Galen. You've pretty much torn the hell out of that old tire," Kyle commented laconically. "Sit down. Let's talk."

"Let it go, Kyle." Galen responded as he walked over to the bench and started to put added weight on the bar. Kyle automatically moved to help his brother. Neither commented on the choice of the hour for working out. Both brothers had developed strategies for getting by. Galen's was to push his body to exhaustion while Kyle's usually involved a visit to one of the seedier local drinking holes. Kyle put the pin on. "I was over at the Court'n House tonight. Someone mentioned that you blew Cam Fawst out of the water in that football toss over at the fair."

"You still hanging out at that dump?" Galen evaded the question.

"Nothing wrong with having a few cocktails now and then, little brother, and some of the skanks who hang out there are pretty well put together and friendly. At least I don't waste forty or fifty bucks on an evening and then not get anything out of it. Besides, you know how it works, if you keep it wrapped, it doesn't count. So, I'm practically a virgin."

Galen groaned as he lay down on the bench. He gripped and released the bar. "Sandra would lose it if she heard you talking like that. You ready?"

"Yeah, whenever. Galen, this will all eventually pass, too. You'll get over it, over her."

Galen braced, about to raise the bar. "Come on, Kyle. I gotta concentrate."

"You did chest this morning, right? You're just tearing muscle up by lifting more now. That's no good… You're just beating yourself up, aren't you? You're one sick dude. I'm telling you, overworking a muscle group is no good for your body."

Galen exhaled in exasperation and rose to a sitting position on the bench. Kyle was well lubricated and ready to talk. There was no way to shut his brother up when he was in such a mood.

"Galen, I know big time athletes work hard, but you've turned into some kind of masochist." Kyle chuckled as he sank back down onto a bale of hay.

There had to be more coming, there always was. There was a lot of bullshit to Kyle. But when you got down to it, Kyle was a good guy and a great brother, the kind of guy who killed himself on a farm that was barely breaking even in order to take care of his invalid father and teenaged brother.

Kyle rested a hand on Galen's shoulder. "You've gotta learn that you can't let things get you down. You just keep going on. That's what it's about… Like Mom dying. There was no reason for it, and you find yourself wondering why God let's shit like that happen. It just don't make sense." He cast his eyes down to the ground. Then, he leaned forward and spat a smooth caramel colored stream onto the dirt floor in front of him. "You just can't let it get you down. We got dealt a crappy hand in life. Shit happens, but we still got each other, you, Sandra, Joe, and their kids, and even Pop, the old bastard. Are you getting what I'm saying?"

Galen met his brother's glance. "Kjersten was at the fair."

"Oh?" Kyle kicked around the dirt in front of him with the fine Ostrich leather boots that he was so proud of having won in an electric bull riding contest. "Once you're at college, you'll forget all about her. The girls will be all over you."

"You don't get it, Kyle. I thought she was the one."

"I thought that she was okay, too… We all did. But it's better that you found out now anyway. And you'll get over her. I'm tellin' you, one semester and you'll have a hard time remembering what she looks like."

Galen snorted.

"Football players are gods at Illinois University. I know what I'm talking about. But don't you get screwed up. You remember what's important and keep your nose clean. You got that? There's no point in thinking about what you shoulda done or what you did wrong. You just gotta let it go. You have a lot to look forward to."

Galen nodded.

"Come on, let's go in. I'm freezing my nuts off."

* * * *

After the drama of the night at the fair, Ben lay in bed and found that sleep eluded him. *Galen. Kjersten. Cam.* Their faces swam through his restless mind. *It's incredible and horrible that Kjersten is with Cam.* And yet, he'd seen the rift develop between Kjersten and Galen. They were his best friends. Of course he'd known that Galen had shut down and shut Kjersten out. And, Ben had been there that night in Chicago when Kjersten and Cam had gotten together. His mind drifted back to that night.

It was a typical Thursday night at the Delta Psi fraternity house of

Milwaukee University. Several couples of the evening gyrated their pelvises together to the heavy primal beat. The basement rooms reeked of beer, in some corners, vomit. Thursday nights at Delta Psi were always the same. They had seemed so cool earlier in the semester. Ben wondered, *Why did I bother to come?* Already more than half way through his sophomore year, Ben was finding the scene a little stale. Feeling way too sober, he glanced around in some disgust.

"Hey, Ben. How you doing?" A chunky red head with abundant cleavage overflowing her army green tank top shouted to Ben through the cloud of cigarette smoke around the keg she manned.

"Good. How about you, Jane?"

"Fine and getting better. You want a beer?"

"Sure." He took the proffered drink, not because he planned on drinking it but because it was the expected prop at such events. "Jane, you are looking fine tonight."

"Yeah, right," she replied, blushing.

"I'll see you around," Ben said.

"Yeah, sounds good."

In the dim lighting, he made out a familiar tall, emaciated figure behind the DJ table so he headed over

"What's up, my man, Ben?" the DJ commented on seeing him.

"Is that you, Walt?" Ben questioned. "I can't tell under the shades."

The DJ pulled off his shades. "How you livin?"

"I'm living large," Ben responded with a slight smile.

"No man. It's livin'. You sound too white. Drop the g."

"Got it." Ben held his hand up for the high five. Walt was about as white as one could get. "Hey Mark."

Mark was short, muscular, and Italian. Together, he and Walt were the best DJs on the campus and were in high demand for all parties.

"Anything interesting tonight?" Ben queried as he leaned back against the wall behind the table piled high with equipment and CDs.

"Nothing too extreme," Mark returned. They studied the crowd. "Looks like Fawst is gettin' busy again tonight." He gestured to where Cam Fawst was all over a tall, willowy blond. Cam had his arms on either side of her up against the wall, his mouth buried against her neck.

"I don't get it," Walt smirked. "Cam treats women like shit, but the chicks are always all over him."

"That's because he's the Coyotes' QB, you dumbass," Mark commented.

"Word," Walt agreed. "This is a new one. She's hot."

Ben studied the couple. There was something oddly familiar in the slender line of the girl's body, in the way she moved. Suddenly recognizing her, Ben experienced a sickening twist in his gut.

"Just a minute," he moved away from the two DJs. He negotiated his way around the crowded room through the cigarette smoke haze, past the other couples hooking up, past the clumps of girls dancing together, past the chugging football players. But he couldn't catch Kjersten's eye. Across the dimness of the room, he saw that her eyes were closed. He glanced around, but none of Kjersten's friends were in sight. So, he hurried back outside to where groups of people were oblivious to the freezing temperatures. In one of the peripheral groups, he glimpsed Lauren Case, Kjersten's friend and roommate. Lauren was cute with a curvy body that was a little on the plump side, a buoyant personality, and a dark bob of hair.

"Lauren?"

"Ben!" She jumped up and hugged him. "It's wonderful to see you," she enthused, clearly feeling a warm glow from the beer.

"Lauren, I need to talk to you." Ben pulled her away. A couple of the girls stared after them.

"I'll be right back," Lauren called back over her shoulder. "Ben, what's going on? Quit pulling me. Let go of my arm."

"I'm really sorry, but what's with Kjersten?"

"What do you mean?"

"She's with Cam Fawst."

"No way! That girl is unbelievably lucky. Where are they?" Lauren led the way back through the maze of sweating bodies into the basement. She moved to the periphery of the dancers until she, too, saw the tall couple. Ben moved up beside her.

"That is some good news," Lauren commented to him. "I knew she would have an awesome time if we finally got her out. She's been moping around for months, ever since she broke up with her high school boyfriend. Then, a couple of weeks ago, I finally convinced her to go to an 'Around the World.' But this is unreal. The Coyotes' quarterback. Too cool."

"No kidding," Ben responded wryly. "Lauren, is she sober enough to know what she's doing?"

"I hope so. I want her to tell me all about it. Cam Fawst is hot."

"Would you get her for me? Please, Lauren. If this is what she wants, I'll leave it alone. I know that she and Galen broke up a few months ago but I just want to be sure that she knows what she's doing."

"Come on," Lauren placed her hand on her hip. "Leave her alone. She looks like she's having a great time. I wouldn't mind being in her place. She's just letting her hair down. She's been repressed for too long."

"Please, Lauren."

"It's just because you're friends with her high school boyfriend, right." She slanted him a glance. "You do know that he dumped her? He's the one who decided that they were done."

"I know. I get it," Ben commented, holding his hands up. "Kjersten's been my friend since we were kids, too. I just want to make sure that she is okay."

"All right. All right. I'll get her."

Ben watched as Lauren made her way over to the dancing couple. She tapped on Kjersten's shoulder, and then tugged her arm. Immediately, he saw the irritation flare on Cam's face at the interruption, but Lauren persevered. In a moment, she was moving back towards him and she had Kjersten by the arm. As far Cam, he stepped away from the dance area and leaned up against a wall, watching them with narrowed eyes. Ben stepped a little further back into the crowd. *I don't need Cam kicking my ass tonight.*

Lauren peered in his direction and finally located him. When he motioned for her to follow him, she nodded. Ben stopped over near the stairwell that led out of the sweaty basement. Lauren followed him, towing Kristen in her wake. Kjersten sort of swayed up against the stairwell wall, and Lauren winked at Ben and jogged back up the stairs.

"Hi Ben," Kjersten smiled all lazy eyed and beer goggled.

"Kjersten, I know it's none of my business, but you know what you're doing? How drunk are you?"

She was still moving in time to the music and not focusing on Ben's face. He grasped her hand. She giggled. Finally, she fully opened her eyes and took in his face, the stern, disapproving set of his features. Then, she stiffened and pulled her arm free of his grip. "Ben, I don't want to talk to you right now."

"Are you sure about this? About Cam? You know he's kind of an asshole and a total player."

"Ben, this is none of your business, never has been." Her words were slightly slurred. "I don't have to answer to you or to anybody else. As for Galen Odgers, he decided that things were done between us a long time ago. He doesn't care what's going on with me. He made that clear enough. Just let it go, Ben. It's over with Galen and me. I know you are his friend, but you're my friend, too."

"Whoa. Slow down." Ben held up his hands in protest. "You're are a big girl, Kjersten, but I am your friend and I'm worried about you. It's just that I've never seen you this drunk before." *And all over a guy who wasn't Galen.*

"I'm not drunk. I'm buzzed." Kjersten smiled and collapsed back into her position back up against the wall. "I'll just stand right here and close my eyes, then maybe everything will stop spinning around."

"Let me take you home. You're wasted. You'll be glad tomorrow if you call it a night now."

"Oh, don't be such a geek," she waved a finger vaguely in Ben's face. "I just want to rest for a minute." Her voice tapered off.

"Kjersten," an unfortunately familiar male voice interrupted them. "You ready to go?"

Ben spun around to find himself face to face with Cam.

"You got a problem with that?" Cam demanded of Ben, clearly not recognizing him.

"Kjersten, do you want me to take you home?" Ben offered one more time.

"The lady is going home with me tonight." Cam put his hand on

Ben's chest and pushed him up against the wall by Kjersten. "Don't fuck with me," he spit the words right into Ben's face while he easily held him there.

"I'm not messing with you, Cam. Kjersten's a friend of mine."

"Yeah, well tonight she's going to be my friend."

"No, I mean. I know her from home, from Eagle River. I know you, too."

Cam's grip loosened slightly, studied Ben's face, then released him totally. Ben sunk back against the wall. "You're the Happe kid. I remember you. You used to do stats at all of the football games, right?"

Ben nodded.

Cam smiled and swung a muscular arm around his shoulders. "I thought you looked familiar, just couldn't quite place you. You used to be shorter. Had glasses, right?"

Ben nodded again.

"That goat beard thing you got growing on your chin threw me off a little, too. So, how's Milwaukee treating you?"

"I like it all right." Ben was throw off balance by Cam's sudden change in mood and focus. "Kjersten, we've been friends forever and she's drunk. She doesn't know what she's doing."

"That's the true beauty of fresh meat." Cam pulled a languorous Kjersten up against him. He kissed her. She draped her arms around his neck and hungrily kissed him back. Cam smiled sardonically at Ben. "Seems to know that she's doing to me. You want to come home with me, sweetheart?" he purred into her neck.

Kjersten nodded groggily and smiled.

"See you around, Happe."

"But I don't think," Ben grabbed Cam's arm.

"Off the threads, Happe. What the heck do you think you're doing? I've cut you some slack, but I don't have much patience. Do you understand me?"

Ben looked over Cam. He observed the thickness of the of the bare forearms, the size of the hands, the breadth of the shoulders, the way the cloth of the short sleeves stretched across Cam's biceps. Then, he stepped back. "I understand." So, he turned and walked the other way.

I'm a coward, a chicken shit coward. But there's nothing else that I can do anyway. Cam would just kick my ass and Galen's not here to back me up, the way he was in high school.

Lauren waylaid him as he made his way out to the car. "Where's Kjersten?"

"With Cam." Ben tried to brush by her.

"But I thought that you said that was a bad thing. Or is it a good thing, now? I don't get what's going on."

"Neither do I."

Ben shoved his hands into the pockets of his jeans. He hated this feeling of cowardice that left a bile taste in the back of his throat. It really wasn't any of his business, after all. It was Kjersten's and Galen's. He couldn't fix anything anyway, so there was no point in beating himself up. Shaking his head and frustrated, he walked off into the night.

Chapter Four

Make up Sex

~ Kjersten ~

The trip to Eagle River that weekend of the county fair was Cam's and Kjersten's first real trip together as a couple and it had been going well, at least Kjersten had thought so, until they'd seen Galen. *That is, since Galen had shown Cam up.*

Right after the whole scene at football toss, she sensed something was up with Cam. He didn't say anything on the way back to the Camaro. Cam loved the car and had parked at the very end of the corn field parking lot, far away from any other vehicles that could ding or nick it. And, when they got there, he hadn't opened the car door for her. She got in. Then, he sat still staring forward, gripping the steering wheel.

"What's wrong?" she asked. "Cam, what's bothering you? Please. Talk to me."

He didn't say a word.

"Cam? Talk to me."

His jaw clenched, but still he didn't say a thing.

She reached out to touch his hand.

He pulled his away. "You shouldn't have embarrassed me like that. I saw the way you were looking at him."

"What?" she sputtered. "You're crazy!"

Cam turned to glare at her. "I know what you were thinking. Were you remembering how his cock felt?"

Kjersten went still, her jaw dropped open in astonishment.

"You still think he's hot for you. But there's no way he'd take you back now. Game over, as far as he's concerned."

Deliberately, she turned away from him. "Unlock the car door now." She fumbled with the handle. "This conversation is so over."

"You can be such a bitch... But you were hot for me that first night, remember? You were all over me and you loved it when I fucked the hell out of you. You were dripping for me and you screamed when you came." He reached down and cupped her crotch.

Kjersten pinched her legs together, resisting his touch.

"Don't you ever embarrass me like that again," he repeated.

"Galen's a friend." To her chagrin, her voice quivered on the last word.

"A friend you used to fuck. You think I'm stupid. You still want to fuck him, don't you?"

She shook her head. "No. You're being a jerk right now, Cam. A total asshole."

Cam leaned closer to her. "You want to know what I think? I think he still wants to fuck you, too. He still wants you, and you want to fuck him, too...That turns me on."

"What?" Kjersten looked at him incredulously. "Are you serious?"

Cam grinned a mean, little smile that didn't reach his eyes, which were dark, hot and hungry. "Totally. Nothing's better than a good angry fuck. If you're so hot tonight, why don't you suck my dick." He cupped the back of her head with his hand and gently drew her closer. "You suck it, and then kiss me, so I can taste my cock in your mouth." He reached out and gently caressed the silken skin behind her ear. "Kjersten, I want to fuck you right now and when I'm fucking you, I want you to look at me. See me. So you can't pretend you're fucking Odgers. You can hate fuck me if you want. I don't care... Aren't you horny?"

"You do know you're crazy, don't you?" Kjersten commented. But her heart was beating faster with his every word. Her nipples tightened and her sex was hot and heavy with lust. "This is totally messed up."

"Don't you want to fuck me now?" He leaned closer to her still, moving his hands up and down her body, arousing her.

"But people can see in the car."

"Nah, the windows are tinted too dark. It's too bad. But I'd like to have someone watch us fuck. I'd like Odgers to watch us fuck. Wouldn't that be hot?" Then, he was kissing her, thrusting his tongue into her mouth, and Kjersten's eyes shut. His gripped her breast firmly and then roughly manipulated her nipple through her bra. She groaned and covered his hand with her own. He reached down between her legs to cup and then grip her cunt. In spite of her anger, or maybe because of it, she thrust her crotch into his grip, a move which seemed to send electric currents shooting up through her. She pushed his shirt aside and bit into the thick chord of his trapezius. That made him even wilder. He reached up and shoved her bra up, exposing the white mounds of her breasts. With the other hand, he unsnapped his pants, pulled his engorged penis out and then pressed her head down towards his crotch. "Suck it."

She licked the swollen head and tasted the pearl of semen beading it. Then, she gripped the base of his cock with her hand, tongued his cock up and down, and began to stroke and suck him simultaneously.

He thrust against her, into her mouth, gently but firmly holding her head to his cock. "I can't take it. I want to fuck you. I have to fuck you."

Nearly growling, he pressed her back into the car seat. He reached away from her and flipped the seat back so it was reclined. Near crazed with hunger, he waited for a moment while she unsnapped her pants jerked them down her hips and off her legs. He reached for his back pocket, pulled out a condom and pressed it into her hand. As turned on as he was, Kjersten tore it open with her teeth and sheathed his cock. He pressed her back into the seat and moved over her, shoving his jeans further down. Now, he jerked her legs up around his neck, and then thrust into her. She screamed and nearly came up off the car seat. But he held her shoulders pinned down. His eyes were closed and he thrust into her slowly, ever so slowly.

"Touch yourself," he demanded. "Your tits and your clit. Make yourself come for me."

The savagery of it, the way he was thrusting into her, the heat and weight of him set her on fire. It was sex, pure and brutal. He was so large hammering into her, she was nearly coming apart. But when he pressed her fingers to her clitoris, it was all over. She touched her clitoris, moving it in small circles that had her nearly crying from pleasure. "Harder!" she demanded. "Grab my tits."

Pulling back and out, he ignored her moan of protest. "I want to fuck you from behind." He flipped her over to her stomach, pulled her body up so she was draped over the back of the seat, hips up and thrust hard into her.

She nearly came then and there, and for a second, her vision darkened. Sensations overwhelmed her, the near claustrophobia of the tight car and the upholstery against her bare knees, then the smell, heat, size of him, stretching her, pounding into her. She came hard and fast, screaming her triumph as he came nearly at the same time. Thrusting, he gripped her hips, pressing ever deeper into her.

"Fuck," he muttered collapsing on her.

"Wow," she muttered from her position over the back of the seat.

But then, he didn't say anything else. After a moment, he pulled out of her, slid the condom off, opened the car door and dropped it outside, then fell back into his own seat. There, he fiddled with his jeans, pulling them up. Without saying a word, he snapped his pants and then, putting the key in the ignition, he started the engine.

Kjersten slid down into the seat, tilting it up straight, then struggled to pull her jeans back on in the moving car. "What's wrong?" She asked, not sure what to make of Cam's behavior.

"Nothing," he muttered. Finally, he glanced over at her. "Were you so turned on because you were thinking about him? Is Odger's cock bigger than mine?"

"Way to kill the moment," Kjersten finally replied, swallowing the lump that had risen in her throat and the tears that threatened. "I thought… No, never mind."

Then, there was nothing more to be said, just the ride home to her parents' house which passed in an awkward silence.

They parted with few words between them.

* * * *

Early the next morning, Cam eased his Camaro up the Solheim's long, narrow driveway. It was palely bright, a cool sort of morning that he associated with the football camps that he'd attended during the summers of high school. He didn't mind early mornings. In truth, he'd always liked the gentle hesitancy of the day before it turned darker yellow and heated up. He liked the feeling that he was getting the jump on people, getting things done. Now, he was ready to pick up Kjersten and get out of Eagle River.

He came to a stop in a clearing before a lodge-like A frame house that was dominated by a glassed front. The landscaping was done in a discreet way to complement the woodsy feel of the home. Cam had been inside the Solheim residence for the first time for dinner the night before. He, Cam Fawst, whose father had ditched him and whose mother had slutted her way around Eagle River throughout his childhood, was dating the richest man in town's daughter and having dinner at their house. Cam had expected that it would feel like he was getting somewhere in his life.

Unfortunately, the whole evening, even before the fair fiasco, had been a disappointment. The house hadn't even been as he'd expected it to be. He had imagined it would be bigger, showier, and more extravagant. The place was nice, but also comfortable and lived in. The Solheims, themselves, had been rather like their home, pleasant, but distant and restrained. Cam had felt out of place with no idea of what to talk about. That is until Kjersten's little brother, Soren, had asked him about football and the Coyotes. He was very comfortable talking about those two subjects.

Cam had been relieved when the evening was over. He hadn't liked reliving that feeling of not fitting in. Now, he waited in the car, not wanting to go to the door. Impatiently, he revved the engine. *Kjersten said she'd be ready.* After a moment, the carved wooden door with the leaded glass etchings swung open. The end of a duffel bag was the first object to appear followed by a long, shapely, denim clad leg. Kjersten reached back and pulled the door closed behind her. She walked quickly over to the car.

"Throw the bag in back," Cam ordered through his half opened window. The hatch popped open with a hiss and a click. Silently, she hurled the duffel bag into the trunk and firmly pressed it closed. She opened the passenger side door and climbed in.

"Let's get out of here."

"I still don't understand why we have to leave so early," Kjersten commented.

"Why? You hoping to see Odgers again?" he demanded suspiciously.

"No. Why can't you let that go? You're the one with the hang up here. Not me. Fine. Let's just get out of here. I'm so done with you right now." The aftermath of their sexual interlude hung heavy between them. "You were the one who brought up that angry sex thing. I just went along with it. So, I totally don't understand why you got so pissed off. If you can't handle it, don't bring it up. I'm so done with you right now."

For the briefest moment, a look of sheer panic flashed over Cam's handsome features. *I don't want to be alone. Not again.* Then, the mask came up again and the smooth charmer attempted to regain control of the situation. "Don't look at me like that, baby. We had a fight." He reached out and took her hand. "You mean so much to me. I get jealous. Sure, it turned me on, but it also made me crazy. We have a good thing going here, you know that, don't you? You're my dream girl. I just couldn't handle it that you were panting after that Odgers kid."

She gripped the car door handle. "I wasn't panting after him. I was at the fair with you, but if you're going to start obsessing about that again, I'll find another ride back to Madison."

"Kjersten, don't be like this. Just stay in the car. I didn't mean it. You know that." Cam's voice grew soft and vulnerable. "Kristy, you know I care about you. Knowing you were with that guy… I freaked out because you mean so much to me."

She hesitated.

Cam could see her lip trembling and pressed his advantage. "You know I need you, baby. We need each other."

He watched as she swallowed hard. He could see the tears building up in her eyes. Cam reached over then and drew her to him. He held her close and stoked her long hair tenderly. "You know we have something special here. I just don't want to lose you."

Kjersten began to sob and buried her face against his shoulder.

"Come on, babe. We're okay. You know how it is, the two of us against the world. Come on now. Get it together. We should get out of here before your family wakes up." Sensing that tide was now going his way, he disengaged himself from Kjersten.

Slowly, she reached to engage her seat belt.

Cam revved the engine and then smoothly slipped into gear. "Let's put this behind us. I'm glad to be getting an early start this morning. Two days in this town is more than enough… I just gotta make one stop over at the diner."

"I don't want to stop anywhere right now, Cam. Let's just get going."

"You just wait in the car. I promised Sal I'd drop by the bar today, and drop off an autographed Coyotes' football, but I don't want to wait around until the afternoon either. So, I thought I'd drop the football off with Gene at the diner."

"That's nice of you," she said and nodded, in agreement.

"Sal and Gene were good to me growing up."

Moments later, they pulled up in front of Green Eggs N' Ham, Gene's diner, which sat directly across the street from the Court'n House, Sal's Bar. The arrangement suited the two business owners well as they were best friends.

"I'll be just a minute." Leaving the car idling in front of the diner, he made his way up to the door. He swung the glass door wide, accompanied by the timpani of sled bells that announced his arrival. Cam found them annoyingly loud and cheerful for so early in the morning. Inside, the diner was still with that Sunday morning, small town peacefulness just before the morning after church rush. The pleasant aroma of dark, rich coffee hung in the air. There was also a tantalizing hint of bacon sizzling on the grill.

"Cam. Cam Fawst." A petite but very pregnant blond in a waitress uniform was moving his way, smiling at him. She looked vaguely familiar, but he couldn't place her. "How are you doing?" The girl oozed enthusiasm and perkiness. "It's so good to see you. It's been forever."

Where was Sal? Who was this chick? This whole thing was taking way too long. It was what you get for trying to do something nice. Still, Cam smiled, unleashing the easy, masculine charm that was his social face. "Honey, could you go back to the kitchen and grab Gene for me?"

"You don't recognize me, do you? I'm Hannah. Remember?" She smiled suggestively and the flash of dimples, the greenish eyes, and the honey blond hair took Cam back to his sixteenth birthday, his sophomore year of high school.

"Hannah. Of course. I remember. The rocket pops." He grinned roguishly. "I remember quite a lot." She had been his birthday present. He had a mental image of a lithe Hannah stripped down to nothing but a pink thong with a bow tied right over the sweet curve of her bottom. After that night, he had called her up, even seen her a couple of times. Then, he'd moved on. She hadn't gotten the message. She'd kept following him around with those sad, puppy dog eyes. That had gotten old real quick. Vaguely, he recalled seeing her with some corn fed farm boy after that.

"Looks like you've been keeping busy since graduation," he said, glancing at her belly.

"Luke and I got married right after graduation," she said, her face beaming. "This'll be our second baby. We already have a year-old girl. Caty's her name. You remember Luke, right?"

Cam had a mental image of a beefy blond guy. "Lineman?"

"Yes. He'll be so pleased that you remember him." She smiled again, seemingly content to chat the morning away.

"Could I get you to grab Gene for me, Hannah? I'm in kind of a rush."

"Oh sure. I'm sorry."

"It was good catching up," he lied glibly. He heard a familiar male voice rumbling somewhere in back. "Gene? Gene? Come on out here," he called out impatiently. *You'd think the guy was performing brain surgery back there.*

"Cool your jets. I'm coming." Gene, the proprietor of the diner, appeared. He was thin, wiry and weathered as always and carrying an overflowing plate of scrambled eggs, sausage, toast, and hash browns. He placed the plate before a down-on-his-luck-looking fellow who sat up at the lunch counter.

"Here you go, Mike. Just the way you like it."

Gene moved out from around the counter and offered Cam his hand and a big grin. "Cam, I didn't know it was you out here. It's been quite a while. I hear you've been doing real good down in Milwaukee."

Cam leaned closer to Gene. "You should check if that guy can pay you before you feed him," he whispered to Gene.

"Nope, none of that for me, boy," Gene chuckled. "I believe that the good Lord intended for folks to look after each other."

"Whatever works for you, man. Anyway, I stopped by to drop this off for Sal," Cam handed Gene a bag. "Could you give it to him, and tell him that I had to get back early this morning?"

"He'll be disappointed that he didn't get to see you in the flesh. Feels like a football. Can I take a look?"

Cam nodded.

"Let's see. My, it's an autographed Coyote football. Sal will be thrilled to get a hold of this!"

"Just paying back an old debt. My mom finally told me that you and Sal paid my football registration until I got into high school. You guys didn't have to do that."

A blush bloomed in Gene's leathery cheeks. "You weren't supposed to find out. It wasn't a big deal or anything. You were a kid who deserved to play ball."

"Well, it meant a lot to me. Thank you."

"You made my day, Cam," Gene commented as he admired the ball.

"Yeah, well, I gotta go now. Get on the road."

Gene glanced curiously first at Cam and then at the idling car which he could see through the diner windows. "You and your lady got special plans for today or something? You're with Kjersten Solheim, right?"

Cam nodded, already backing towards the door. "Something like that. Thanks Gene. See ya."

"It was good seeing you, Cam. You don't come home near enough."

"Well, goodbye." He made his way out of the diner without looking back.

Chapter Five

The Pride of Eagle River

~ Galen ~

Galen realized that he was awake, had been for several minutes. He turned to face the clock, five of seven. Kyle had let him sleep in, and he'd slept hard, and felt groggy and heavy as a result. The light that eased in through the shutters was a gentle yellow-gray. His left leg tingled with pins and needles. Slowly, he moved it, only to find that it was buried under the dead weight of Heidi, the Odgers' ancient boxer. Heidi turned her head and gazed at Galen soulfully with her dark eyes.

"All right, Heidi." He stroked the silky head. "Two more minutes." The dog rested her chin back down on the coverlet. Galen lay still, savoring the peacefulness of the morning and the decadent sensation of sleeping in.

The house was absolutely silent, but that wasn't unusual in and of itself anymore. Kyle was never around and Pop wasn't exactly a talkative kind of guy. The old house only felt like a home when Sandra and Joe and their brood stopped by.

His mother always said that "morning was the time to face reality," to deal with life. So, Galen dwelled on the events that had transpired the previous evening. *I handled it all wrong. I didn't even talk to her. The break up was my fault. But why did she have to get together with Cam Fawst?* The thought that she might actually love Cam Fawst twisted and coiled in his gut. He couldn't stand thinking of Cam's hands on her, touching her.

Shit happens. Whole mountain ranges of it. Sometimes it seemed as if Galen's whole life had gone to shit. *We've been through so much together. I don't want to lose her as a friend. Maybe I already have.* He longed desperately to speak with her. *I gotta speak with her, even though it's too late.* There was nothing that he could say or do that could take anything that had happened back. *Still, I gotta talk to her. I just can't let it go like this. I can let her leave Eagle River with it so messed up between us.*

Resolved, Galen got up and threw some clothes on.

He found the kitchen as disastrous as usual, the used microwave trays from the previous evening lay crusty on the kitchen counter while some dirty dishes were stacked in the sink. Jim Odgers sat reading the previous day's *Eagle River Eagle Eye* at the kitchen table, oblivious to the chaos and filth around him.

"Mornin', Pop."

"Morning. There's coffee in the pot."

Pleasantly surprised to find the coffee made, Galen dug around in the cupboard until he located a clean mug. He poured himself some of the coal black, acidic, jet fuel that passed as coffee to his father. "After the milking, I'm gonna go into town for a while."

His father didn't respond.

He could tell that the old man had had another rough night of it. This morning, his eyes were bloodshot and his expression more hangdog than usual. *Wonder where he hid the booze this time?*

"What's going on in town that's so all fired important this time of morning?" Jim still didn't look up from his paper. Galen saw that he was reading the obituaries.

"I want… I need to talk to a girl. Before she leaves."

"Some girl can't wait until chores are done?" Jim didn't look up as he turned the page of his newspaper.

You could do some chores, Galen reflected. *Then it wouldn't be an issue.* But his father had shut down on life long ago, and that wasn't going to change any time soon. "Kjersten Solheim."

The only sign that Jim had registered what his son had said was a brief raise of his eyebrows. His chin moved slowly down as he scanned the Classifieds. *Not that he would ever take a job. No, Pa can sit around the house all day moping while we work like dogs. He always said he'd "earned the right." Sure.*

"Your Mom always did like that girl… Haven't seen much of her around here lately." He turned another page.

"I guess so."

"Where's she going to school?"

"Milwaukee University."

The two men, one old, one young, sat in silence, sipping coffee. It should have been a peaceful moment, but it wasn't. It was electric with unspoken words and tension. After a moment, Galen got up and put some water on for oatmeal.

"You want something to eat, Pop?"

Finally, Jim looked up from his paper. "I ate that crap almost every day for the twenty some years your mother and I were together 'cause she said it was good for me. Now she's dead, and there ain't any point in worrying about what's good for me and what ain't."

Galen glanced at his father in surprise. *The old man was being downright talkative.* "Can I have the Sports Page?"

"Go ahead." Jim pushed the remaining sections of newspaper over.

Galen located the section he wanted and began to read.

"You and that Solheim girl used to go together, right?"

"Yeah." Galen listened unsure of where this was going.

"Didn't work out for you, did it?"

"Nope." Just hearing the words spoken out loud made him angry and hurt at the same time.

"That's what I thought," Jim smirked. "Don't waste your time on women. They just let you down."

Galen wasn't one to stand by and hear his mother insulted, especially by his worthless father. "You're the one who let Mom down. Ever since the accident."

"Jessica left me before the accident. You think you're so smart. Did you know that? The only reason we didn't get divorced was because I was in such bad shape."

"Mom took care of you for years."

"She didn't treat me like a husband ever after that."

"Maybe 'cause you didn't act like one."

"Don't you disrespect me! That's somethin' else she taught you."

I am so done with this conversation. Without another word, the younger Odgers finished his breakfast, made some futile efforts at straightening the kitchen, and then headed out to the milking parlor to give Kyle a hand.

The two brothers finished up about two hours later. Then, Galen showered, changed, and drove into town, to the Solheims.

As he pulled into the long driveway, George Strait's "Famous Last Words of a Fool" was playing on the radio. He clicked the radio off. He didn't need a poignant, tear jerker of a song to make things worse. Just driving the familiar driveway was enough to bring back the memories of the countless times that he'd biked up this same driveway to this same house. *I wish I could make it right. I gotta make it right.*

He paused for a moment and stared up at the house. *Are they still asleep?* He took a deep breath, opened his truck door, jogged up the steps leading to the front door and rang the bell.

No one came to the door.

He listened for a sound from within. *Nothing.* He rang the bell a second time. Glancing nervously at his watch, he shifted his feet. Still, no one came. He'd turned to go back down the steps when the front door swung open. Mr. Solheim stepped out. Nick Solheim remained the tall, slender, elegant man he'd been since he'd come to town years before. But this morning, he looked tired and care worn. He reached up and smoothed the still thick, white hair back from his brow. He didn't look happy to see Galen, but he didn't look upset either.

"Mr. Solheim, good morning." Galen held out his hand.

"Galen," Solheim said and took the proffered hand. "I've been reading about your exploits a lot these days in the Eagle Eye. You've become the pride of Eagle River."

"Thanks, sir," Galen responded awkwardly. "I'm really sorry to bother you so early in the morning."

Solheim waited for Galen to continue, then said, "I was already up. Is there something that I can do for you this morning?"

"I… I wanted to speak with Kjersten. Is she around?"

Mr. Solheim's face shifted, was troubled for a moment. "She's already gone back to school. She left early this morning."

"Oh." His heart sank. "I thought maybe she'd come home for the weekend."

"So did we. Apparently, she had to return earlier than she had originally planned. I'm sure that her mother will speak with her this evening, would you like her to deliver a message for you?"

"No. That's all right. Maybe I'll give her a call or something."

Mr. Solheim retreated back over the threshold to the door. "It was good to see you, Galen. I understand that your college prospects are looking good."

"Thanks, sir. Well, yeah. I gotta get back. Thanks again."

"Good bye now."

Galen turned and walked back to his truck, opened the door and climbed in. *Kjersten was already gone and I didn't get a chance to talk to her. I was too late, again.*

* * * *

The Court'n House bar and restaurant opened at noon on every Sunday. By twelve thirty, when the obligations of church and family breakfast had been satisfied, a decent crowd invariably formed to watch the afternoon's sporting events.

Sal moved slowly, decorously, like a reigning monarch through his hazy, smoke-filled domain. He greeted everyone assembled at the round tables by name, as he gracefully navigated his bulk around in such a way as to avoid blocking any view of the big screen.

Ben shouldered his way to the end of the bar. "Sal?"

"What can I do for you, Benny?"

"Could I please use your phone for just a minute?"

Sal went over and rummaged behind the bar again. He set a black touch tone out in front of Ben. "Here you go. You didn't forget the rules, did ya, college boy?"

"No long distance and under two minutes," Ben recited. "I remember. Thanks." He picked up the receiver and dialed the Odgers' number.

"Odgers."

"Hello?" Ben asked.

"Yeah."

"Galen, it's me. The Twins game starts in half an hour. Get over here."

"You're shouting in my ear."

"Sorry. They have the pregame show blasting here." Ben pressed his hand against his ear not pressed against the receiver.

"I don't know if I'm up for it today, Ben."

"Come on, Galen. Everyone's here. You should stop by. I'm only going to be in town for a couple days."

There was silence for a long moment. "Okay. I gotta couple of chores to finish up then I'll be over."

It was early in the third inning when Galen finally showed up at Sal's. His buzz cut blond-brown hair was still damp from the shower. He wore a faded blue t-shirt on which the Copenhagen tobacco emblem had faded to almost a memory. His neatly pressed but washed out and patched Wranglers defined his long, muscled legs.

"Glad you made it, Galen," Ben commented when his friend appeared at the bar.

"You could have saved me a seat."

"You know how it works." Ben gestured to the men sitting on both sides of him. Both had pitchers of beer on the bar before them. "A root beer drinker doesn't have much say here."

"Gotcha." Galen leaned up against the bar.

"Galen boy, we haven't seen much of you lately," Sal commented. "The only way I hear about what you're doings is by talking to that brother of yours, or to one of his lady friends. What can I get you?" Sal's ears and bald head were red and glowing from frequent trips to the kitchen and his shirt sleeves were rolled up to reveal his hairy, black forearms.

Galen's face eased into the familiar crooked, wide, one dimpled grin that Ben remembered from their childhood but that had been scarce in recent months. "I could really use one of your Sunday specials with the secret sauce."

Sal took a step back and bellowed through the swinging door that led to the kitchen: "Another special, Maria."

"And another one for me, Sal," Ben called out.

"Maria, make that two… Happe, you want the sauce?"

"Please."

While they waited, the two friends sat and watched the baseball game.

"You heading back to Milwaukee soon?" Galen finally asked.

"Next Wednesday. Mom and Dad are taking me down."

"Here you go, guys." Sal appeared with two plates filled with his trademark hot beef sandwiches and fries.

"Thanks, Sal."

"So good," Ben moaned in anticipation before he sunk his teeth into the layers of soft roast beef.

"Whole game been like this?" Galen muttered between mouthfuls.

"Yeah. Twins suck this year. Don't you ever read the paper or watch the news?"

"It's baseball," Galen countered. "Besides, no one is whacked out about stats as you are." Contemplatively, he toyed with a large batter dipped fry in his ketchup. "Kjersten took off early this morning."

"That's what I heard." Ben studied his friend's deliberately blank expression.

"I stopped by the Solheims. I wanted to talk to her. Wish I knew why she took off so quickly."

"Cam probably wanted to get going. He always thought that this town is a hole. He just came back to show us all what a big man he is now. And as far as Kjersten goes, well, what can I say?"

Galen glared at Ben. "What? What were you going to say?"

"You won't want to hear it."

"No, go ahead."

"You want me to be honest with you?"

Galen nodded.

"You never gave Kjersten a chance. After everything, I mean. She's my friend, too. I don't like that she's dating that jerk. But you ended things with her. You shut her out."

"You mean after Mom died," Galen stated flatly, his voice calm and noncommittal. He wouldn't meet Ben's gaze.

"I should have said something then, but you were all clammed up. You didn't want anyone hanging around you, including me. What did you expect her to do? Sit around and wait until you got your head worked out?"

Galen said nothing, just fiddled with his straw in his glass of pop. "I was messed up, I know. But I didn't think that she'd hook up with him. Why couldn't she just wait?"

"Wait for what? For you to decide you actually wanted to talk to her. You told her it was over, remember?" Ben observed his friend carefully. "But none of that matters now anyway. That deal is done. You've gotta get her out of your mind."

"It's just that Mr. Solheim said that he'd expected her to stay all weekend. I wonder what changed?"

"It doesn't matter. Quit thinking about her. It's too late."

Galen stared angrily across the room. He stuffed a fry in his mouth. "Why does everything have to change?" he asked morosely. "Why does everything have to go bad?"

"Look, I'm your friend and I'm going to be honest with you. This didn't just happen to you, not like your mom getting sick. That just happened. But this, you did this. You gotta let her go now. It's over." For a moment, Ben was silent.

"I know, it's just…"

Suddenly Ben reached across the table and gripped Galen's arm. "Check it out. This is just what you need."

"What?"

"There are some girls over there at a table a little off to the right. Don't make it obvious you're looking."

Galen shook his head. "Come on."

"Seriously." Ben kicked him under the table. "They're cute. The Kjersten thing is done. That ship has sailed. Get over it. Please, for me, look at them."

Galen turned his head, as if to get a better angle. He caught sight of a table of three girls who were all bent together, whispering, glancing their way.

"I met the blonde one at the fair," Ben continued. "Her name is like Sarah. I don't know any of the others, but none of them are half bad either."

Galen turned back to the TV screen, while Ben continued to glance over at the table with the three girls.

"Galen," Ben prodded his friend's shin with his toe. "They're looking over here.'"

"So?"

Ben kicked him harder now.

"Ow. Would you quit kicking me. I'm trying to watch the game."

"No, I'm serious. They're checking us out."

Galen slowly dragged his eyes away from the screen and to a sweet smile and dimples. Without thinking, because his brain had just totally shut off, he smiled back. The girl giggled and turned away to whisper in her friend's ear. Her hair was a curly brown mass that bounced and swayed with her every movement. In fact, the whole girl was bouncy. She was petite but well-rounded beneath the cropped top of her sunflower yellow T-shirt. He caught a glimpse of tanned, soft tummy when she leaned over closer to another girl. Suddenly, Ben kicked him again.

"What the heck are you doing?" He reached down to rub his shin.

"You're staring."

"They're staring, too." Galen turned back around. *The brunette was the cutest of the bunch.*

"Let's go over there," Ben whispered conspiratorially.

"No way."

"They want us to. Come on."

"I'm watching the game."

"Look. See how they keep turning our way. They want us, man."

"Uh-uh. No way."

"You've been busted. They know that we were checking them out.

Besides, this is the perfect opportunity for you to get over Kjersten. I'm going over there with or without you. Come on, Galen. I'm your best friend and I'll only be in town for the weekend. I'd do it for you. You just sit there and I'll do all the talking."

"But—"

"But, bullshit. I'm going over there with or without you."

"It's the seventh inning. You don't want to leave now."

Ben ignored Galen. His entire focus was on the table of girls. A taller auburn-haired girl grinned and gestured for him to come over. The two others dissolved into giggles.

"I'm going."

"You do that. I'm gonna finish my hot beef."

"You'll come over then, won't you?"

"Yeah, sure, Ben. All right."

In short order, Ben was on his feet and over at the girls' table. Galen took a bite and watched as Ben bent to speak to the girls. Then, he was heading back with the cute brunette in tow. Galen hurriedly wiped at his mouth with a bar napkin.

"Galen, Mallory here has something to say to you." Ben winked at Galen.

"Galen Odgers," she began, putting her hands on her hips. "I have a score to settle with you."

Galen took a sip of pop, to wash down the hot beef, which he promptly aspirated on, and blew out his nose. Ben pounded him on the back. Galen coughed, snorted, let out a burp, and then turned scarlet with mortification.

"You're all class, Galen," Ben guffawed.

"I think you must have me confused with someone else," he finally managed to respond to the girl. "I don't think that we've ever met."

"No, you're the guy who ruined my homecoming dance last year. You Warriors killed our Knights, remember?"

Galen nodded.

"My boyfriend was the captain of our football team, and he was a jerk all night because we lost so badly. So, you see, it was all your fault. You owe me," she finished with a playful smile.

"I'm sorry. I didn't mean to make problems for you and your boyfriend," he stammered, the tips of his ears now tomato red.

"Silly." Mallory leaned up against the bar right next to him, engulfing him in a cloud of some tangy, floral perfume, her leg almost touching his, the curve of her full breast just at his eye level. "I'm kidding, don't you get it? Actually, Galen," her voice grew softer and husky, "I've wanted to meet you ever since that game. All the girls in Webster did, want to meet you, that is. Why don't you come sit with us?" she suggested. "We'll be here until the end of the game."

"Sounds great," Ben said eagerly.

"Yeah," Galen echoed, rising to his feet. He followed Mallory's hair flipping saunter back over to the table. There they pulled up chairs and made introductions. They sat together for the rest of the game and for a good half hour afterwards. To his great surprise, Galen found that he was enjoying himself. The three girls laughed and smiled at whatever came out of his mouth. Ben was in rare form, telling jokes and stories.

They were all standing up to leave when Mallory grasped Galen's hand. She pressed a scrap of paper into his hand. "Call me," she mouthed as the girls wandered off.

Galen and Ben were getting up, ready to leave when Sal clapped a meaty hand on both of their shoulders. "Hey boys, have you seen my new football?"

"No," Galen answered.

Sal walked to the bar and returned carrying a football carefully. "Look at this beauty. It's autographed by all of the Great Lakes University Coyotes. Cam stopped by and left it for me."

"Can I have a look?" Ben reached for the ball eagerly. Galen stood looking on. After a moment, he shoved his hands into his pockets.

"What do you think?" Sal was puffed up with pride. "I just hope Tom stops by tonight. He'll get a kick out of this."

"That's great, Sal," Galen murmured, not even looking at the football. "I gotta get going. Say 'hi' to coach for me."

"Sure, Galen. Glad you came today."

Ben was still enthralled by the football, but looked up as Galen began to walk away. "I'll call you tonight," he directed at his friend.

Galen nodded and waved, but kept going.

"What's with him?" Sal asked.

"He's just got a lot on his mind." Ben responded.

Galen made his way out of the bar. The burnt golden, late afternoon sunlight was cleansing after the smoke-filled darkness of the Court'n House. He kicked at a pebble with a battered brown roper boot. The pebble launched a few feet then bounced several times. He stepped forward and kicked it again. He couldn't predict which way it would bounce. *Life's like that, unpredictable.* Sometimes he could forget about Kjersten for a little while, but then something always came up that remind him that she was gone. *That she was with Cam and done with him.* He leaned down, picked up a rock and whipped it as far as he could down the street. He stared after it, but didn't see or hear where it landed, then he made his way back to the truck.

Once inside, he reached over and flipped the radio on. The Nitty Gritty Dirt Band was singing about fishing in the dark. The happy rhythm tripped its way across his battered soul with sharp, puncturing, highheeled boots. Slowly, he exhaled and rolled his window down the rest of the way. The air tasted cool, crisp, and with a freshness hinting of the coming fall. Galen wasn't ready to go home yet. The song played on and he was aware of a gradual loosening in his chest, an infinitesimal easing. *Would Kjersten be easier to forget in another place, where he wasn't constantly reminded of her? Reminded that it was his own damn fault.* Suddenly, he wanted to be somewhere else, somewhere other than Eagle River, where he could forget and live a life like none of it had ever happened, where he could be someone else, someone he invented. Suddenly, his college path was clear. He was going to turn down the scholarship offer from Milwaukee University. *I'm not going to sit on the bench and watch Cam Fawst play even to be near her. Heck, that would probably make things worse. It's time to get on with my life. I'm going to be an Illinois University Bearcat.*

Chapter Six

Catching Up

~ Tom ~

The cemetery was peaceful. The plots were well spaced and most of the monuments. The plots, even the older ones, were tidy and well-tended. Wild flowers and arranged flowers moved delicately in a gentle breeze. This soft, rustling was the only sound.

Tom had always thought it was too quaint, too pretty for a cemetery. But then, he had been used to the relative anonymity of a big city graveyard where there always were a good number of neglected and forgotten plots, where some of the headstones were sunken in, or standing aslant and on some the lettering had been rendered almost unreadable with age or graffiti. He made his way slowly through the headstones that bore messages like "Harriet, Beloved Wife and Mother," and to "Tommy, You Will Always Be a Part of Us," and "Ingeborg and Oliver, Together for Eternity. We Love You, Mom and Dad." These days, he moved with a slight hitch in his step due to a rigidity in his left knee.

For Tom, the family names on some of the headstones matched with the youthful, vibrant faces of some of the players on his current football team. It was a truism of small town life, some families simply stayed put. In his years in Eagle River, Tom had grown accustomed to this and other aspects of small town life. Now, he was a part of the town, no longer just a stranger or someone simply passing through. Sure, it had its drawbacks, but this little Northern Wisconsin town was the first place where he had ever found peace, a place that felt like home. When he was young and restless or stupid, if he was honest with himself, he had never understood how people could live their whole lives in one place and know all the same people for that whole lifetime. Now, he could see a warmth, a confidence, and a sense of knowing who you are that you could derive from such a life. Tom had finally grown roots.

He sat down on the stone bench at the foot of the plot. After a moment, he leaned forward with his elbows resting on his thighs. He observed that the flowers around the edge of the grave were delicate, well-tended, and brightly cheerful. Their scent was cloyingly sweet. Tom shook his head. *Jessica had never cared for tended, tidy flowers.* His girl had always preferred natural, untamed looking flowers, the Golden Rockets that lined the highways throughout the Midwestern summer, the daisies and Queen Anne's lace that flourished in the prairie. She'd had a special fondness for great smiling sunflowers even though they were domesticated.

"They seem more alive than the other flowers," he remembered her saying. "See how they follow the sun."

He'd just smiled back at her, unsure of what to say. She often left him at a loss for words, and he didn't know a damn thing about flowers. He stood there for a few moments, just thinking about her, about them, about what had been. Then, he began to talk softly to her as was his habit.

"I'm still keeping our secret, though I'm not sure why anymore, except that Galen has already been through so much. I've kept it for nearly twenty years now… You know, keeping it is easier now. I've gotten used to it. You know if I'd had my way years ago, I would have printed it on every road sign around Eagle River, painted it on the water tower, had it announced on the radio." But these feelings were just something else that he'd had to bury with her, this woman he'd loved so much, who'd hurt him so much. Even today, he continued to sneak in and out of this cemetery, as he had in and out of her life.

"Jessica, could I tell him now? Is this the right time?" But the grave maintained its stubborn silence.

Tom rubbed at his forehead with a forefinger and a thumb. He ran his clenched fingers back through his still thick, wavy, silvering hair. "I still don't know if it was the right thing not telling all these years... Jessy." Her name on his lips was still a plaintive cry. Memories of an unforgettable day years before filled his mind. Overwhelmed, he knelt down by the side of her grave.

He'd gone out to the farm to see her after lunch on a week day while her two kids were still at school. They'd made a habit of stealing an hour together on many such afternoons. On that particular day, when she met him at the door, he handed her a bouquet of roses.

She took them and inhaled them with her eyes closed, savoring the scent.

He pushed the door closed behind him. "They're beautiful. Just like you." This time, the words, so corny and trite had been heartfelt. The red of the roses were exquisite against her red gold hair and fair, lightly freckled skin.

Her eyes opened and met his, and he was jolted again by their caramel warmth. "I can't stop thinking about you," he said.

"I don't believe you," she'd said and smiled that siren smile that drove him crazy. "I know you've been with more beautiful women. Younger women."

And he had. It was true. "But...that was before. Before I met you. And none of them compared to you." The words were heartfelt. There was an earthy sensuality to Jessica Odgers that intoxicated him. He reached a hand out, brushed back her hair, and caressed the nape of her neck. He stepped closer. "Everything changed when I met you." He took the roses from her and set them down on the table. Then, he drew her up against him, savoring the feeling of her against him, the warm cinnamon scent that was so uniquely her. Then, they were kissing, her mouth, open beneath his. He pressed her against him. She was a tall woman and his cock pressed right against the juncture of her legs.

"I want you. Now," he nearly growled the word, lost in the heat, the passion of this woman who was so right for him.

She groaned and bit him lightly on the neck. Then, there hadn't been further need for words. She shoved her panties to the ground and he'd unzipped his fly, and he'd taken her right there, fully dressed, standing up, with her back pressed against the wall behind her and her feet supporting her, flat against the wall on the other side of the narrow hall. He'd fucked her hard, and she'd met him stroke for stroke, grinding up against him and it had been glorious.

Afterwards, they slid down the wall, and he had held on to her, tenderly cradling her in his arms.

"You're going to come away with me, right?"

She'd nodded. "I'll tell the kids tonight."

"Will your ex care?"

She'd snorted, a short unladylike sound. "Jim only cares about his next drink."

"Even if we take the kids with us?"

"I don't really care. He hasn't thought about Sandra or Kyle or me in years. It's been over between us since just after Kyle was born. He's a sick man. I feel bad about it, sure, but I can't let him bring all of us down."

"Have you told him about us?"

"Not yet. But the paper work for the divorce should be done in a week or so. Then, it will be finished, and remember I kicked him out long before I met you."

"Then, let's go out tonight. Bring the kids. We'll celebrate."

Tom flinched against the pain of that memory. That had been the last time that he had ever made love with Jessica. It had also been the last time that they had ever discussed a future together. For, that same afternoon, an inebriated Jim Odgers had driven his truck into a telephone pole, nearly killing himself and inflicting serious damage to his brain and his body. That single act had changed everything for Jessica and for Tom. Jim had been in a coma for months while Jessica had continued to run the farm. Months later, when it became apparent that Jim would never be able to live on his own, Jessica had irrevocably broken things off with Tom, even though she was visibly pregnant with his child.

Chapter Seven

What Goes Around Comes Around

~ Cam ~

Cam tossed his keychain up and down as he sauntered into the alley just behind the bar, the Nasty Habit. He glanced up at the apartment window where he'd spent a handful of nights over the past few months, but the lights were off.

He'd parked the Camaro a couple of blocks away, as was usual. *Don't want word to get out about me being here. Don't want Kjersten to find out about Cat. It really was Kjersten's fault any way. I wouldn't have hooked up with Cat at the bar that night if Kjersten hadn't been giving me the cold, icy treatment since coming back from that weekend in Eagle River.*

"Why don't you ever just park on the alley?" Cat had asked him once as they lay naked together on the couch in her tiny apartment which was over the bar where she worked. She was tall, lean, with great legs, short red hair, some tattoos and she always wore black. *It was her legs in those skin tight, black leggings that did it for me that first time.* He hadn't been able to stop thinking about them wrapped around his waist. *Besides, Kjersten was being such a bitch. Still I don't want anyone who knows me to see it here.* The black car was kind of conspicuous with its vanity plate that read "GOLDN ARM."

"I'm not just a booty call, for you, am I?" she'd asked as she threw one long leg over his waist, straddling his naked body.

Dumb bitch. Of course you are. What do you expect? So, he distracted her by nibbling on her full lower lip. She was a good, uncomplicated fuck when he needed one, when he needed to get his rocks off, and couldn't deal with Kjersten. He'd been with her four or five times in recent weeks and on this particular night, he enjoyed the anticipation of heading up to her apartment over the bar. *Cat gets that it's just sex. She gets it.*

He was exactly on time as usual. That could sometimes be a problem, because she tended to be late. It was her thing and it drove him nuts. But this time, it seemed that she was ready for him. The door to the apartment was unlocked and Cam caught the pungent scent of an earthy incense as he swung it wide.

"Cat?" he called.

There was no answer. *She should be home.* He'd called her an hour before, told her that he needed to see her. But she hadn't agreed at first.

"I have things to do this evening."

"I can think of things we can do to each other," he'd replied teasingly.

"Tonight doesn't work for me. I have some studying I want to get done."

"Why? Come on, baby. I want you. Tonight." He didn't take Cat taking classes seriously. *Maybe she had some other guy over. No, not likely.* His arrogance dismissed that aberrant thought.

"Look, I've got work and school going on. You can't just call me and expect me to drop everything because you want to get laid."

"Why are you being like this?" He was getting irritated. "I thought that we have fun together."

"Fine. All right. I'll see you tonight," she had agreed, albeit reluctantly.

"Cat. Babe, where are you?" Cam closed the door slowly, his voice barely audible over Janis Joplin's wailing. There were two candles lit on the coffee table. By them, he saw a dark shape move away from the cloaking shadows of the long curtains that covered the French doors that led out onto the small, rusted balcony. *She was here. She certainly knew how to set the stage,* Cam observed with satisfaction. "Cat, I've dreamed of you these past few nights. I want you, Cat." He moved a step farther into the room.

"Stop," she ordered abruptly, still no more than a shadow. "Don't move."

Her husky voice turned him on. *This is hot.*

"Cat." He moved closer. He still couldn't make out her face in the dimness of the room, but he could see her tall, long shape just beyond the small couch.

"I'm going to fuck you right there on that couch."

"You have no patience." She purred the words. "It's been a while, so I want to enjoy this." She moved into the soft dome of light cast by the candles. She was wearing a black tank top with no bra, short shorts, and was barefoot.

Cam inhaled deeply when she slid her hands down her narrow ribcage to her hips, where she rested them. She moved a step closer to Cam. "Is this what you want, Cam?" Her whispered words excited him. She took a step closer still.

"Well, you aren't getting a thing." Suddenly, her voice was shrill and angry. "Bill, Terry, you wanta help me with this garbage?"

Suddenly, the overhead light flicked on and two body-builder sized bouncers from the bar downstairs stepped into the room.

"What the hell do you think I am? Your whore?"

Still stunned by the abrupt reversal in the situation, Cam started to back up, but the two bouncers moved up behind him and grabbed his arms.

"What's going on? What the hell do you think you're doing?" Belatedly, he began to struggle, and he was a strong guy, but the two steroid-filled meatheads held him with relative ease.

"You wanta know, you piece of shit? You call me and say you want to see me. You think that I'm dirt, that you're some big, fancy quarterback." Cat got right up in his face. "I know you've got some other girlfriend. Does she know you've been coming over here? You don't call me, except when you want to get off and that shit doesn't fly with me." She was livid and she open handed him hard across the face.

"Cat, you've got it all wrong. Get these guys out of here and let's talk." He grunted as the one on his left began to twist his arm. *Not my throwing arm.*

"No way. You blew it. Game over. Now you get the hell out of here and don't come back. I made a mistake with you, but that's over now. I learn from my mistakes. You should, too." With her hand in a claw, Cat reached out towards his crotch. Cam, guessing her intent, tried to pinch his legs tightly together. But she expertly grabbed his balls and twisted hard. "I'm so done with you." She relished the way the color drained from his skin, but he didn't cry out. "Get him out of here, boys."

Cam fought the waves of nausea that swamped him as the two goons dragged him down the steps and back into the alley. He didn't struggle. The truth was that he didn't know if he could have made it down the stairs, or even stood up without some help, his balls were hurting so badly. Predictably, when they got him out the back door and into the ally, the bouncers worked him over, punched into his body, his chest. Cam couldn't breathe. Uppercut. Another right, straight to the abdomen. He rolled onto his stomach, tucking his throwing arm underneath. *Protect the arm. Don't let them break it.* Then, the world exploded into jagged shards of red and black.

Chapter Eight

Reflections

~ Kjersten ~

Kjersten sat curled up on her bed and picked up the mystery novel that she'd started the night before. After rereading the same paragraph three or four times, she set it back down. Her mind was going a mile a minute, spinning in circles. *Should I call Cam? No, I don't really want to talk to him.* Things were awkward between them, had been since the trip to Eagle River. The truth was that she didn't really want to see him.

But Cam was right. I was looking at Galen at the fair.

Still, that didn't justify Cam being a dick. *I looked, but I didn't do anything about it.* The argument spun round and round in her head, until though she knew it was the wrong thing to do, because she felt guilty, she picked up the phone. She dialed Cam's number, there was a click and then a "Hi." Cam's voice rang out over the line.

"Hi, Cam..."

"I'm out right now," the message continued. "But leave a message, and if you're lucky, I'll get back to you."

Kjersten slammed the receiver down and stared at the phone. *I should have known. He was almost never at home at night.* He always had some glib excuse about where he'd been, working out or with the guys, but she knew that Cam didn't have a lot of close guy friends. Everyone wanted to know him or be seen with him, but he managed to keep himself somewhat aloof, to not really belong to any one group. This had endeared him to her. Sometimes, he did seem like a lonely, little boy.

He's probably seeing someone else. But the thought didn't bother her as much as it should have. She realized that it was actually a relief not to have to see him. *Grim thought.* She had never been one to take cheating lying down by any means. She had always been very possessive when it came to Galen, her only other real boyfriend. Thinking about it, she had also been far more sexual with Galen than she was currently with Cam. She'd actually been quite horny. They'd worn each other out. But not anymore. What had happened to her? *When had sex become a chore?*

And it wasn't just Cam. *It's not like he's a bad lover.* It was something with her, too. She remembered that at first with Cam it had been fireworks and earthquakes. But not anymore, not in quite a while. The truth was that she just didn't get into it with Cam. It was something to be gotten through and then lay on the bed awkward, wary, wondering what he was thinking, and, as she admitted for the first time, hoping that he wouldn't stay the night. *We never know what to say to each other afterwards.* Unfortunately, that often ruined the act, itself.

Impulsively, she went down on her knees beside the bed. She pulled out a plastic box from underneath her bed. She opened it up. It held a couple of framed photographs of her family members and some high school shots. There was one of Ben, Galen, and herself, arm in arm, at her graduation. *So much has changed.* Kjersten set it aside. She had brought them with her from her home to adorn her dorm room. For the first few months, they had, even after she and Galen had broken up. The pictures had come down when Cam had entered her life. He had taken the pictures down, tossed them on her desk. "It feels like all of Eagle River is watching us," he'd said.

There was an element of truth to it, so Kjersten had dutifully left the pictures down and then put them away, but after that the room never felt like her own. *That was the start of the compromising.*

Next, she pulled out a thin stack of opened letters that Galen had written to her during her high school years when she'd been away at summer camp or for spring break in Vale or Aspen. It still hurt too much to read them. Next, she removed a couple of newspaper clippings and a folded magazine. It was a *Wisconsin State Journal*. The cover shot was of Galen, his arm was drawn back in the classic quarterback pose, his face was lean and determined, and his eyes, targeted on some distant receiver. Finally, there was a dried corsage. She held it in her hand, running her fingers along the pink satin ribbon. It slid smoothly through her fingers. It was from their first dance together, at that long ago homecoming. *That first dance. The first time they'd held each other.*

Chapter Nine

Anticipation

~ Galen ~

The day had finally arrived. Galen had thought about, dreamed of it for so long, it didn't seem possible that it was finally here. The Eagle River Warriors were set to play in the Division Two State High School Championship game in Camp Randall in Madison against the Milwaukee Jefferson Wildcats. It was by no means a perfect day for football. The November afternoon was chilly and the overcast sky promised rain.

The night before, when Coach Murray had walked his team through the gates of the storied football stadium for their pregame practice, Galen's heart had pounded.

"I can't believe that we're going to play here!" Troy Kendy, one of the Eagle River receivers who was frankly impressed, voiced Galen's own thoughts.

"This place is huge," one of the other boys echoed. "And there's going to be TV stations here, too. Think about how many people are going to see us play."

"This is where the B-b-badgers p-p-play," Seamus Duffy, whose stuttering worsened significantly whenever he was nervous, managed to get out.

"No shit, Sherlock. You must be some kind of genius or something," Troy mocked. "Hey, Galen, you'll probably play a game here next year when you're a Bearcat. I woulda chosen the Badgers myself. Who wouldn't want to be a Badger?"

Galen didn't respond. *Be cool.* He was very aware of Tom Murray's eyes on him. *The rest of the team is losing it. I gotta keep it together. Be a leader.*

"You boys can drop the ball here as well as anywhere else," Coach Murray stated flatly. "All I see is a football stadium. You're football players, here to do a job. We're not some damn tourists. So, quit gawking around. Yeah, this stadium is big, but you boys gotta remember we're here to do a job. You know what the Badgers do here? They play football. There isn't any magic to it. What are we here to do?"

No one answered.

"I said, what are we here to do?" Murray's voice grew loud and commanding.

"Play football." A few desultory voices responded.

"I can't hear you."

"Play football!" This time, the voices were loud and clear.

"All right then. You boys remember that. I won't put up with any star struck bullshit from any of you. Do any of you corn fed farm boys get what I am telling you?"

There were a few nods here and there. Galen just stared silently around at Camp Randall.

"Just remember, boys. People come here to play football. If you're here as spectators, then you're wasting my time and yours, and I'm going to be pissed that whole four hour ride home. It's good we're here today to get the gawking over with. Let's go do the grand tour."

Most of the boys eagerly trooped off after Tom. Galen, alone, remained standing where he was. He allowed the strap from his bag to roll off his shoulder. The bag dropped to the ground, and he pivoted about, taking it all in. The red brick walls, the fields, the stands. Exhaling slowly, he tugged at his Vikings baseball cap. *Would Kjersten come to the game? Please, God, let her come and please let me play great.* His next thought was less charitable, *Cam Fawst never made it to a State Championship Game in high school.* He shook his head. *All this stuff is making me crazy.* He couldn't let his family and Coach Murray down, and he wouldn't let Eagle River down. *Keep your head clear. Be focused. Forget about Kjersten and Cam.*

"Hey Galen," Troy called to him from the tunnel to the locker room. "Coach wants you down here now. You aren't going to believe

* * * *

Cam shifted in his stadium seat. "Kjersten, I still don't understand why you'd want to come to a high school football game in this crappy weather."

"It's the State Championship game. Everyone from Eagle River is here, today," Kjersten beamed, waving to another friend. "It's awesome."

In response, he grunted. He glared up at the sky from which a misty rain was beginning to fall. "I can think of about a hundred places that I would rather be."

"Come on, you love football."

"Playing it, not watching high school kids."

"High school kids from your home town, and you asked to come. Hi Lauren! Hi Maddie!" Kjersten waved to friends from Eagle River. "I'm going to go talk to them, okay?" She glanced over at him with some concern.

"Yeah. Sure," Cam decided to let her off the hook. Today was the first time that they'd been out together since Cat and her goons had beaten him up. Afterwards, Cam had lain low for a few days, claimed he'd had the flu. He'd stayed out of the weight room and out of public until his face had looked normal. *Thankfully, I wasn't seriously hurt. That would have sucked.* He hadn't pressed charges or pursued it in any way. Doing so would have brought him some seriously negative attention from the press. *But Kjersten hadn't called, not once, the whole week. Things are going south with her, too.* This was why he'd called her, because now that he was losing her, he wanted to hold on. She'd blown off his invitations at first, but when he'd called on this particular morning, she'd mentioned that she was going to the Eagle River and Milwaukee Jefferson game and he said he was, too. Once he said that, there was no way that she could gracefully back out of going with him.

It's not going well, Cam acknowledged. The tension between them was palpable. *Now she wants to ditch me.* He tilted his head, allowing the water to run off his brim. Then, after adjusting his coat, he sat down, and pulled the brim of his hat lower over his eyes. *This totally sucks.*

A few minutes later, the game began.

The Milwaukee Jefferson Wildcats kicked off. After a decent kick return, the quarterback kept handing off to the tailback. The Wildcats made steady gains. Five yards and then eight yards. They steadily advanced. The Wildcat tailback, Richardson, aided by a big ox of a fullback, kept pushing through. Suddenly, he swept right and took off. The way was clear in front of him. He practically flew for thirty yards. Touchdown!

"Cool," Cam sat up a little straighter. "That's more like it." He glanced over to where Coach Murray stood with his player. *The Warriors are in trouble*, Cam noted with some satisfaction. Sure, they were his high school team, but he had never made it to a state championship game with them, and he didn't like to be shown up, especially by Odgers, who had always seemed to be coming up behind him, getting all the love. *It'll be fun to see him knocked down a notch or two.*

The Wildcats kicked off to the Warriors. The receiver made it to the thirty-yard line before he was stopped, his green and white uniform lost under a pile of orange and black much larger ones.

Then, Odgers jogged onto the field. Cam couldn't resist looking over at Kjersten. She had stopped speaking with her friends and was watching the field. *Bitch. She still wants him.*

Galen's long, lithe frame dwarfed more of the other players, and he moved with the loose limbed grace of the natural athlete. *Fucker. Why does he have to look so good?*

Odgers dropped back. Immediately, Cam noticed the intended receiver, a little dude, but he could move. The receiver beat his man. Odgers threw and it was a beautiful, spiraling textbook throw. Cam and everyone else in the stadium held their breath, and then the receiver dropped it. *Yes!* Cam was into it now.

On Eagle River's third play of the game, Odgers dropped back, and planted the football right in the middle of the fullback's chest. The fellow charged nine yards before being tackled.

It was fourth and one at the Warriors own thirty-nine-yard line. Cam watched Murray send in the kicking team. Cam recognized that this wasn't the time to go for it, but he could see Odgers was pissed; he ripped off his helmet angrily and walked over to the bench.

"Here we go," Cam chuckled.

Kjersten sat down next to him.

"Where did your friends go?" he asked, not looking away from the game.

"I want to watch the game."

"You mean watch Odgers."

"Don't be a jerk."

The punter shanked the ball off his foot.

Cam burst out laughing. "I could make that kick."

"They're high school kids, Cam. This is your old team. You should be pulling for them."

"Oh, get over it, Kjersten. I don't give a shit about Eagle River."

"What about Coach Murray? He was good to you."

Cam ignored her comment, but still sought out Coach Murray on the field. He could see that Coach was starting to blow, too. He was pacing, "He's gonna throw the clipboard," Cam muttered.

"What?" Kjersten asked.

"His team's falling apart. Coach is gonna lose it and throw the clipboard."

The Wildcats got the ball. Stung perhaps by the embarrassment of the past few minutes, the Eagle River's defense made them work hard for every gain. Orange and black clad receivers even got stuffed a few times, but they were eating the clock. Suddenly, Richardson, the Wildcat running back, broke for another twenty, scored, and then the quarter ended.

Cam watched as the team huddled around Coach Murray.

Kjersten, following his gaze, commented, "Coach Murray looked out for you. That's what you told me."

"You don't know shit about anything, Kjersten. He recognized that I was going to be a good ball player. I won lots of games for him."

"Don't be so rude. No, there was more to it than that, and you know it, Cam."

"Nah, he didn't do anything for me that he wouldn't have done for his other players." He slouched back in his chair. *Especially for Galen Odgers. He thought I was something special until Odgers came along, then, he didn't even see me.*

The Warriors were a different team in the second quarter. The defense managed to hold for two series, then the Eagle River offense began to make some plays. On their next possession, through a combination of short passes and runs, the Warriors advanced to their own forty-five-yard line. With a minute and twenty seconds left in the quarter, an Eagle River receiver put the burners on. He took off, streaking down the side line.

"They gotta get something done now," Cam commented.

Odgers stepped back and threw a huge, arching bomb straight at the receiver. The football hung in the air for an endless moment. It was a perfect throw and the outcome seemed preordained. The ball and the intended receiver moved in harmony. Closer it came, and closer still. The receiver reached out his hands. The ball hit them and bounced off. The receiver continued in full stride. The ball hit his outstretched hands again. And bounced off again. The receiver made contact once more. He allowed the ball to fall back into his body. And then, it was his. He streaked unimpeded into the end zone and then proceeded to do his version of the end zone shuffle. He had scored! The Eagle River fans went nuts.

Cam whistled low. *Odgers could really throw the football.* He glanced over in the stands to where the scouts were sitting. He recognized a few of them. *They're looking at the Odgers kid like he's turkey dinner.*

"Wow," Kjersten murmured. "That was quite a throw."

"For a high school kid." He pretended not to be impressed. "Let's see your Galen boy try to do that in a college game where he wouldn't have all kinds of time in the pocket."

She glanced over at him. She met his glance. "He's not 'my Galen,' but that was a good throw and you know it."

"If you're so hot for him, why don't you just go back to him?" The jealousy and bitterness seeped through his words. "Oh wait, he dumped you didn't he?"

Determinedly, Kjersten looked back at the field and Cam watched the muscle clench on the side of her jaw. "Yes, he did."

"Still not over him, are you? I could find a hundred girls who'd give anything to be with me and you're still hung up on this kid. Is it because he was your first? Is that it?"

"It's because he wasn't an asshole all the time." Kjersten stood up. "I'm getting a ride home with Maggie. Cam, we're done. Over," she gestured with her hands, like she was flicking him away.

"Sit down. Don't you embarrass me by walking away. You just love to make a scene."

She just walked away and didn't bother to respond.

Bitch! I'm not going to give her the satisfaction of following her. She can just forget it. Acutely aware of the eyes of Eagle River on them, he sat back down in his seat and watched the field.

The game had gotten exciting. With the score at seventeen to eight, the two teams began the fourth quarter. Murray held his breath during the kick off. Then, the miraculous occurred: A Wildcat fumbled on the return and the Warriors recovered at the twenty-four-yard line.

The Warriors made a couple of nickel and dime plays, not really getting anywhere and running down the clock.

Cam glanced at the clock, too. *Not much time was left.*

Odgers stared determinedly down the field. He checked out the defensive formation of the Wildcats.

"He's gonna throw," Cam muttered sitting up. "He has to throw."

The Wildcats were clearly expecting him to throw, too. The ball snapped to Odgers who dropped back, looking for a receiver, but they were blanketed. Then, his eyes fixed on the end zone, he started running.

"Quarterback sneak!" Cam yelled, but the Wildcats clearly could not hear him.

The Wildcat defensive line began to scramble when the players realized that Odgers was making a run for it, but it was too late.

Odgers was rocketing along toward the end zone. His stride grew with every step. His long legs devoured the yardage remaining.

Cam sucked in a breath. *The kid was not only blessed with a golden arm but rockets for wheels! It just wasn't fair. Why did a kid like that have to have all the breaks and I don't get shit? Kjersten is still hung up on him. Even Coach Murray loves the kid.* Odgers was nearing the end zone, but Cam saw a defender coming fast. The two hit hard. Odgers' feet were down, but he had come short of the end zone. Still, Cam had had enough. In disgust, he got to his feet and headed up the stairs and out of the stadium.

* * * *

The game was over and Eagle River had lost. *I feel weird. That last hit was rough.* Galen pulled off his helmet and his eyes travelled over the crowd. *I won't look for her. I won't!* Still, his gaze was fixed on the stands. He glimpsed Ben making his way down. Then, Ben's figure was blocked out as a camera was shoved into his face.

"Have you made any decisions about next year, Galen?" A blond reporter demanded.

"What do you think of Milwaukee Jefferson and Marvin Richardson?" another demanded.

Galen ignored the questions that rained down on him. His entire attention was focused on the stands. He'd seen Ben, but where was Kjersten? *Had she come?* He saw Ben turn back, as if hearing someone calling for him, and then he moved back up into the stands. He watched as Ben stopped and stood talking to someone. The person rose and Galen made out that familiar tall, slender shape and that fall of silvery hair. *She's here! Kjersten came!* He watched as she stood up and followed Ben.

"That was awesome!" Seamus, an Eagle River defensive end, pounded Galen on the back.

"We lost," Galen commented, still staring up into the stands. He couldn't be sure because of the distance, but it seemed as if Kjersten was looking right at him, too.

"Good game, boys, good game." Coach Murray pushed his way through the crowd. "Galen," Murray clapped him on the back. "You worked hard. Nothing to be embarrassed about. There's no such thing as a good loss, but we played hard."

Galen didn't respond. *Where had Kjersten gone? Would she speak to him or just leave?*

"What's with him?" Murray gestured at Galen.

"I don't know, Coach." Seamus shrugged.

"Make room. Make room." Coach Murray interpreted the blank, searching expression on Galen's face. "The boy took quite a hit. Give him some air!"

Galen felt Coach propelling him along towards the bench, but his attention remained fixed on the stands. *Kjersten.* He couldn't make out the features of her face, but the way that she carried herself and moved remained the same.

"Galen, boy, you in there?" Coach Murray placed his hands on his shoulders, pushing him down into a seated position on the bench.

Galen felt strangely detached and separate from his body. *It feels like I'm in a dream.*

As he watched, Kjersten tentatively raised her hand and waved.

He tried to raise his arm to reciprocate, but it felt heavy. *Too heavy to raise.* When he didn't respond immediately, her arm dropped.

"Galen. You all right?" Murray squatted down right in front of Galen, blocking his view and tilted his chin up. He looked into his eyes, trying to make him focus on his face. "You hearing me okay? Nod your head… Where's the trainer?" Murray shouted as he stood up.

"Let me through," a thin, hard bodied, older woman pushed her way through the crowd that had formed around the bench. "What's your name, young man?"

He shook his head, trying to clear out the cobwebs. "Galen Odgers. I'm okay."

"I'll be the judge of that. You took quite a hit on that last play. Look at my finger," the trainer ordered, holding her index finger just in front of Galen's eyes. "Now follow it with your eyes." She ran a few other quick tests on him and then stood up.

"Is he okay?" Murray asked.

"I think so. His eyes are tracking correctly. Still, we need to check him out," she explained to Murray.

"Yes, absolutely," Tom agreed.

So, Galen sat on the bench, doing as he was told. Then, when the trainer was satisfied that he was in reasonable condition, he rose to his feet and followed Murray and the trainer down to the locker room. The entire time, he couldn't stop thinking: "I wish she knew I tried to wave back."

Chapter Ten

Bearcat

~ Galen ~

On a bitterly cold Friday evening in January, while Galen toweled off following his shower, he could hear bits of the raucous conversation downstairs. He made out Kyle's tenor and Sandra's loud, joyous laughter, as well as squeals of joy from her children, but he couldn't make out the words. He rubbed his head vigorously, and buttoned up his pale blue shirt. Next, he pulled on a clean pair of Wranglers, a pair of socks, and then grabbed a boot brush and swiped at the most offensive crud on his Ropers. Perfunctorily, he combed the half inch of hair that covered his head, and splashed some cologne into his hands and then onto his neck and his face. Galen liked to smell good, particularly after an evening of work in the cow barn. Then, he headed down to the kitchen.

"That you, Galen?" Coach Murray's voice boomed out in greeting as Galen strolled into the kitchen.

Coach was sitting near the front door, stogy in hand. The kitchen was unusually clean looking and smelling. With guilty pleasure Galen noted that Joe, Sandra's school teacher husband, who was compulsively tidy, had been at work.

"Thanks for cleaning up, Joe," Galen commented to Joe who was runner thin, blond, and chronically cheerful.

"No biggy. But you guys gotta watch the dates on some of the stuff

the confirmed alcoholic lined his sunken cheeks. Jim stared directly into his oldest son's eyes with an identical pair of bright blue ones. "You don't know nothing." Slowly, he turned. "I'm going outside for some air. It stinks in here. Don't hold dinner for me." He turned and limped out of the room.

"It's the truth. Everyone knows it." Kyle said defensively. "He hasn't done a thing since the accident. It's not like he's not capable. He could do something, but he chooses not to. But I'm done with it now."

"He does have brain damage from the car accident." Sandra defended her father.

"And from the drinking," Galen put in.

"Sandra, you know Pop shut down on life years ago, even before the accident," Kyle said.

"I don't know why Mom stayed with him," Galen said.

"Maybe she felt sorry for him," Tom offered.

Sandra glanced sharply over at Tom. "He's right, you know," she explained to her brother. "Mom didn't think he'd survive without her."

"So she took care of him until she got sick, too." Kyle said. "I still think she would have been better off without him. We all would have been."

"Just let it go, Kyle," Galen broke in.

"Things are going to change now," Kyle announced. "I've given up enough years of my life for this farm. Thing are going to be different."

"What do you mean?" his brother asked.

"Well," Kyle began.

"Are you all ready to eat?" Joe broke in, responding to his wife's raised eyebrow prompt.

"We do have a guest," Sandra reminded her brothers.

"The ribs are ready."

"Yes, let's eat," Sandra agreed. "Let's not talk about this now. We have a guest."

"I'm hardly a guest," Tom commented.

The subject was dropped. So, following dinner and a couple of hours of after dinner conversation, Galen wandered out to the old horse barn, to be alone. He had always felt at peace there. As a kid, he had liked to listen to the sounds that horses made at night; the gentle snorts and the dull thumps of their hooves in the straw. The horses were long gone now. Kyle had been forced to sell the two Belgians that they'd raised as a 4H project several years before. He hadn't wanted to, but he couldn't afford to keep the two hay burners around when they weren't used much except at Christmas time to give wagon rides at a nearby Christmas tree farm. Galen still missed the sweet, warm smell of their big bodies, the aroma of dusty, salt-sweaty, furry bodies. There was still a hint of it in the air, but almost overpowered by the reek of diesel fuel and exhaust that lingered in the enclosed space. Galen walked over to the empty, cobwebby stall and leaned his elbows up against the bottom half of the Dutch door. He had run to this place that horrible night his mother had told him that she was no longer in remission from the cancer.

In tears, he had run of the house and then to the barn. There, he had buried his face in Jethro's coarse mane. But she'd come after him.

"Galen, nothing's certain. I don't take what those doctors say as Gospel. They don't know everything. Only God does. It's going to be okay." Jessica Odgers had reached out to touch her son, but he'd pulled away, sobbing fiercely.

"Mom, it isn't fair. It just isn't fair." He had hiccupped between words. "You just got done with all that chemo stuff and surgery. You should be okay."

"I was better, honey, for a while. But it just didn't last. The cancer has already spread. It was too late. The doctors just didn't know it. It's gone all through me." Her amber brown eyes had filled with tears, but his mother had remained composed. "Galen, you gotta be strong for me. I need your help. So, please don't turn your back on me now. I'm here right now." Her voice had caught, she swallowed a sob. Then, she'd reached out, pulled her youngest son to her, and hugged him fiercely. He had hugged her back desperately, then had buried his face in her shoulder and sobbed bitterly.

"I love you, Mom."

"Honey, I love you, too."

They'd held each other and cried until there were no tears left.

That still open, gaping wound deep inside him ached at the memory.

But it was a familiar sort of ache. *I feel close to her out here still.*

Mom. Mom, I need you. We all do. Pop's drinking himself to death. Kyle's all torn up inside. Sandra and Joe seem okay, because they have the kids and she's always been strong. I wish you were here. We're all falling apart without you. I miss you.

Galen closed his eyes and pictured her as she'd been before the cancer: her tall, athletic form, the laughing eyes, the dazzling smile. She had always been moving, never still. Everything she had touched had seemed so full of life.

Mom, help me. I don't know what to do or even if I am making the right decisions. This thing with Kjersten is eating me up inside. I want it to stop hurting. But I just don't know how to fix things, after how I treated her. I cut her out of my life. I was hurting so much. I don't know how things got so screwed up. But how could she hook up with him?

Chapter Eleven

Fight

~ Cam ~

Cam groaned as he turned over on his bed. His whole body still ached from a particularly rigorous work out in the weight room on the day before. Half awake and half asleep, Cam's mind drifted over people and events from his life. *Cat! Bitch! What a bad deal. She should have known that it was just sex. I never pretended otherwise.* He repressed the slightest twinge of guilt he always felt when he considered his own mother and guys who had used her. *Kjersten... don't want to go there. Don't want to deal with all of the emotional bullshit. If she had been easier going, I wouldn't have hooked up with Cat. So this bullshit is sort of her fault. Football, yes. That's a good thing to think about.* His mind drifted back over the years of football, college and then back to high school, back to Eagle River, to being a Warrior.

It was a cool April afternoon with a bite of frost in the air. *Tight.* A seventeen-year-old junior, Cam Fawst felt tight with the cold. Spring Captain's practice had started after school just the week before, and it felt good to be out tossing the pigskin again, to be in charge of the Warrior offence.

"Nice job, today," Coach Murray patted his back as he passed through the locker room.

"Thanks, Coach," Cam accepted the compliment. "You gonna come out and help tomorrow?"

"You know I can't," Coach protested. "The summer contact days will be here soon enough. We should have a decent team next year. A lot of players are coming back."

"Yes," Cam agreed, wanting to prolong the conversation. *Coach treated him like he was special on the team and like he cared.* Cam liked to think that there was more to it than that he was the starting quarterback.

"How are the freshmen looking?" Coach asked.

Immediately, the image of the tall, lanky freshman, Galen Odgers, popped into his head. *The kid had talent. He could really throw the ball and he was patient.* Cam shrugged his shoulders noncommittally. "They'll be all right."

"What about Odgers? The kid has an arm, don't you think? And he can see the plays developing. You can't coach that."

Cam tasted bile in his mouth. "Odgers is okay. But he's a pussy."

"You think so? I haven't seen it, and I watched him play middle school ball. I think the kid is one cool customer in the pocket. Too bad there aren't any decent receivers in that class."

"Odgers may look decent against other freshman, but he'd get eaten up in a varsity game."

Murray eyed him. "I'm not so sure about that. But don't be worried about him taking your job. He'll back you up in the varsity games this year, and he'll play JV. He just needs some reps now. I want you to look out for him, sort of mentor him. Okay?"

Cam nearly ground his teeth in frustration. "Sure."

Coach Murray headed off.

Cam was still taking his gear off when he heard Galen and the other freshmen come in. Except for Galen, they all gave him a wide berth. Because they were both quarterbacks, Cam's and Galen's lockers were located right by each other.

"Hey," Galen offered as he passed by Cam in the narrow space.

Cam just nodded in acknowledgment.

Galen started to take off his pads and hang them up in his locker.

Cam bit his cheek in annoyance. *The kid bugged the crap out of him.*

Why did everyone, even Coach Murray, have to like him?

"Move your stuff over," he barked at Galen. "This is my spot."

The kid said nothing, but he did as he was told, sliding down the bench as he bent down to take off his cleats.

Cam glanced at him in annoyance. "You know how it works on this football team. It's the upperclassmen's job to teach you freshmen the ropes."

Galen eyed him warily.

"Since you think that you're a quarterback, let me explain your job. You will help bring in the equipment at the end of every Captain's practice. You got that?"

Galen nodded his head, but didn't look at him.

"And you will carry my bag to the locker room at all games and practices."

Galen glanced down and kicked his cleats off. "No." He shook his head.

"What?"

"I said 'no.'" He looked right at Cam. "That's bullshit."

Cam took an aggressive step closer. "What did you just say to me, Odgers?"

"I said," Galen's voice was calm, but his stance was ready. He leaned forward slightly, as if braced to take a hit or throw a punch. "Carry your own bag."

The kid was obviously spoiling for a fight, was angry about something. I'm in the mood to make his day. Cam took another step forward and glowered down at Galen. He drew his hand back and pushed Galen's shoulder hard.

Galen was ready for him. He launched himself up at Cam, tackling him at the waist. They crashed into the lockers.

Cam heard someone yell, "Fight! Fight!" But his vision was filled with red heat and all he wanted to do was kill this kid. He grabbed him by the neck and slammed his head into the ground. Then, he took a punch to the side of the head and fell back.

"Coach!"

"Fight!" someone yelled.

Vaguely, as Cam fought, he was aware of people gathering around of shouting and pushing. Galen was strong and quick, and the contest was proving tougher than he'd anticipated. Then, he felt a strong hand gripping his shoulder, pulling him off, holding him back.

"That's enough!" Coach Murray held Cam up against the wall. "What's wrong with you, two? For Chrissakes, you are on the same team!"

Cam stood there panting. He glared over at Galen. *The kid's mouth is bleeding. Good. Serves him right.*

Still, Galen didn't look cowed. In fact, he looked defiant. And furious. He also looked ready to go again.

"The rest of you, get out of here." Coach waved his arms. "Get out now! Now!"

The other players were clearly reluctant to leave, but they followed Coach's orders. Cam and Galen were left alone in the locker room with a clearly irate Coach Murray.

"Cam. Galen. Sit on the bench now. Let me make myself clear." Coach was so upset, he was spitting. He gesticulated, throwing his arms wide. "Cam, I've never seen you pull something like this before. He's a freshman. You could get into trouble for bullying."

"He didn't bully me," Galen wiped at his bleeding lip. "No one's going to bully me."

"What is this about?" Coach demanded.

Cam glared over at Galen, but the ninth grader didn't say a word.

"What is the problem, Cam? You're the junior here. Next year, you're the team captain. You should know better."

Cam just shook his head. *If Galen wasn't going to say anything, he wouldn't either.*

Coach frowned as he looked from Galen to Cam and back again. "All right, if that's how it's going to be, let me make myself clear, neither of you are more important than this team. Any more problems like this and you are out. Off the team. Period. No discussion. Do you understand me?"

"Yes sir," Cam ground out.

Galen nodded.

"Now Galen, go hit the showers. I want a word with you, Cam."

Cam glanced down at the ground, waiting for Galen to get up and leave.

Once they heard the door to the showers swing shut, Coach stood square in front of Cam. "What was that all about, Cam?"

"Coach," Cam help his hands wide. "I don't know what his problem is."

"Leave him alone, Cam. I don't care if you don't like him, he has a lot on his plate right now. Do you know his story?"

I don't give a shit about his story. My mother is a town joke and I don't have a father. For a moment, Cam was silent as he ruminated. *Why do you give a shit about that kid, Coach? What about me? I've run through walls for you, Coach!* Cam swallowed a lump which lodged in his throat. He didn't trust himself to speak. *Get a grip. It's not like he's your dad or anything.* But that was the problem. Sometimes he wished Coach Murray was his dad. Heck when he'd been younger, he may even have pretended that was the case.

"His mom is dying of cancer."

"That sucks," Cam admitted. "But that doesn't mean he gets to be a little shit and mouth off to me."

"Cam, I would think that you of all people would understand how a boy feels about his mom."

"Don't bring my mom into this."

"Like you, Galen has been mostly raised by his mother."

"He has a father. I know he does."

"His father," Coach seemed to choke on the word, "is an alcoholic. He had a car accident years ago and hasn't been worth a damn since."

"At least he has a father."

"Come on, Cam. Quit feeling sorry for yourself. A lot of us have been there for you and this kid needs help now."

Cam felt the anger rise up in him. *Why is he defending that little shit? What about me? I didn't have an easy time of it. Coach, why don't you care about me? I'm not just another one of your players. I thought I was special to you.*

"Look, I'm not asking you to be best friends with Galen, just don't go after him. He's hanging by a thread right now."

"Yeah," Cam said and glanced away. "Whatever."

"I want your word that you'll leave him alone,"

"Coach, I don't give a shit. I'm outta here after one more year anyway." He relished the hurt he saw on Murray's face. He rose to his feet.

"Cam..." Murray appeared to be struggling to find words. "You know that I'm here for you too, right?"

"Sure," He spat the word flatly. *Why do you treat that kid like you care about him? I'm so done with this place. I'm done with being the town slut's son. I'm just done with it all.*

"Cam?" Murray asked.

"I got stuff I gotta do tonight."

"All right. We'll talk another time."

Cam awoke abruptly, flinching against the pain which swept through his body. *Odgers.* The guy had haunted him for years. Coach loved the kid and even his girlfriend couldn't seem to get over him. It was a nightmare. *When's it going to be about me? Just me?*

Chapter Twelve

New Friends

~ Galen ~

Galen stared down the field, trying to find an open receiver, but no one was open. He danced back to avoid a lineman coming right for him. He shimmied left. Still, there was no one open. He started to run. Just out of the corner of his eye, he made out a body hurtling towards him, then he hit the ground hard and lay there sucking air. Thankfully, this was the final play of the game.

He rose to his feet. For once, he was relieved that the game was over. This Wisconsin High School All Star football game had been rather one sided. His team had been smaller, weaker and slower. It hadn't even been a good battle. Galen loved football, loved to play the game, but this had proven to be something of a disappointment, and not even one member of his family had been able to come, though Ben had come. Pulling off his helmet, he wiped his dripping brow on his jersey as he made his way to the sidelines.

"Yo, Odgers," an unfamiliar voice called out to him.

He spun to face Marvin Richardson, the highly recruited defensive back from Madison Memorial. Richardson had sacked him several times in the game.

"Yes?"

"Damn! The Bearcats are going to be pretty fierce with the two of us next year." Marvin grabbed Galen by the shoulder pads and hugged him.

Why is this guy hugging me? Where do I put my arms? Weird?

"Just think, me, Marvelous Marvin Richardson and Galen Odgers on the same team. No one is going to be able to touch us."

"What?"

"I'm going to Illinois U, too." The immaculate white grin flashing in that chiseled, black face was contagious. Galen felt himself grin back. Marvin kept his arm around Galen's shoulders as they continued down the tunnel towards the locker rooms.

"The way I see it, you and I got to get to know each other. 'Cause we're like brothers now. We gotta stick together"

As they made their way down to the locker rooms, Marvin did all of the talking and Galen just listened. He saw that Ben stood waiting for him just outside the door.

Ben glanced curiously at Marvin, but addressed himself to Galen. "Tough game, huh?"

"Yup. Some good players out there."

"You got that right," Marvin broke in.

Ben was nonplussed, unsure of how to respond to the presence of Richardson, Galen's nemesis in the state championship game and now in this all-star game. "How long do you think you'll be, Galen?"

"Probably be a while yet. We have to talk to the reporters. The whole nine yards. I wish I could pass on it."

"What are you talking about," Marvin admonished. "This stuff is just as important as how you play. From now on, the scouts are going to be looking at us to see if we are potential pros. You gotta play the game… What's the name of your boy here?" Marvin held out his hand to Ben. "I'm Marvin Richardson."

"I'm Ben Happe."

"You going to Illinois U, too?

"No," Ben shook his head.

"That's too bad. Cause you're going to miss out on going to a school with a National Championship football team. Well, it was sweet meeting you guys. Galen, be seeing you in Chicago. Take care of that arm." With that, he sauntered out through the opposing team's locker room door.

Both Galen and Ben stared after him.

Ben was the first to recover his composure. "What was that all about?"

"I guess we're going to be teammates next year."

"Wow. That guy is certainly not lacking confidence."

Galen nodded, chuckling. "We're bonding, I guess." Then, he caught sight of a group of journalists moving as one body towards them. "I'll see you in a little bit," he said to Ben. "Let me get some of this gear off and talk to them."

Ben nodded in understanding. "I'll be here."

* * * *

Kjersten picked up the phone, then set it down on the receiver. She picked it up once and stared fiercely down at the numbers. Slowly, hesitantly, she dialed the eleven digits. The phone rang once, twice, three times.

"Odgers."

Kjersten recognized Kyle Odger's voice. "Hello. Is Galen there?"

"One minute… Ga-len," she heard him shout. She heard some distant incoherent answer and then Kyle said, "You have a phone call."

"Hi, this is Galen."

"Hi Galen… It's me. Kjersten." Her hands felt clammy and her heart was racing.

"Kjersten?"

"Yeah, um hi. How are you?"

For a moment, he didn't answer.

"Well, uh, I didn't mean to bother you… I mean, if you're busy."

"No, I'm not busy… Don't go, Kjersten. I wanted to talk to you, too. I stopped by your house that day after the fair, but you'd already left."

"I left early that morning."

"How come?"

"There were ... reasons. You really came to see me that morning?"

"Yeah, I did."

"Oh, I didn't know."

"Your dad didn't tell you?"

"No, he didn't."

"Why?"

"Why what?" Galen asked.

"Why did you come by?"

"When I saw you at the fair, I wanted to talk to you. But you were with Cam."

"Yes."

"Are you still with Cam?"

She hesitated for a moment. "We broke up."

"Oh," he paused for a moment. "Really?"

"Yeah, it just wasn't working."

"So, how come you called today?"

Kjersten shook her head. *I'm done chasing after you. If you want to get back together, you are going to have to come after me.* "I was just calling because you're one of my oldest and closest friends. I want us to still be friends." The words cascaded out of her.

"Friends?" Galen's response sounded cold even to him.

"Yeah. Do you agree?"

"Sure."

"I'm glad to hear it." The silence dragged. "I heard that you are going to be playing football next year at Illinois University."

"Yeah."

The silence dragged on awkwardly. "Um, I'm sorry that you won't be coming to Great Lakes. It would have been great to see you around."

"The Coyotes already have a quarterback."

"Well, maybe we'll run into each other in Eagle River some time. I'm planning on going home more often now." The line went silent once more. *How do I get through to him?* Nothing came to mind. *Galen obviously doesn't care about me. Say something,* her heart silently screamed.

"So, we're friends then?" He interrupted her musings with the blunt question.

"I was always your friend, Galen. You're the one who didn't want me in your life anymore."

"I know," he hesitated, but couldn't resist adding, "but things were messed up then and I never thought you would get together with him. We made fun of him in high school. Remember?"

"It's not like you haven't dated other people," Kjersten protested.

"Yeah, but he's such a jerk. He's *the* Cam Fawst, and he's his own biggest fan. He is all he thinks about."

"I agree with you." The words were out of her mouth before she could stop them.

"Then, why were you with him?"

"Galen, I was a mess when you just cut me out of your life. I was lonely and miserable, and he can be charming. He seemed to care about me when you obviously didn't... Look, I already told you, I don't want to talk about Cam. I just called to make sure that you and I were still friends."

"Sure. We're friends."

"Well, see you."

"Bye."

Feeling immensely dissatisfied, Kjersten set the phone back down. *That didn't go at all the way I wanted it to. I'm totally over Cam, but clearly Galen isn't.*

* * * *

Galen heard the click of the receiver being set down. *Why had Kjersten called him? Did she really think that he would simply forget it all, sweep it under the carpet? Let's be friends. If that wasn't a crock of shit.* There was no way they could ever be "just friends," but he'd used those same words on her when he had cut her out of his life after his mother died.

He waited for it to come, the satisfaction that she'd called, that he had real evidence that he still mattered to her some. But it never did. He felt even more hollow and empty than before. He stared down at the receiver desperately wanting to take back his coldness, wanting to really talk to her, the way they had before everything had gone so wrong. *Should I call her back? But what could I say? That I still love her? That I cannot stop thinking about her.*

Suddenly, the phone rang. He snatched it up.

"Hello?"

"Hi, is this Galen Odgers?" It was a female voice, but not the right one.

"Yes?" His pounding heart began to slow. He swallowed disappointment.

There was a feminine giggle. "I don't know if you remember me. We met the other night at Sal's. In Eagle River."

"Oh yeah, Sally. Right?"

"You did remember." She sounded pleased. "I was just wondering if you want to get together on Saturday night? I'll be in Eagle River, staying at my Aunt's."

Even though Kjersten and Cam were broken up, she'd said she wanted to be `friends' with me. I am not sure that she wants anything else. She certainly hadn't said so. Friends?

"Well? Are you available?" the girl asked again, sounding nervous.

"Yeah. Sure… What?" *Still, she called me. Obviously, friend or not, Kjersten still thinks about me.*

"What do you want to do? Wanna go to the drive in Saturday night?"

"Yeah." *Maybe Ben knew what was going on with Kjersten. I'll call Ben.*

"That'd be great," the girl had tittered. "I'll see you Saturday. Around seven?"

"What?" Galen finally tuned into the conversation.

"The drive in, Saturday, right? Or did you just remember you have something going on?"

He nearly groaned into the receiver. Hearing the disappointment in her voice and aware of his own part in it, he said: "No, Saturday sounds good. Where can I pick you up?"

As Sally rambled on, he tuned out. *Kjersten. How do we get back to where we were? Can we ever go back? Has too much happened already? Is it too late?*

When the conversation with Sally was finally over, Galen placed the receiver down. *Damn.* He hated himself for his deliberate cruelty to Kjersten. *I don't want to go out with Sally. I want Kjersten. But there's no way to go back and fix things. Is there?* It was like he couldn't help himself. The pile of shit just kept getting bigger and the mosquitoes swarmed. *How had it all come to this? Now I have a date with one girl while I can't stop thinking about another girl.*

Chapter Thirteen

Training Camp

~ Galen ~

Galen hauled his two duffle bags out of the bed of the pickup. *I can't believe I'm finally here at Great Lakes University training camp.* He had graduated from Eagle River High in June and summer had flown by with training and working. He had been so busy he hadn't had time to think. And then suddenly, it was mid-July and time for the football players to report for the pre-season.

The ride from Eagle River down to Chicago had been a quiet one for the two Odgers brothers. They hadn't exchanged more than a handful of words by the time that they pulled up onto the downtown Chicago campus of Illinois University.

"Here, give me one of those," Kyle hefted the green bag onto his shoulder.

Galen grunted in response.

"You haven't said two words since we stopped in the Dells. You scared?"

"Nah," Galen said and shook his head. He felt anxious. There were knots twisting in his stomach. *It's just something else to get through, but I'll survive it.*

The two brothers made their way out of the parking lot towards the dorm. The campus was green with summer lushness. It was also relatively empty. Some students were around for the summer term and all of the football players were on campus for training camp, but that was it. The air was heavy and damp, like inhaling a wet blanket, and the Odgers' t-shirts clung wrinkled and damp to their backs. The pickup didn't have any air conditioner, and the drive had been more than six hours long. Galen sniffed at himself. "I stink."

"College kids stink the same as you or me," Kyle mocked and then let out a low whistle. "Check out the scenery."

Galen eyed the two long-legged coeds in cut off shorts and bikini tops who roller-bladed right past them on the side walk.

"The blond was checking me out! Did you see that?"

"In your dreams, Kyle. She was probably wondering if you were a stalker."

"No way. She was definitely checking me out. I think that I'm going to like visiting you here, little brother. Chicks dig me."

Kyle's familiar lewdness elicited a weak smile from Galen.

"Excuse me." Kyle waylaid a girl with books in her arms who was just passing them. "Is this Walker Hall?"

"Yeah, you're in the right place. The third building, there." She pointed across the quadrangle. "That's where the football players live. You a ballplayer?"

Galen nodded.

"Well, I'll see you around." She smiled at Galen.

"Thanks."

"See what I mean?" Kyle elbowed Galen.

The brothers made their way through the entrance foyer and checked in at the front desk. There, they got Galen's room assignment, and headed up the steps. The dorm was new and spacious, though rather utilitarian in decoration. They proceeded down a hall, past a lodge which was occupied by several groups of young guys to room one thirteen. Galen unlocked the door and swung it wide. It was a decent-sized room with two twin beds, two dressers, two desks, and a big window.

"Not bad." Kyle looked around, appraising the accommodations.

"Haven't met the roommate yet," Galen reminded him bleakly.

They stowed away his few belongings quickly. As a finishing touch, he pulled out a rolled up poster.

"Kyle, tell me when I have it straight," Galen requested as he held up the poster against a wall.

"That's okay, there."

Galen taped the poster to the wall and stepped back to admire his handiwork. It was an old poster of Johnny Unitas, the legendary Baltimore Colts quarterback, in the classic quarterback pose with his arm drawn back. It was an old poster, frayed at the edges and faded in color.

"Can't believe that you brought that piece of crap all the way from home. You should have a Packer poster up," Kyle muttered. "Hell, at least go with the Vikings."

"Coach gave me the poster. It's lucky."

"Whatever. Well, it looks like you're about all set. You got a while until your team meeting. You wanna give me the grand tour?"

"I can try. I can't promise you that I know much more than you do. This place is huge. Wait until you see the athletic facilities. The weight room is unbelievable. They've got everything."

Suddenly, the dorm room door swung wide to reveal a mountain of a human being. The man standing there was six five, and easily three hundred and twenty-five pounds. He was fleshy but underneath the fat was serious bone crushing muscle. A Bearcats baseball cap covered his shaved scalp. He was sweating profusely despite the air conditioning in the dorm. "You Galen Odgers?" a deep baritone rumbled.

Galen nodded.

"I'm Moe Johnson and I'm here for the team to welcome you and see that you get around okay. You'll be my project this week."

"You're in deep shit," Kyle muttered, clearly amused by this turn of events.

"What did you say?" Moe queried, as he moved his bulk into the room. The room suddenly felt very close and tight. Moe moved up to Galen and held out his hand. With relief, he gripped it firmly and shook.

"I'm Galen's brother, Kyle. Pleased to meet you." Kyle smiled up at Moe and Moe returned the smile. Moe's smile was brilliantly white against the blackness of his skin and impossible not to reciprocate.

"You two finding your way around so far?"

"We were just going to go out and look around some," Galen commented.

"If you need anything, let me know. I'll help you out. I'm gonna look out for you."

Galen nodded gratefully.

"Don't forget that there's a team meeting tonight. I'll see you then. Good meeting you, Kyle."

Moe closed the door after him as he left.

"He seems like a good guy. In no time at all, you'll fit right in," Kyle reassured Galen. "You already know one player."

"Yeah," Galen sighed and collapsed back on the twin bed.

"That thing's about a foot too short for you."

"You're not kidding." He stretched out in order to show how his feet dangled over the end of the bed.

"You oughta ask if they have any of those extra-long ones. You know what I mean? They probably do."

"I'll take care of it, big brother. Don't worry about me."

"Yeah, you're a big boy now." Kyle looked somehow dismayed at the realization. "Come on. Let's get going. I want to be back on the road before dark."

Chapter Fourteen

A Chance Meeting

~ Kjersten ~

A few months later, on a bright but still cool October afternoon, Kjersten sat reading a romance novel at a table in the window of a sub shop that was popular with the college set in Milwaukee. She didn't glance up when the bell jingled because the door had opened.

"You doing some heavy reading, I can see," a familiar voice teased.

Kjersten spun around to face Ben, and a blush crept up the pale column of her neck. "Ben!" She jumped to her feet, hugging him. "You know I've always loved romances. Especially cowboy ones."

Ben laughed. "Yeah. I remember you dragging Galen and me to all of those rodeos. Little britches, semi-pro, pro. It never mattered as long as you got to see your cowboys. You only quit going when you figured out that girls couldn't participate in most of the events. Thinking back, you never did mention that you wanted to go to see the cowboys."

"I didn't think that would have gone over well with either you or Galen."

"True." Ben chuckled, taking a seat at Kjersten's table. "Do you remember that rodeo in Medford when the calf's neck was broken? You went nuts. I thought you were going to run down into the arena. We never went again."

"It seemed so cruel to rope the poor little guys around the neck, then flip them off their feet…" She shivered at the traumatic memory. "What have you been up to lately, Ben?"

"Well, I'm a communications major now. I want to get into broadcasting."

"I think you'd be great at it."

"I've always loved sports, just never been very good at them. How about you? You still pre-vet?"

Kjersten nodded. "I needed a break from Organic Chem."

"Hence the heavy reading," Ben commented. "You'll be a good vet. Galen always said that you had a way with animals."

"Thanks. Mom and Dad weren't too pumped at first. They wanted me to go into business or pre-law. But I realized that I want to work with animals."

"Sounds like you really have things together."

"Yeah, well, I guess it takes some of us longer than others. Have you been home, lately, Ben?"

"I go home at least one weekend every few months."

"Do you see anyone when you're back?"

"I've seen a couple people," Ben equivocated.

"Like whom? Come on, Ben. Just tell me."

"No way. You have to ask the question if you want the answer."

She grimaced. "Fine. How's Galen?"

Ben grinned. "He's good. He likes Chicago and Illinois University. But that's not really what you want to know, is it?"

"Since I've obviously left myself wide open here, I might as well get this over with. Is he seeing anyone?"

"Galen's dated some, but I don't think that he's gotten serious with anyone. Could be he still has feelings for an old flame."

"Give me a break, Ben. You aren't still trying to patch things up are you? Galen got over me a long time ago… You know, I did try to call him a few months ago. He wasn't very friendly."

"What did you expect?"

"He broke up with me, remember. I wish that I could take some things back, fix things, but everyone makes mistakes. He made some big ones, too."

"I was glad to hear that you broke up with that jerk Cam."

"He is a jerk. You're right. Lesson learned. It's good to see you," Kjersten shook her head and smiled. "What's up with you? You seeing anyone?"

"Nope. I can't find anyone who can keep up with a dynamo like me. Actually, I just don't seem to have any luck. There aren't that many girls who find a trumpet playing Communications Major all that sexy."

"I don't believe you. I've missed you, Ben," Kjersten said.

"I've missed you, too, Kjersten."

While she sat chatting with Ben, Kjersten's thoughts kept drifting to Galen. No matter how much time passed, she couldn't stop thinking about him, even though their relationship was ancient history.

Chapter Fifteen

Dreams of Days Past

~ Galen ~

He heard the alarm go off and sought to ignore it.

"You gotta get up, man," Marvin Richardson shook his shoulder. "Let's go eat."

Just two more minutes," Galen pulled the pillow over his head, closed his eyes and slipped away into his memories...

The engine of the snowmobile burned hot against his calf and its roar obliterated every other sound. The icy wind bit into him where it penetrated through his clothing, helmet, and even his balaclava. It tasted like snow fresh with a faint hint of diesel. Dimly through the heavy snow, sixteen-year-old Galen could make out Kyle on the snowmobile ahead of him. It was one of those truly amazing winter days when the snow was brilliant and white and the air tasted so fresh and cold that it burned one's lungs.

"Hold on," Galen shouted back to Kjersten, who, seated on the back of the snowmobile, was gripping him tightly. He was aware of every inch of her body against his, of her heat. The feel of her was thrilling.

"What?" Kjersten shouted back.

He turned his head. "Hold on!"

Galen felt her nod against his shoulder. He revved the engine. The snowmobile rocketed forward in response. He muscled the surging monster off the path, around Kyle on the Odgers' old snowmobile and then back on. Galen waved as he passed his brother. Predictably, Kyle flipped him the bird.

Kjersten laughed and he felt it pulsing against him and through him. Mr. Solheim's snowmobile was top of the line, powerful and fast, much faster than Kyle's, which had been assembled from the refuse of other wrecked machines. His cheeks burned with the combined effects of the wind chill, the speed, and the ten below zero temperature.

Faster, he kept going faster. He waited for Kjersten to make some gesture of protest but she didn't. Her arms gripped him ever more tightly and he could feel the softness of her breasts pressing into his back. He felt incredible and she was totally with him, egging him on. *Lean into the turns. Give it gas. Don't hold back.* It was awesome. Galen felt awesome. They were practically flying, swooping through the winter wilderness.

Suddenly and unexpectedly, the path took a sharp right turn. He had a moment of objective clarity when he recognized that he was going way too fast to take the corner smoothly. He saw the pine trees as he bore down on them, inexorably. He swung the snowmobile hard into the turn. He felt the roaring machine fly out from under him, then felt every bone in his body disintegrate on impact with the earth.

He didn't know if he'd been knocked out. Suddenly, he was staring up at the grayness of the sky peeking through the pine branches. He struggled to breathe under the crushing weight that was pressing down on his chest. *Breathe, small breath, in and out. Don't panic.* Slowly, the weight lessened. Gradually, he became more aware of his surroundings; of the coldness of the snow against his neck and cheek. He began to move each limb carefully, to make sure nothing was broken. *Limp. Sore as hell. But nowhere near dead and nothing broken. Kjersten! Where was Kjersten? Was she okay?*

"Kjersten?" His voice came out in a raspy whisper that he could barely hear himself. "Where are you?" He managed to sit up. He saw her body, tossed like some brightly colored, discarded rag doll against the white of the snow. She was not moving.

Galen began to crawl. Every inch sent needles of pain shooting through his body. He tasted the coppery saltiness of his own blood. He probed the tear in the inside of his cheek with his tongue.

"Kjersten?" He got right beside her, but she still hadn't moved. Galen felt the panic, the fear pooling in his stomach. "Kjersten." He was afraid to touch her, to move her. *What if she was seriously hurt?* "Kjersten?" Then, he realized that her chest was moving up and down. *She was breathing.* He felt an enormous surge of relief. He took her hand as her eyes fluttered opened. Her eyes moved wildly about. She began to suck and choke for air. Galen saw the panic, the tears in her eyes.

"It's okay. You had the wind knocked out of you. Breathe slowly in and out. It'll pass."

She followed his coaching and slowly the fear diminished in her eyes. Gradually, her breathing calmed and slowed. He watched the tears streak their way slowly down her cheeks. He pulled his gloves off and brushed them gently away.

"Galen?" Her voice was a shaking rattle, as she reached up and gripped his hand. Galen felt a sob forming in his own throat. He collapsed back down onto the snow beside her and embraced her carefully. She patted his shoulder. "I'm okay," she whispered with a weak smile.

"I could have killed you," he choked on his own words. A world without her, in which he had hurt her gaped before him. "I could have killed you," he repeated.

She nodded. In a hoarse whisper, she muttered: "From now on, I'll drive the snowmobile."

Despite the discomfort that encompassed his body, despite his awareness of the near tragedy, he felt himself begin to laugh. She, too, began to giggle. Then, they lay back in the snow, weakly laughing while cringing and holding their bruised ribs. They laughed until the adrenalin, fear and the excitement subsided. Finally, they settled down.

"Where's Kyle?" Kjersten asked.

"He must have turned onto another trail. He should have come up on us by now."

"Well, I hope we don't have to peel him off a tree on the way back... So much for your lightning fast reflexes," Kjersten teased Galen.

"Nah, his snowmobile probably broke down. You wouldn't have been able to make that turn either. We were going way too fast."

"You were going way too fast," Kjersten corrected him dryly. "I've never wiped out on a snowmobile. I should have listened to your brother's warning. You are a terrible driver."

"I doubt anyone could have handled that turn."

"You sure couldn't."

Galen noticed the small cut oozing blood on her cheek. Automatically, he reached into a pocket and pulled out a handkerchief. "Mom always puts these things in my pockets. Never made much sense to me. Until now." He picked up some snow with the handkerchief, allowed it to melt in the heat of his hand, then pressed it so gently to her cheek.

Kjersten's eyes were riveted on him as he held the handkerchief to her cheek and stared back. He felt his breathing go shallow again. She leaned towards him. He saw her eyes close. Then, he felt the butterfly brush of her lips on his. Her lips began to move against his, slowly, delicately. Just as Galen began to savor the delicate sensation, Kjersten pulled back. He opened his eyes in time to see the warm color flood her cheeks. Then, he lifted her hands and moved them up to rest on his shoulders. Next, he pulled her body closer to him. Leaning, his head down to hers once again, his lips encountered the more yielding softness of hers. He nibbled on her bottom lip and felt her lips move in response. Her tongue…

"Galen. Come on, man. Wake up."

Galen shook his head, resisting the masculine tones invading his memory. Desperately, he reached back with his mind to that elusive January day years ago that was already drifting just out of his reach.

"Galen." A hand jostled him impatiently. "Wake up."

He felt it slipping away. The memory, the sensations, all slipping away, eluding him as only a half forgotten memory can. *Gone.*

With a sigh, he opened his eyes to face the new day.

Chapter Sixteen

Another Birthday

~ Tom ~

Tom Murray looked out over Pleasant Meadows graveyard. *It was Jessica's birthday again. Another year come and gone without her. Where did time go?* He laid the bouquet of lilacs on the plot. "I know you love the smell of lilacs. The ones you planted at the back of your house are a wall now. I saw them when I was over at the house for dinner with Kyle, Sandra and her family and Galen, of course."

Every spring, it was with a tugging poignancy that he observed the lush purple-blue blooming of the lilacs. It took him back to that last argument they'd had, when she'd ended things between them so many years before. For a moment, he closed his eyes, remembering. It was all right there, as if it had happened only yesterday.

Tom reached out to touch the softness of Jessica's cheek. "You can't mean that. Not now."

"Especially now, Tom." Jessica grasped Tom's hand. She took it in her own. "I love you or I did love you for a while." Tears pooled in the large, green-brown eyes. "But we can't change everything just to suit ourselves. I have two other children." Jessica exhaled slowly. "And I have a husband who is no position to take care of anyone."

"Because of his own stupidity. Jess, don't do this to us. I need you." Tom's voice quivered. "I can't live without you." His tone grew desperate.

Jessica Odgers' face hardened. "You can and you will. Don't blame me or threaten me. We're both adults here. We both knew what we were getting into. This is where we've ended up and that's all there is to it." She put her hands to both sides of his face and stared into his eyes. "You'll be just fine. You've always been fine. Jim, he's not fine now."

"Odgers did it to himself. We deserve a chance. You were done with him before the accident. We were going to be together. He's not even a good father."

Jessica pulled away from him. "I know and I don't want this to end any more than you do, but what can I do? He won't even be able to take care of himself. What will the kids think if I leave him now? It wouldn't be right."

"You threw that worthless bastard out. Now, he wrecks himself and you think you have to take care of him. For Christ's sake, I know how hard it is to stay sober. You think he's going to stay sober now, after that accident? How will it be for your kids to grow up with an even more worthless alcoholic father?"

"They've been growing up with a drunk for a father for years. But they don't need to have a mother who'd leave a disabled man to run off with her lover."

"But that baby's mine." He looked down at her belly.

"Tom." Jessica's voice was softer. "You say that you'll stay in Eagle River for a while, but I have no way of knowing whether you will be gone tomorrow, whether you will just take off when things get too dull for you here, when you get bored with me. No, don't shake your head at me. Consider your track record. You've never stuck. Why should I believe that you will this time?"

"For Christ's sake, it matters. I'm good with kids, you know that. We'd be fine. I get along well with your other kids."

"We've been magic for each other, but you're not a family kind of guy… I don't want this to get ugly now. It just wasn't meant to be, the day to day and the forever part, that's just not you."

"Give me a chance… Wait a minute, you're bullshitting me." Tom grabbed Jessica's arm and pulled her up close against him. "What is this?"

"You don't have any roots here. I can't just drag my kids all over the place. Not after all that they've been through, and Jim needs me now. This baby needs me. You don't need me. You don't need anyone."

"What the hell do you mean by that? I need you. I love you, Jess. I want this baby."

"Tom, you'll be okay on your own. You're a survivor. Jim clearly isn't and there's Kyle and Sandra to think about."

"What about me? What about you? You think that you are so noble, giving up your little weakness for your family. But you're wrong. You are incredibly selfish. You got some good cock. You've been satisfied, and now you want to wash it all away. Forget about it. You can't just close your eyes and hope I'll disappear. You say you choose this life. Well, I sure as hell don't."

"Tom, stop, please." Jessica's voice was infinitely tired. "I don't know what to do. Maybe this is wrong. God, I don't know, but I don't know any other way. I have to take care of my family."

"What if I stay here in Eagle River? You could pass me in the street once a week for the rest of your life. Do you honestly believe that you could forget me then?"

"I could never forget you, Tom. Not now, especially not now with this baby I'm carrying."

Tom pounced. "Are we just going to pretend that he or she doesn't exist?"

"You'll have to."

"I could just tell Jim the truth about you and me."

"I already have. He understood or didn't care. I don't know. I'm not sure what he understands at this point."

"Understood what? That his wife fucked the living shit out of another guy and is now pregnant by him. Oh yeah, that would go over great with most guys."

"I can't hear this. You just want to hurt me." As she drew her tear drenched face up, Jessica faced Tom unflinchingly.

For the first time, he saw a coldness in those exquisite eyes meeting his own. There was a distance now. Jessica Odgers always arranged life so that it worked out as she wanted it to. She was no victim. Tom realized then that she wanted their relationship to end.

"I can't believe what a cold, selfish bitch you are."

"Stop it, Tom. It's over and you are just making a fool of yourself."

In shock, he stared at the chiseled lush beauty of that so familiar face, a face that had smiled in love at him and rarely spoken in anger. But he recognized that she had already cut him out. For her, the time for sentimentality was clearly over.

"I'm going now, Tom."

"You'll come crawling back."

She hadn't even bothered to answer. She had walked to the hotel room door, exited, and closed it firmly behind her.

As Tom straightened up, resting his hand on the grave marker, his right knee buckled. Automatically, he shifted his weight off of it. He had seen Jessica often enough after final confrontation, at school functions, at Galen's football games. But that episode had been the end of *them*.

"You know, Jess, at first I stuck around Eagle River to prove you wrong. Then, I stayed because it was the only place that ever felt like home. And I got to see our boy grow up and to be a part of his life, even though he doesn't know I'm his dad. I want to tell him. It doesn't kill me like it used to. You always said I'd know when the time was right to tell him. I'm not so sure that that time will ever come, but I also don't know if that boy would've turned out so well if I'd actually had a hand in his raising. You certainly did a fine job.

"We all miss you." He swallowed hard. "Sandra's kids are getting big, but I guess that you know that. Galen's about done with his first year of college. The boy did okay. Didn't embarrass us at all. He's gotten thick with some kid from Milwaukee, a running back, and he's gotten to play some ball, too.

"I'm doing all right. I have a decent team this year, not like last year's but decent." He traced with his booted toe in the dirt. "Look I'm going to stop beating around the bush. I'm here to tell you something. The reason I stopped by today is that there is this woman. I know that you're probably thinking 'another one.' But it's not like that, not this time. I really like her. Her name is Maggie. She's the new girls' volleyball coach and she's taken over a couple of my Phy Ed classes. She's cute. High energy and real bouncy. She's an athlete, too. She even beat me at tennis. Well, we've been dating for a while now." He took a deep breath. "I think that I'm going to ask her to marry me. Maggie's not you and I'm not trying to replace you. But she and I, we do okay together. I don't want to be some lonely, old man living alone. You showed me that family is important. Maybe Maggie and I can be family to each other. I don't deserve this shot, I know. But I lost you. Twice. Maybe God is cutting me some slack. I just wanted to tell you… She's the first woman I've cared about since, well, since you." He stared off into the distance, hesitating. Then, he brushed his fingers gently on the headstone, shoved his hands into his pockets and then, his stiff knees, limped slowly away.

As he was walking back to the car, a gentle breeze drifted over him. It carried the oh-so-familiar scent of lilac with it.

Chapter Seventeen

Bethany's Men

~ Cam ~

With single minded enthusiasm, Cam Fawst dove into the stack of chicken wings. They were super-hot, just the way he liked them. He savored each tender limb, attempting to block out his mother's staccato chatter from across the table.

"When I told Jerry," Bethany stroked one long red fingernail down the lime silk sleeved arm of her companion, "that my son was the Coyotes' quarterback, he said that he was just dying to meet you."

Cam examined Jerry distastefully: the slicked back gray-black hair, the stubble darkened cheeks, the slightly pot-bellied frame. The guy positively reeked of oil. His wavy hair glistened in the bar light, as did his shirt and the black material of his pants.

Jerry pulled the thick cigar out of his mouth. "Yeah, I can't wait to tell the guys. Can you get me some really prime seats for a game?"

"Could you do that for Jerry, honey?" Bethany wheedled her son. "It would make your Mommy very happy."

"Yeah sure, I guess I could do that." The whole familiar dinner scene with his mother and her current flame made him want to puke. "Just give me your address. I'll send you some." *Maybe in another life time.*

"I'd really get a kick out of that."

"Wouldn't that be wonderful? It could be like a father-son outing,"

Bethany gushed.

"Your real dad ever come watch you play?"

"Cam's father is dead," Bethany stubbed her cigarette out.

Cam studied his mother curiously. *So my father is dead.* This was the first that he had heard of it, but he didn't really feel anything. The subject of his biological father had been closed throughout his childhood. After all, Cam's father had ditched them both. How did Bethany know that this particular ex had died? Had she kept in touch with him all these years? Still, Cam let the subject go. It wasn't something that he wanted to discuss in front of Jerry.

He hated how Jerry's hands moved continuously. The man had big, black haired hands with obviously manicured nails, and he sported several chunky gold rings. "So, Jerry," Cam sought to redirect the conversation. "What do you do?"

"I have diversified business interests."

"Jerry's an entrepreneur. He owns a chain of beauty parlor and tanning salons all over the Midwest. He calls them `Bounce and Body: A Complete Salon.' That's where we met. I went in for some hair color and came out with a guy." Bethany giggled.

Jerry patted her hand.

Cam cringed.

"How long have you two been seeing each other?" *Might as well pretend to get into the spirit of the evening.*

"Two wonderful months now," Bethany answered.

Cam hoped this one wouldn't stand the test of time.

"How's your love life, honey? Cam's always been such a lady-killer, but lately he's been serious with this girl from Eagle River." Bethany pronounced the name of the town distastefully.

"Your high school sweetheart?" Jerry questioned, but didn't wait for an answer. "I played the field while I was in college. I played a bit of ball, too. I don't want to pump my own tires or anything, but I was pretty good."

"Kjersten and I are done." Cam ignored Jerry's comment and answered his mother. "Have been for a long time."

"What happened, honey?" Bethany queried. Jerry looked irritated that the conversation had veered away from him.

"Just didn't work out."

"I thought you really liked her. Kelly or Kristen was her name, right?"

"Kjersten," Cam corrected. "But you of all people should know how things go," he countered. "It's just over. That's all there is to it. It didn't work out."

Bethany looked more puzzled than angered by her son's rudeness. "You seeing someone else?"

"No. Well, yeah, I guess so."

"So tell us all about her."

"There's not much to tell. Her name is Julia. She's an exotic dancer." With sadistic anticipation, he waited to see how this would register. His mother's face didn't change at all. She wore the same cheerful, heavily made up mask. He knew there was real beauty under that mask. His mother had always been a good-looking woman, but life had weathered her and worn away some of her beauty.

"A hot number?" Jerry queried lecherously in his gravelly voice.

"Come on, Jerry. You're embarrassing him." Bethany gently nudged her date. "I think she's a very lucky girl to catch a guy like my Cam. You know what would be fun? Maybe we could double date sometime. Because of Jerry here," she patted his hand, "I'm down here in Milwaukee a couple of times in a month."

"You could be down here all of the time, Bethany," Jerry muttered. "I've asked your mom to come live me."

"Why don't you?" Cam asked. "You've always hated Eagle River."

Bethany glanced at her manicure. "My business is there."

"Mom, you're a realtor. You can work anywhere. Besides I'm down here. There's no reason for you to stay in that crappy, little town."

She finally looked up and met her son's gaze. "Maybe you're right. Maybe it's time for me to finally get out of Eagle River."

"That's my girl," Jerry patted her thigh under the table. "We'll get you moved in right away."

"Let me look into it, Jerry. I have to think about this one. I will want to start out in a place of my own."

Mom has no plans of moving in with this joker, Cam realized with satisfaction.

"Well, what's the point of that?" Jerry argued.

But Cam tuned them out. He had heard what he needed to hear. *This was just a temporary relationship, like all of the others.*

Bethany Fawst had never shown much taste or discretion in the men she dated. She had been so out of place in Eagle River, a rare single mother with a reputation for being fast in a town too small to keep anything quiet. She had always liked to party, and she had hung around with a lot of loser guys over the years. Cam remembered too many evenings that were indistinguishable from this one. Different guys. Different bars. Always the same story. She would throw herself into love and their lives would mesh with that of some stranger. Then, she would throw herself out of love, and they would never see the guy again. Then, the cycle would start over again. Cam had spent much of his life being embarrassed of his mother and of her behavior. There was only one time that it had been different, only one guy whom his mother had dated that he'd ever given a damn about and that had been Coach Murray. Cam's mind drifted back to that long ago day when he had met Coach for the first time.

Coach had come into his life when he was in fifth grade, a ten-year-old. He'd come home after school to see a fancy, black pickup truck in the driveway at the duplex where they lived. Cam's heart sunk, and he dreaded meeting his mother's new man.

Using the key, he'd walked in the front door to see a big, muscular guy seated on the couch beside his mother.

"Here's my Cam. Cam, honey, come say 'hi' to Mr. Murray."

Cam didn't say anything. He just eyeballed this new man in his mother's life. Of course, he recognized him. He was Tom Murray, former NFL player, head coach of the Eagle River Warriors.

Tom rose to his feet and held out a hand to the ten-year-old boy. "Call me Coach."

Skeptically, Cam had taken the proffered hand, and that had been the beginning. For the few months that Bethany and Coach dated, he didn't make up to Cam or buy him gifts like some of his mother's other boyfriends had. Instead, he just treated him like one of his players. Coach knew how to treat a kid with decency and respect. He was the first grown man that had ever treated Cam that way.

Then, one evening, Coach had stopped by to pick up Bethany for a date, and she wasn't ready yet. Cam was hanging out on the porch.

"Hi Cam. What's up?"

"Nothing," Cam swung his legs off the end of the porch.

"A babysitter coming to watch you or something?"

"Nah, I'm too old for that."

"Oh. You have any plans for the night?"

"I was just gonna bike around"

"You're a big kid," Coach eyed him up and down. "You play any football?"

Cam shook his head.

"Why not? Football is awesome, kid."

"I don't know…" He hesitated and then looked up at Coach. "The other kids go with their dads." Cam's voice trailed off.

For a moment, Coach didn't say anything. He just studied the boy on the porch steps in front of him. Then, he said, "Follow me, Cam."

Hesitantly, he rose to his feet and followed Coach's long-legged walk over to the back of his pickup. Coach opened his truck door, reached behind the seat, and pulled out a football. He tenderly cradled it in his arms and then tossed it into the air. His eyes were bright with excitement. "Come on over here."

"What are we going to do?" Cam asked.

"Throw the pigskin around, kid. Don't you and your friends ever throw around a football?"

Cam shook his head. When Coach tossed the ball his way, he tried to catch it. But he fumbled it and it fell to the ground.

"Open your fingers and pull the ball into your chest. Watch it. Okay? Now, throw it back to me."

Holding the football in his hands for the first time, Cam gripped it hard. He allowed his fingers to slide over the smooth, slightly pebbled surface. *It feels good, right.* He took the ball in one hand, drew his arm back and threw it back directly at Coach.

"Hey, good throw. Now, keep your eyes on the ball."

Cam caught the next one and then grinned at Coach. "I caught it!" he shouted with excitement.

"Yeah, you did. Now, throw from the shoulder and point the football where you want it to go. All right, send it back to me."

They threw the ball back and forth. Coach provided some gentle direction throughout. About twenty minutes later, Bethany came out. "Hi boys, oh isn't this nice. You're playing together… Tom, are you ready to go?"

"Give us a few more minutes, Bethany. Your boy has an arm," Coach commented as he lofted the ball back to Cam.

"Tom, I'm hungry," Bethany whined. "We were going to go to the Water's Edge, right? That new fancy place? I'm ready now."

"Aw, Bethany I'm all hot and sweaty now. We need to talk about this kid of yours. He should be playing football. Why don't you have him signed up for YMCA football? He could be playing Y league now."

"You know how busy I am, Tom," Bethany commented. "I don't know if I could get him to practice."

"One of the other parents can pick him up. Team sports are good for kids, Bethany. This boy should be playing sports. I know some of the guys who manage Y leagues. Give me the go ahead to see if I can get him on a team."

Cam had ended up going to dinner with his mother and with Coach at Sal's diner that night. True to his word, Coach had gotten him on a Y football team. Even after Coach and Bethany broke up a few months later, he had continued to take an interest in Cam. He'd come to most of his youth football games, and then, of course, all of the high school ones. *Coach wasn't my dad, but he was the closest thing that I ever came to having one. He was someone to look up to, someone who seemed to care. But then Odgers had come along.* Coach had continued to be involved in Cam's life, but he'd also been close to Galen, and that just rubbed Cam wrong. *Why couldn't I be the only special one?*

Bethany, of course, had moved on to another guy, and then another. And despite all of the guys, all of the rough times, he could appreciate that she had always done her best by him. She had supported the two of them on her own and he respected her for that. She had held her head up in a town that looked down its nose at her. He looked over at her now. As was usual, she had too much make up on and her hair was a very unnatural shade of burgundy with some highlights. *She'd never been like the other Eagle River moms.* But Bethany had never let him down on the important stuff like keeping a roof over his head and food in his belly. *She'd always been there for me and I owe her for that.* The rest of his childhood, his life in Eagle River, he could try to put behind him, but not Bethany. *Not Mom.*

Chapter Eighteen

New Year's Eve Disaster

~ Galen ~

Galen turned off the ignition outside the Court'n House. When he stepped down out of the old truck, he observed the winter's night sky. It was a midnight vault with pinpricks of stars sloping down to a smoothly carpeted, snow covered world. He took a deep breath and the bitingly cold, winter fresh air invigorated his senses. It was New Year's Eve, time for fresh starts. *It feels grand to be home and out of the city, even if it's just for two days.*

With ebullience, he swung open the door to the Court'n House. He stepped into the front brassy country music, beer, sweat and cologne that always assaulted one at the door.

Ben was already bellied up to the bar.

Galen clapped him on the back. "Hey, man."

Ben choked and then spit out the beer he'd been drinking. He coughed, choked and grinned. "You made it."

"I wouldn't miss New Year's Eve at Court'n House," Galen agreed. "Especially since this is the first year that I'm legal."

"Let me get you a drink." Ben waved to get Sal's attention.

"Just a beer."

Ben nodded with a grin. "That's right, you're legal now. Sounds good."

When Sal glimpsed the two of them at the bar, he sent over a pitcher of beer. In the spirit of the holiday, Ben and Galen chatted, caught up on old times, greeted old friends and drank. As the evening progressed, the faces they saw grew a little blurred and unfocused. The bar became stiflingly warm with holiday spirit, booze, and warm bodies. Kyle eventually showed up. He was as always, ready to party. Billy Ray Cyrus was booming out a plea about his achy heart on the jukebox, and usually the song annoyed Galen, but not tonight. On this night, it sounded happy and right. Some line dancers were attempting to get something going on an edge of the dance floor.

Hot. Galen noticed that his face felt tight and warm. His smile grew larger still, stretching the muscles of his face to their limit. Tom and Sal were off to the side of him, arguing over the Packer's possibilities for the upcoming playoffs. Faces swam in and out of his focus. People clapped him on the back and bought drinks for him. He even managed to gag and choke his way through a couple of cigars.

"It's Cuban," Sal had explained with a reverent expression, as he'd rolled it between his fingers right by Galen's ear. "Listen to it. Smell it. It tells you a story about sunny days and tropical nights, rum drinks and bikinis. It's all there."

Galen had done as directed, but the cigar had tasted just like any other cigar to him. In his intoxicated state, he had ended up inhaling deeply the pungent, hot cigar smoke and came up choking and gagging.

"Not quite the smoothie yet, are you, Galen?" Gene had teased while Ben pounded him on the back.

"Easy, Galen. Enjoy it. Savor it. Don't devour it," Kyle had advised. "You smoke a cigar with style, like a gentleman."

So, there Galen was, leaning up against the bar, a stogie in one hand and a Jack and Coke in the other when he caught a glimpse of a fall of blond hair and a familiar tall, slender form. *Kjersten?* His entire focus was on the movement of that long, pale hair. *She was here. She had come. To see me?* Warmth flooded through his body and immediately pooled in his groin. He moved towards her, honing in on his target through the gyrating bodies, the floor swayed and undulated with his every step. Standing right beside her, her back toward him, he caught a whiff of her soft scent. *Was it lilacs?*

"Kjersten." He reached out and for the first time in more than three years, touched her, just her shoulder, but he was aware of the contact throughout his body.

Surprised, she jumped and spun to face him. She smiled her beautiful perfect smile, the same one that he'd once imagined was only for him. *That didn't turn out to be the case.* But then he squashed that jealous thought. *Kjersten is here now. With me. Not with Cam.*

"Hi, Galen. Happy New Year." She bit her lip nervously. *She looks amazing.* His eyes went to her lips which were overly full and had felt so good back when they slid up and down on his cock. "Galen?" She was staring at him strangely. "You okay?"

"You're beautiful." He reached out and drew her into his arms. A stunned Kjersten stiffly allowed herself to be held. Galen reveled in the feel of her body against him. Tall, slender, and soft, she felt so right, the way that she always had. He nuzzled his lips into the silky, lilac-scented softness of her hair. *God, she is even better than the dreams.* "I've missed you."

Her body eased from rigid and resistant to his embrace, to hesitantly soft and pliant against him. "Galen," she whispered his name in a throaty voice.

He leaned back and reached a hand out to cup the warm, softness of her cheek. "Kjersten." He began to gently sway against her. "The music." He leaned back into her and lost himself in the feel of her form against his.

"Let's at least get on the dance floor," she whispered back. "Everyone's watching. Do you think that you can handle a two-step? Or are you going to fall down as we try to get to the dance floor?"

"I can make it." He held tightly onto her hand, pulled along by the slightly hazy vision of swaying pale hair and an effervescent smile that she turned on him when she swung around to protest his slowness. *She seems happy to see me.* Once there, she took him by both hands and drew him onto the dance floor. There, she stopped and released him, and put her arms around him in the posture of country dancers.

Unsatisfied with the distance between them, he pulled her

completely up against him, muffling her protests. He rested his hands in the small of her back, just above where her ass began to round out. Once again, she relaxed in his arms. He slid his fingertips down and stroked and kneaded the firm curves, as the sides of his arms brushed against the full breasts that were pressed against his chest.

He felt himself grow harder still. Distantly, he noticed other couples attempting to country dance around them, but he just shut them out and swayed to his own rhythm. He burrowed his lips through her hair and into the warm groove at the side of her neck. There, he tasted her with his tongue. She tasted salty, sweet, hot. He felt as much as heard her soft moan. She tilted her head further to the side, accommodating his gentle nuzzling. He felt her nipples tighten against his chest. *Kjersten wasn't wearing a bra.* She felt so good against him, so right.

The song ended and though she drew back, as if to step away, he held her tightly, refusing to let go, oblivious to everyone around him.

Then, a romantic waltz melody began to play and John Michael Montgomery was singing about Texas ladies and dreaming. His warm, velvety tones and the smooth magic of the waltz intoxicated Galen and, it seemed, Kjersten as well. Now, he loosened his grip on her, moved back into a correct waltzing stance, and winked at her while she smiled radiantly up at him. Galen closed his eyes and his feet began to move effortlessly into the steps that they'd learned together in his mother's kitchen a lifetime ago.

Around and around they turned. Despite all of the alcohol he'd consumed, Galen's muscle memory ensured that the two of them moved lithely and skillfully together, long legs lean, elegant forms in smooth motion. They had learned to dance together, practicing endlessly before the exacting eye of Jessica Odgers in the weeks before Kjersten's Junior Prom.

Galen's every nerve ending tingled, hot and alive. This was far too hot, too pulsing to be nostalgia. His strides grew shorter. Soon, he no longer bothered with footwork. His movement returned to a body-on-body sort of swaying.

The song slowed and then came to an end. Too lost in the moment, Galen began to slide his hands up and down her sides, caressing her.

Kjersten pulled back. "Galen, people are staring."

"Let 'em stare."

"I don't think." She detached her body from his and the feeling of separation was almost physically painful for Galen.

"Let's get out of here."

"What?"

"Come on, baby," he protested as he followed her.

"Baby?" She pivoted and practically spat the word at him. Her face transformed, losing the soft, aroused look it had worn before. She stared at him incredulously. "Who are you talking to? I'm not your baby. I've never been your baby. Who do you call 'baby?' I'm Kjersten, remember? Not some football bunny! You're just drunk!" She pushed him with both hands on his chest and stormed off.

"Whas wrong?" he slurred the words. Then, shook his head, attempting to clear it. *Why was she being so difficult? What's her problem?* He started to follow her, but she was moving too fast, and the floor had kept shifting under his feel in the most annoying way

She paused to speak with a girlfriend of hers.

What was that girl's name? Amanda? No, Margo. They both turned to glare at him. Still, he started to follow after her.

Then, a hand clapped down on his shoulder. "Galen, how about a game of pool?" Coach's face swam into view. Coach deliberately steered him away from the two women. "Better yet, why don't you sit down and take a load off."

"But Kjersten… I need to talk to her. Need to."

"You're drunk, Galen, no question about it. You are officially bullet proof," Tom evaluated as he propelled the younger man over to a bar stool. "You are way too far gone to be dealing with knots as complicated as that one. Let it go for tonight. Don't do anything stupid. You two got everyone talking with that dance you just had. Don't stoke the flames." He pushed Galen down on a bar stool. "You got the rumor mill turning. You need to add to it by having her slap you?"

"Why would she slap me?"

Tom rolled his eyes expressively. "You were getting a little frisky for being out on a dance floor in Eagle River." He chuckled. "There's too much history between you two. You're not going to work through all that during one dance."

"We were getting along fine." Galen pushed Tom's hand away.

"That's why Kjersten walked away from you," Tom commented dryly. "For tonight, let it go. You're in no condition to try to fix this. Trust me."

Still, he stared longingly over at Kjersten. *What did I say or do wrong? How did I mess things up again?*

"Galen." Tom stood right in front of him, trying to get his attention. "There was something I wanted to say to you tonight, something I wanted to tell you. This is probably not the right time, but I'm not sure that there ever really would be a 'right' time. There hasn't been in twenty-one years." Tom eyed him anxiously. "Maybe its better that you're a little worse for the wear, maybe that will make this easier to swallow."

Even through the swirling fog that clogged his thoughts, Galen recognized that Tom was uncharacteristically unsure of himself. He was searching for words, obviously doubtful of what he was trying to say, or how he was trying to say it.

"It's about your mother. Your mother, you see her and me… well…"

"What?" Anything about his Mom caught Galen's attention. "What about Mom?"

"Your mom was special, and she and I," Tom paused.

Galen glimpsed Kjersten heading towards the bar door.

"Focus, Galen. I need you to pay attention."

But Galen clearly wasn't. Tom shook his head. He scrutinized Galen for a moment and then stood up from his bar stool and tossed a couple of bucks on the bar. "Come on, Galen. Get Ben and let's get out of here. I'm going to drive you home. You need to sleep this one off."

Hey, Kyle," Tom called Galen's brother, who was busy putting the moves on a rather weathered-looking blond at the other end of the bar. "Can you give me a hand with your brother here?"

Kyle waved back. "Yeah, give me a minute."

"But it's not New Year's yet," Galen muttered. "Happy New Year," he shouted. "Where's Kjersten? Where did she go? I need to talk to her."

He pivoted around, searching for her.

"No, we're getting you home now."

"No," Galen muttered. "You don't understand. I have to talk to Kjersten. I want her. You don't understand."

"That's enough, Galen. The door's this way."

"But I want her!"

Tom grabbed him by the arm and turned him around. "Listen, she's gone. Left. If you ever want to have a chance with her again, let me take you home now. You can't do anything about it tonight."

The words seemed to penetrate Galen's alcohol fogged brain. "She's gone."

"Galen," Ben said as he patted his buddy on the back. "Kjersten already left."

"Gone," Galen echoed the word, then slowly followed Tom and Ben out through the pub door.

* * * *

In the middle of the night, Galen awoke to a foul mouth and the feeling that a steel band was tightening inexorably around his temples. Carefully, he opened his eyes to assess the situation. He recognized that he was lying on the living room couch at his childhood home and that he was fully clothed. Holding his head as he slowly sat up, he was very aware that he felt like he'd been run over by a truck. *It's still dark outside. What time is it?* The stench of cigar smoke and booze clung to his hair and clothing tweaked his stomach. Taking a deep breath, he braced himself for the inescapable pain of getting to his feet. Awkwardly, painfully, he drew his arms down and pushed himself groaningly up. His pulse throbbed in his ears.

Still holding his forehead, he focused, on recollecting the events of the previous night. *Kjersten.* He focused. *Oh, God, no.* He groaned, completely mortified; he'd been a total idiot in front of her again, in fact, in front of the whole town, and the worst part about the whole thing was that he could remember almost all of it.

He rose heavily to his feet and stumbled to his bedroom. Slowly, awkwardly, he stripped and kicked the offending garments into a far corner, pulled some old, soft sweats out of a drawer and put them on. The material was comforting, warm, and fresh smelling next to his skin. It was a start to feeling almost human.

Next, he dragged himself in the direction of the kitchen. He was dehydrated, downright parched. He needed a glass of water, some aspirin, and then some sleep. *I acted like a jerk. Think. Think of what to do. How can I make up for how I acted? For what I said?* He groaned as he made his way down the hall. He could see that a light was already on in the kitchen.

He staggered his way in to find a surprisingly clear-eyed Jim Odgers already seated at the kitchen table. Surprisingly, he had a big mug of coffee on the table in front of him.

It hurts to think. Galen staggered over to the fridge. "Hi Pop." *Something to drink. Kjersten.*

"You're up early," Jim muttered.

"Did you go to bed last night?" Galen asked. He was very familiar with his father's Canadian Windsor habit.

Jim shook his head. "Doesn't look like you did much sleeping either," Jim said. "There's hot coffee in the pot."

"You make it?" Galen glanced over in surprise. His father never bothered himself to do much these days.

"I use it as a chaser for the Windsor."

He shook his head, but coffee sounded good so he went and got a mug from a cabinet. He poured himself cup of thick, black coffee.

"Thanks, Pop." He kept his eyes down. *I'm not up for any father-son bonding, and I really don't want to talk.*

"Rough night?" Jim questioned.

Galen grunted, not quite sure how to handle this midnight interview with his usually taciturn father.

"Been there myself once or twice."

Galen had to fight to keep from snorting at the blatant understatement.

"I been meanin' to talk to you, Galen. You know of all you kids, you were the one that bugged me the most. I never did like your looks. You were always kind of spooky, all quiet and big eyed, watching me. But I want you to know…" The older man paused, then continued, "I think you're gonna do all right with your football. It's a crime that a man can make a fortune playin' a game when a man can't hardly make a decent living farming no more, but that's how the world is. Like that Tom Murphy. He's a worthless piece of crap. Never did a full day's work in his life."

Galen sat stunned by chattiness of a man who, for most of his life, barely managed to be civil.

"You listenin', boy?"

"Yes, sir."

"Your mom spoiled you. I always told her that but she wouldn't hear it." For a moment, it appeared that Jim was lost in memories.

Galen just waited, cradling the mug in his hands, shivering with the after effects of his night of overindulgence.

"You're looking rough." Jim chuckled. "Never did have much respect for a man that couldn't handle his booze or fists. You still ain't much of a man, despite being a fancy football player and all."

Galen allowed the cruel remark to wash right over him. It was a skill that he had relied on throughout his childhood.

"Pop, I'm gonna take a shower."

"Slow down, slow down. I got somethin' I've been wanting to say to you. I know you don't have much respect for me. You think I'm a drunk, which I am, that I've been worthless since the accident, which is also true. I've been a shitty father. I'll admit it. Don't try to bullshit me. I know what you and your brother and sister think… Did Sandra tell you that she's been taking me to a doctor? Yeah, I've been seeing a shrink. The doc told me that I have depression problems, manic depression. That jerk is making a hundred bucks an hour to tell me something that I've known for years, that I'm blue, sometimes for no reason at all, and that's why I drink. The drinking dulls things when they seem too bad. I think it's because my brain doesn't work right that I didn't know that I had it good for a while, what with your mom and Kyle and Sandra. Then, after the accident, my brain worked even worse."

"You don't need to tell me any of this, and I don't really want to hear it."

"Listen up. I'm not making excuses. I made my choices, but now I want to set things straight, have my say. The doc has me on some pills, but the liver is shot and so are the lungs. I'm not gonna live much longer and I can't change what's past. But I do want to take care of some business."

Galen rose abruptly, knocking his chair over as he did so. His hangover had eroded even the little pity that he felt for this man. "You've never had anything worthwhile to say to me before. Let's not waste each other's time now."

"Sit down and shut up. You're gonna hear what I gotta say." Jim slammed his fist down on the kitchen table. The rheumy eyes were firm and unyielding in the wrinkled and sun damaged face. The thin, proud features from which the skin hung limply suddenly revealed their resemblance to Kyle's. "I know I ain't done right by you kids."

Because of the uncharacteristic quiver in his father's voice, Galen sat reluctantly back down.

"Your mama was fourteen years younger than me and so pretty and alive. I still don't know why she married me. Jess thought I was something fine at first, because I'd served in the military overseas. We were married real fast, before she figured out that I was just a farmer and an ornery cuss at that. I knew better, but I let her anyway. Then, when things got bad for me, well she stuck by me for as long as she could. You know your mother was like that, always taking care of sick or weak animals. You remember that damned three-legged cat? It followed her everywhere. Your mom was wrecked when I drove over it."

"That cat always slept under the trunk. You just were too drunk that night to remember to check."

"Don't interrupt me, boy. I was just like that cat, worthless. You know your mom and I had split up before you were born? We were heading for divorce, then I had that accident."

"When you nearly killed yourself."

"You know the story. She took me back and took care of me." Jim's voice was matter of fact. "But things were over between us after that... Sometimes I think I should have died in that accident. You all would have been better off without me. I know Jess would have been. I always thought that when we were split up, there was another man, someone she never got over."

"We all turned out fine." *No thanks to you. I am so done with this conversation.*

"I'm not done. Just wait."

"What are you getting at?" Galen felt the hair at the back of his neck rise up. "What is this really about, Dad?"

Jim leaned forward and grabbed Galen's wrist. "We've never liked each other much. You were always a mama's boy, and close to that damn football coach who was always sniffing' around after your mother. They thought I didn't know, but I did. But there was no point in bringing it up when she took me back. I wasn't in any condition to."

Galen pulled his arm away and leaned back from his father, trying to avoid the spittle shooting out of the man's mouth

"You and your mama are both the same," Jim's tone was bitter. "She thought that I was blind and deaf, too. But I knew about it all along. There are no secrets in this family that I don't know. You think you're so smart. You don't know nothing. But I know! I know!" This final exclamation was punctuated with an outburst of shrill laughter that dissolved into a hacking cough. "I may already be dead to you all, but me and this farm, we're still here. That's not going to change no matter what Kyle thinks. He's just like his mother, too, with his plans and his secrets. But I know. I know!"

Galen stared at Jim despairingly. *The old man's gone, lost in the hateful, tormented world of his own mind.* This strange conversation had just come to an abrupt end. "Night, Pop. Thanks for the coffee." He rose to his feet.

Jim Odgers merely grunted in response, lost in his own thoughts.

As for Galen, he slowly made his way back down the hall to his bedroom. *What a fiasco.* He shook his head. *Pop's mind is gone. Who knows how long he'll be able to live out here with Kyle out working all day? He's just not well in the head anymore. Crazy.*

Upon reaching his room, he lay back down. *Should I call Kjersten and apologize? But it's already so late*, he rationalized. He didn't want to disturb the entire Solheim house. *Calling her now will just make a bad situation worse.*

Chapter Nineteen

An Unexpected Phone Call

~ Galen ~

That night slipped by, and so did the following morning, and the right moment to call Kjersten never came. Then, it just felt too late. *What can I say? That I was in idiot... She knows that already.*

Galen returned to school after the weekend a more somber, serious young man. One afternoon, he was listening to a melancholy love song on the radio when, suddenly, the music was cut off.

"Hey, What'ya doin'?"

"Can't stand that country shit," Marvin scowled. "It ain't got no beat. All it is is whining. 'My wife left with my best friend. My truck broke down. My dog ran off, so I'll just ride my horse.'" He had a smooth tenor and he did a slick job of mimicking the typical country western twang. He shook his head in disgust. Then, tuned the radio in to some rap.

"Not rap. I just don't get rap," Galen groaned.

"It's about attitude and you gotta get yourself some. What're you doing up here in the middle of the afternoon?"

"I gotta get this paper done."

"It's Sunday."

"Yeah, and it was due on Thursday."

Marvin eyed his friend. "You been blue for a long time, man. What's been up with you?"

"I just wish that..." Galen muttered and then his voice trailed off.

"What?"

"This weekend, the whole campus is a ghost town. Everyone is going home."

"But not us," Marvin commented as he lay down on his bed tucking his arms behind his head. "Chantelle's coming down to spend it with me."

"Guess that means I'm on the couch in the lounge."

"Do you mind?" Marvin questioned.

"Nah." He paused for a moment. "You're a lucky man. She's a cool girl, and hot, too."

"She is fine," Marvin agreed with relish. "But don't you go getting ideas."

"Of course not. I thought that I had something special with someone once," he sort of stumbled over the words. "But I messed it up, and then she moved on."

"You'll find a special gal someday. You just gotta get out more."

Galen shook his head in response. "That's low yield."

"No, I'm serious. A special lady isn't gonna come hunt you down. You gotta go out and find her. It's not like chicks don't dig you. You just gotta sift through them a little bit. I've seen what happens with you. You go out with a chick a few times, maybe mess around a little bit, then you decide that something is wrong with her. You don't give anyone a chance. Every time you meet a girl, it's like you've already decided that it's not going to work out. That's no good."

"Yeah, I know," Galen responded. "But I blew it with the one I wanted."

"You need a lady," Marvin repeated. "My momma would say it's all about balance. You need more balance in your life. It can't all be football and school."

"I suck at balance," he countered. "I also suck at relationships."

"And dancing. You definitely suck at dancing."

"Hey," Galen protested, throwing a pillow at Marvin.

"By the way, you get your message on the machine?"

"Nope, didn't check it."

Marvin tapped the machine.

Tom Murray's familiar tones filled the air. "Galen. Big news! I'm getting married and Maggie wants to have a big, old fashioned wedding. It would mean a lot to me if you could come and be one of my groomsmen. It'll be in May, six months from now. Give me a call."

"I can't believe it." Galen gaped.

"Who's that?"

"My high school coach. The one who played pro-ball, Tom Murray. I'm surprised he's getting married. He seemed like the confirmed bachelor type to me. He was always dating some lady, but rumor had it that he was mourning some long lost love."

"Kind of like you," Marvin observed.

Galen thought about it for a moment. "Yeah, I guess you're right. And now he's getting married."

"You gonna go?"

He nodded. "Yeah." *Would Kjersten be at the wedding?* He was afraid to hope, afraid of being disappointed. *This time, I'm going to speak with her, make it right. Who knows if there ever will be another next time?*

Chapter Twenty

Girl Talk

~ Kjersten ~

Kjersten stood rigidly, staring skeptically at her reflection in the mirror. Schooling her features to be expressionless, she eyed the strapless, pleated, deep plum, chiffon bridesmaid dress. *It is Maggie's day,* she mentally repeated to herself.

"You look lovely. There are no other words to describe it." Irma, the stout seamstress oozed. "That dress was designed for exactly your build."

It's really not that bad. It was just that her chest and shoulders felt very bare, and the skirt was super short on her long legs.

"Maggie, are you sure you won't reconsider the hats? All of the girls would look so lovely in them. It would really help solidify the color scheme."

Kjersten swallowed, one wore what one had to when one was a bridesmaid, but there were limits.

"No," Maggie demurred, catching the looks of horror on the faces of Kjersten and the other bridesmaids. "I think we'll just go with the dresses. Mom, are you absolutely sure that this is the dress?"

"Darling," Serena Hellstrum cooed frostily from her arm chair. "Ripened cranberry is your color. Your blond petiteness will stand out so enchantingly with this color framing it. It will also look charming on

Maddy and Sam," she insisted, gesturing to where her two granddaughters sat. "You said that you wanted me involved. If you are going to undermine my every suggestion, well, then I…"

"No, Mom. I really do want you to be involved."

Sam giggled and buried her Skittle stained hand in the folds of her full skirt. She smiled an enchanting eight-year-old gap toothed smile. Her far more sophisticated twelve-year-old sister, Madeline, sat demurely with her ankles crossed flipping through the latest preteen magazine.

"They do look adorable." Maggie was clearly torn. "It's just that I worry that the style of the dress is a little, I don't know…" She waved her hands in front of her chest. "What do you girls think?"

Serena Hellstrum leveled her martial gaze at Kjersten and the two other bridesmaids who were present for the fitting. The corsets on the three girls had their bosoms cascading over the tops of their décolletage, particularly on Tami, who was a little heavy set.

"Whatever you want, Maggie." Tami volunteered. "It's your day."

"I don't know. It just seems to have gotten a little out of hand… I would really have preferred for the whole thing to have been a little less…" Maggie searched for the word.

"You certainly had `less' the first time around. In fact, you had nothing at all. You went to the court house. Remember? It broke my heart. I just wanted this wedding to be special." Serena sniffled. "You didn't even invite your father and me to your first wedding. It still hurts to think about it. My only daughter eloping."

Maggie rolled her eyes at Kjersten. "All right, Mom. We'll do it your way."

Serena rose with a triumphant smile. "There are some details that you and I need to go over. We need to talk about the music for the service and the flowers that the bridesmaids will wear in their hair."

"Mom, I'm sorry to cut you off, but I'm having lunch with Kjersten today. She's only going to be in town through the weekend."

"Oh, all right then." Serena looked irritated at having her plan disrupted, but she was too pleased with Maggie's capitulation concerning the wedding plans to put up much of a fight.

"Can you take the girls, Mom?"

"It's almost time for Power Rangers, Gramma. We gotta hurry."

"Fine." Serena beamed at her grandchildren. "We'll have grilled cheese sandwiches, girls. And while you watch your program, I'll work on the invitation list. Has Tom finished his?"

"I hope so," Maggie answered. "Thanks for taking the girls, Mom."

"Come with me, my little chickadees." Selena claimed the two children after they hugged their mother.

Maggie turned to her bridesmaids and offered them a weary smile. "Thank you guys for being such sports."

"Any time," Tami, a childhood friend, responded with a smile.

"Are you kidding? I'm so excited," the other woman, a teacher and Maggie's coworker, agreed.

The women chatted back and forth as they changed back into their own clothes.

"Well, at least this is done and done is good." Maggie commented to Kjersten after the others had left the fitting room. "Carrie is the only one who remains to be fitted and her dress will have to be shipped to her in Chicago. What a circus," she exhaled slowly.

"Better you than me," Kjersten teased.

"Oh, it'll be you one day. You'll suffer." Maggie smiled and, as always, Kjersten found it contagious. Maggie was the kind of person who was always bursting with energy, with plans. She lit up every room she entered.

"So, how long have you and Coach been together?"

"Well, the girls and I came to Eagle River six years ago when I got the job at Eagle River High. We didn't get involved for the first three years. I was still going through my divorce, but then," she hesitated.

"The attraction proved irresistible," Kjersten teased.

Maggie took Kjersten's arm. "I'm so glad that you are back in town. I've missed you, girl. And it's so fun that you're all grown up now."

Kjersten smiled, too. "I've missed you, too."

"I don't know about you, but I'm famished," Maggie said. "I would much prefer running a marathon to this wedding stuff."

The two had made their way to Green Eggs and Ham, Gene's diner.

"Hey there," Gene greeted them from behind the register. "Be right with you folks."

"We're in no hurry, Gene." Maggie called back.

They took a table facing the street in the glassed in front of the diner. Maggie groaned. "I was hoping that it would be prettier outside, maybe some flowers up. It's just so dreary," she groaned.

"It'll be a beautiful day," Kjersten asserted. Don't worry.

"I just hope that everything goes smoothly. I want Tom to enjoy it, and it's gotten to be such a big mess what with my mom taking over."

Kjersten squeezed her friend's hand. "Everything will be fine. Just approach it like a volleyball game. I remember that you always told us to focus on the game, but remember that it was just a game, an hour out of our lives. The wedding is just a day, your day, but only a day. Besides, Coach Murray adores you."

"When did you get so wise? I'm supposed to be the mature teacher type. That university must be doing you some good."

"Ladies," Sal's booming baritone interrupted their conversation as he appeared tableside. "You two ladies ready for the big event?"

"Just about, Sal. How about yourself?"

"I'm just getting all the loose ends together." Sal wore a guilty expression.

"Sal, you know that Tom and I agreed that a stag party is out. You had better not be planning anything like that."

Sal was now obviously chagrined.

"If I hear that you have strippers down at your place, I guarantee that I will personally storm the place with some of the most anal members of the PTA, without their husbands, and you know exactly which ladies I am talking about. You'll lose half of your Monday night football crowd."

"Aw come on, Maggie. As the best man, I have to organize something. It just wouldn't be right for old Tom to finally get hitched without a proper send off."

"I'm serious. I don't want any funny stuff, nor does Tom."

"Would you agree to me getting some of the guys together for a couple of beers in the evening? Maybe a little poker? Just close friends, more like family. I was going to invite Tom to golf with me in the early afternoon. There won't be any funny stuff going on. I know that you could make my life a living hell, what with you and Mary being friends and all."

"You're making me sound like a shrew."

"You know I think you're wonderful. Can't think of anyone I'd rather see Tom hitched to. But I also know that you don't take any shit… I just want to make my intentions clear."

"That sounds fine to me," Maggie agreed.

"Well, good then... Kjersten, it's good to see your pretty face back in town."

"Thanks, Sal. It's good to be back."

"I'll leave you ladies to each other. I got a couple of roast beef sandwiches that are demanding my attention." Sal returned to his stool at the lunch counter.

"Sal's a good guy," Maggie observed with a grin. "But you have to give a man clear black and white limits, or they will walk all over you."

"I think you're right about that one, Maggie. That's a lesson that I've had to learn the hard way." Kjersten fiddled with the salt shaker on her table.

"Don't we all. I never realized how much planning a wedding would be." Maggie groaned as she rubbed her hands nervously together.

"It'll be wonderful. Don't worry. By the way, I know who your bridesmaids are, but you haven't told me who Coach chose as groomsmen."

"Tom has a bunch of old football playing buddies that he wants in the wedding party. Sal's the best man. And I already told you that Galen Odgers and Cam Fawst are going to be the ushers. I am sorry, I know that it may be awkward for you, but Tom has always been really close to both of them. They are like sons to him."

"I'll be fine," Kjersten reassured Maggie, despite the sinking feeling in her gut. "It's all ancient history."

"Tom will keep both of them in line. You sure that you'll be okay?"

"I can handle it."

"I wanted to ask you about something, Kjersten," Maggie said, hesitantly toying with the edge of her place mat. After a moment, she raised her eyes decisively. "You knew Galen's mom, Jessica?"

"Yes. Sure. I spent a lot of time at the Odgers' farm when Galen and I were... when we were kids," she finished lamely.

"What was she like? Jessica Odgers?"

"What do you mean?

Maggie was embarrassed. "I've heard a lot about her. I'm just curious."

"I liked her. She was kind of like you, tough and strong, able to stand on her own two feet. She was very pretty with all of this red gold hair. She was a lot younger than Mr. Odgers. She worked the farm by herself with the kids after her husband's accident. You know about all that, right?"

"Yes. But what was she like?"

"Mrs. Odgers wasn't a normal mom type at all. She was really alive. She was very outdoorsy, into hunting and fishing. And she was a hard worker. The grounds of the farm were always immaculate, even though the house was always a mess. It used to drive Sandra crazy. She's a very tidy person, you know, everything in its place. Mrs. Odgers didn't care about the indoors. She always wanted to be outside, doing something. I think she was a little frustrated. No, actually I know she was really frustrated with her husband. I remember she said that she got married really young, before she knew what she really wanted from life. But she loved her kids. They were her life... Is this the sort of thing you wanted to know?"

"That is exactly what I wanted to hear."

"I remember when I was about fifteen, it was a snow day, so we were off from school. As you know, school is almost never called off in Eagle River."

Maggie nodded.

"But that night the temperature stated to fall. It went to minus thirty degrees. Something happened with the pipes at school. They exploded, I think. When I found out that we had the day off, I had my mom drive me over to the Odgers.

"I remember that it was unbelievably cold outside and the sun was incredibly bright and blinding off the snow. Galen and I had talked about going sledding when we spoke on the phone, but then, when I got to the farm, he said it was too cold to go, but I still wanted to."

"You've always been so flexible," Maggie teased.

"I know, I know. I'm a work in progress. Anyway, when Mrs. Odgers came in from milking the cows she said she would go sledding with me. In the woods behind the Odgers' house is this almost sheer drop that leads down to a creek. There are pine trees all over this thing and you have to dodge trees when you sled, but you can really get some speed going down. When you hit the creek, it's frozen on top, so you shoot right across it. It feels like you're flying. That day, Galen stayed inside while Mrs. Odger and I went sledding.

"It was such a rush. I remember that the icy air burned and we went so fast that I was blinded with tears. We went down again and again, though snow got into our boots and our faces went numb. Eventually, Galen came out and joined us. Finally, when I had lost sensation in both my hands and feet, we went in. But that's the kind of person that Mrs. Odger was... I don't mean to babble on. I'm sorry."

"Oh no. I'm interested. You are the first person who has given me any idea of what she was really like."

"She was the kind of person that people felt strongly about, but why are you so interested in her?"

Maggie gazed at her young companion. "You know how close Galen and Tom are. I believe that Jessica Odger's death was one of the things that really drew them together, so I was curious about her."

Kjersten studied her friend, but decided not to push the subject. She had always been close with Maggie when she'd played volleyball for her. They'd grown closer still because Kjersten had often babysat her girls. Once Kjersten was in college, their relationship had grown into a true friendship. Maggie was open, definitely not the sort to keep things to herself. *If she was not being forthcoming, she probably had some worthwhile reasons.*

"Well, that's enough of that," Maggie commented. "So, tell me, what have you been up to?"

"Nothing too thrilling. Pretty much same old, same old. Just school."

"Are you seeing anyone?"

"No. I'm taking a break from the whole dating thing. I need to get my own act together." *Besides, I can't have the guy I want, and any other would be a poor substitute.*

Maggie nodded. "I felt that way for a while after my divorce."

"Can I take your orders?" A waitress had appeared at the table.

Chapter Twenty-One

Exes

~ Kjersten ~

"It's freezing. Hurry up."

"I'm trying," Kjersten shivered. "My fingers are frozen."

Lauren stared at the plume of smoke that was her breath. "Remind me why we decided to go to school in the Arctic Circle? We could be at the University of Florida right now, drinking margaritas and having gorgeously tan hunks rub oil all over our bodies."

"I don't know if they have any hockey players in Hawaii," Kjersten commented dryly as she swung the door open.

"Hey, I'm over the hockey player thing. Now, I'm into tennis players."

The long, sterile halls were dimly lit and the white tiles of the roof and the shadowy gray walls extended in two directions. The girls' footsteps echoed weirdly through the empty, dimly lit corridors.

"This would be the perfect location for a pursuit scene in a Friday the Thirteenth movie," Kjersten observed as the two women walked quickly to the Genetics classroom.

"It is pretty creepy here at night," Lauren acknowledged with a shiver.

"Look, the lights are on," Kjersten observed, gesturing at the small, rectangular window that glowed brightly in the darkened hallway.

"Somebody else must have flies hatching tonight." She opened the door.

After the cold, inhospitable darkness of the hallway, the genetics lab was brightly lit, comfortably warm, and reeking of a sickly sweet, sticky odor that was reminiscent of rotten bananas.

"What is that smell?" Lauren groaned. "I think I'm going to yak."

"That's ether and banana," Kjersten explained. "You'll get used to it in a sec, then you won't even notice it."

"Banana?" Lauren echoed questioningly.

"Yeah. That's what the little buggers eat." A very tall girl, who was red headed and fully dressed in black commented from her seat down at the table.

"Hi, Cat," Kjersten greeted her classmate. "You know Cat, er, Cat, don't you, Lauren?"

"Yeah. How's it going, Cat?" Lauren acknowledged the other girl.

"Good. See this stuff?" Cat held up a scoop of blue powdered crystals from a bag. "Just add water and Voila! Wonder goo. They eat it and they live in it."

"You science people are so gross," Lauren groaned.

"My problem is that I can't sort the flies very well. They all look pretty much the same to me. When I do get them differentiated, it takes me so long that they start to wake up. Their little legs start to twitch. So, I ether them again and again and before you know it, they're dead," Cat observed.

"Let me see." Lauren jumped up from her seat and ran to where Cat bent over the microscope. "Wow, the little legs are moving. That one... He's walking. Oh wait! He just lifted off."

"Could you pass me the ether?" Cat said.

"I'll bring it over," Lauren offered. In her rush, she hit the bottle and it tipped over. She righted it quickly, but a pool of it had spilled. Cat grabbed two towels, one for her face and the other for the spillage.

"I didn't realize that it was open," Lauren apologized. "Can't we open a window or something?"

"No, they're locked. Try not to breathe the stuff."

"Does it make you high or something?"

"I don't know about high, but I always feel a little brain dead in this room," Cat remarked.

The little group moved to another one of the long, narrow tables. Kjersten got to work sorting her flies.

"I can't believe your parents spend a couple of thousand dollars a semester so that you can play with bugs," Lauren remarked.

"I spend a couple of thousand dollars each semester to play with dead things in Anatomy and Phys," Cat offered.

"The life of the bio major," Kjersten remarked.

"That is so vile." Lauren shuddered. "Please, let's talk about something else. I can feel those Ranch Pringles that I snarfed starting to work their way up."

"Now that's gross… Hey Cat," Kjersten called out, not lifting her eyes from her microscope. "You're a reporter for 'The Turnip,' right?"

"The Turnip?" Lauren questioned.

"It's an alternative student run paper," Cat explained. "Haven't you seen it? It's in the Student Union and everywhere on campus. And yeah, I am."

"Oh," Lauren commented.

"Whatever happened to those frat boys who exposed themselves pissing out of a window?" Kjersten asked.

"I heard something about it," Lauren commented. "Do you know all the juicy details?" she asked, her eyes alight with curiosity.

"These guys got tanked one afternoon a few weeks ago," Cat explained. "They were all hanging out on their porch. Two women were walking by. The guys started to yell stuff, whistle and catcall. The women yelled back at the guys. So, one of them pulled down his pants and pissed out the window, several others did the same."

"Idiots," Kjersten commented.

"Then what happened?" Lauren asked.

"Well, the women called security. They said that the Frat guys had 'brandished' their penises at them like weapons, in a threatening manner, and that they felt violated. Anyway, it looks that the guys are being held responsible and made to face disciplinary actions. Jerks. I think they were some kind of athletes, maybe wrestlers. The whole macho, male bonding thing goes to their heads, and they treat women disrespectfully."

"Not all athletes are like that," Kjersten commented.

"No offense, Kjersten, but the jocks you've dated haven't exactly been role models," Lauren commented.

Kjersten shook her head and rolled her eyes. "No offense taken. Cam was a jerk."

"Cam? Cam Fawst," Cat shook her head reflectively. "Been there and done that, too. Sexy, but a total asshole."

"You were with him, too?" Lauren questioned incredulously. "That guy gets around."

"Yeah, he used to come into the Nasty Habit, where I bartend. Turns out, he was seeing both Kjersten and me at the same time."

"What a pig!" Lauren commented.

"We figured it out at the beginning of the semester. By then, both of us were done with him so it didn't really matter. We just bonded over it," Kjersten commented. "The best part is that Cat had two bouncers kick his ass."

"No way. That is so cool. What is it with that guy?" Lauren questioned.

"Well, he is hot," Cat remarked. "He has an unbelievable body. I'll admit he rocked my world. We had fun together. Then, I figured out that I was just a booty call for him, that he had a real girlfriend. So I had two of my friends kick his ass. Not kill him or anything, but at least give him something to think about."

"Was Kjersten the girlfriend?" Lauren asked.

Cat nodded.

"Cam's like a drug," Kjersten said. "He gets you hooked. He's an asshole, but there's something about him. He comes across all cocky, but there's also this lost little boy look in his eyes."

"Yeah, well, he's going to have to grow up now." Cat observed. "I heard from a reliable source that Cam is going to be a daddy. His current girlfriend is pregnant."

"Are you serious?" Kjersten was shocked.

"Yup. That's what I heard," Cat responded. "I sort of know his current."

"Guys, I feel a little weird," Lauren interrupted. "Not quite high, but definitely funky. You sure that the ether won't affect us?"

"It shouldn't," Kjersten answered.

"Kjersten has to see Cam again soon. They are in a wedding together."

"You serious?" Cat questioned, her dark eyes, bright and sardonic.

"And the best part is that Galen Odgers is in the wedding, too," Lauren commented.

"Galen Odgers," Cat stated. "That name sounds familiar."

"He's another guy that I used to date," Kjersten admitted.

"Who is he?" Cat asked.

"The quarterback for Illinois University," Lauren responded.

"We all come from the same home town. We're all in a wedding together," Kjersten said and shrugged.

"I am impressed." Cat smirked. "I've got to start running in your circles. You doing some kind of comparative study or something: `QBs of the Big Ten.' Ow, you didn't just kick me, did you, Kjersten?"

Kjersten had pink creeping up her neck, but she laughed. "Galen went to my high school, too."

"And you were the head cheerleader or the homecoming queen, right?"

"Nope. Co-captain of the volleyball team. I am definitely no cheerleader or homecoming queen. It's a complicated story, but Galen dumped me, then I hooked up with Cam. Low self-esteem at the time, I guess. I had a hard time being alone."

"So which one was better in the sack?" Cat questioned with a mischievous grin. "I mean, I know how Cam was, but what about Odgers?"

"Galen and I were the first for each other. We learned things together. We experimented together. We knew how to touch each other. The sex was pure magic." Kjersten's eyes drifted closed.

"And what about Cam?" Lauren prompted.

"He's … forceful. He likes to be in control. He looks at you likes he wants to devour you and then, he does."

"You are so right," Cat commented. "You're getting me all hot and bothered now."

"But I have to see both of them at this wedding and I don't have a date," Kjersten continued.

"You know I'd go with you if I could," Lauren said. "But I have to go home that weekend. I promised my mom."

"Which weekend are we talking about? Cat asked.

Kjersten glanced at her hopefully. "The third one in April. We'd go up on a Friday night and be back on a Sunday."

"If you want someone to go with, I'll go," Cat offered. "This sounds too delicious to miss. Besides, it would be fun to see Cam again. He'll freak if I show up."

"Let's do it," Kjersten responded with a twinkle in her eye.

Chapter Twenty-Two

The Pontoon Ride and the Reception

~ Kjersten ~

Tom and Maggie's wedding day afternoon proved to be cool, gray and drizzly. After the ceremony at the Faith Lutheran Church in town, all of the guests went to the Silver Beach Marina where they were to take a boat over to the Eagle River Lodge. Tom and Maggie had already departed while the wedding party gathered under a green and white striped awning, waiting to embark onto another waiting pontoon boat that was to carry them to the reception.

Kjersten, whose shoulders and upper chest were bared in the bridesmaid gown, shivered. "I wish we could go on the next boat ride," she muttered to Cat, who stood at her side wearing a short, form-fitting black dress.

"Yes, but the wedding party has to get over to the lodge for pictures. You are in the wedding party."

"I know, but look who's on our boat," Kjersten muttered.

Cat just chuckled, eying Cam and Galen and their dates. "This is exactly what I was hoping for."

"Let's get on last," Kjersten suggested. "That way everyone else can get settled down and seated."

"You mean Cam and Galen and their dates, right? Come on. Have some fun. Cam does look hot in his tux. He is great eye candy," Cat murmured.

Kjersten nervously shook her head. Thankfully, she hadn't had time to speak with either ex before or after the service. Unfortunately, there would be forced intimacy on the boat for the next twenty minutes or so. She took the step down into the pontoon boat and Cat, whose tight skirt prevented her from separating her legs, followed a moment later.

Cam nodded to Kjersten as she made her way to the bench under the Bimini top. His date, a tiny, top-heavy cheerleader type in a painted on sequined dress was tilting precariously sideways on a bench seat. She already appeared to be totally tanked and miserable. But Cam was paying no attention to her. His eyes were lasered in on Cat. "What are you doing here?" he demanded when she drew abreast of him.

Cat, who was his equal in height, glared right back at him. "I'm here for the wedding."

"You bitch," he snarled. "You're lucky those guys didn't seriously hurt me. I could have pressed charges against you."

Cat put one hand on her hip. "That would have gone over well. I can see the headlines, 'Cheating Coyote Quarterback Beaten Up by Night Club Bouncers.' You can bet I would have told the whole story, if anyone had been interested."

"You two are here together?" Cam snarled.

Both Kjersten and Cat smiled.

"About a year ago, we discovered that we had a lot in common," Kjersten stated.

Cam had the grace to blush, then he shook his head and deliberately turned his back on the pair of his former lovers. "Classic," he muttered.

As they moved further down the large pontoon, Kjersten gripped Cat's hand. "That was so awesome," she whispered.

"This trip was so worth it," the other woman responded with a satisfied grin.

"She the pregnant one?" Kjersten mumbled to Cat, gesturing at Cam's date with some concern.

Cat shook her head no.

Just then, Galen and his date appeared on the dock. He handed his date carefully into the boat. Cam and Galen exchanged curt nods and then proceeded to ignore the other.

"Chivalry has not died," Cat pointed out, taking a seat beside Kjersten at the far end of the benches, one from which someone had already wiped the water off.

Galen's date was a tall sporty-looking brunette. Once they were onboard, the couple moved down to the end of the pontoon where Cat and Kjersten sat. Taking possession of the bench opposite them, Galen covered the bench with his overcoat for his date and she sat down. He avoided making eye contact with Kjersten. "I'll be right back," he commented to his date, then went to help the other bridesmaids on board.

Galen looks delicious. He was wearing his dark blond hair longer than Kjersten had ever seen it, and it had a wave. It was combed back and styled. His body had grown thicker and taller, and the way that his pants fit on his muscular thighs nearly made her mouth waterwhen he walked to the front of the boat, where the other guys in the wedding party were congregating. Kjersten stared hungrily at his ass. *It looks so grabable.*

Cat caught Kjersten ogling Galen's ass and winked. Kjersten blushed and looked away. Cat rolled her eyes at Kjersten expressively.

"Hi, I'm Sarah," Galen's date gushed.

"I'm Kjersten."

"Cat."

"Where are your dates?" Sarah asked.

"We came together," Cat offered.

"Oh," Sarah responded. "I'm so okay with that. I think it's great that you feel comfortable enough to come together."

"No, you don't understand," Kjersten broke in, seeing the amusement on Cam's face.

But then Cat took her hand. "You know how it is, Sarah, you try new things in college, right? We found that we liked it."

Sarah's eyes went wide and Galen, who had just returned, chuckled.

"Kjersten." Galen said, finally acknowledging her.

"Galen. It's good to see you." *And it was. Her heart was suddenly pounding.* "How are you?"

"Fine. I mean, good. And you?"

"Good, too." *Think of something clever to say. Or, just say something. Anything.* But nothing came to mind. They both looked away from each other.

Once everyone was loaded, the boat pulled away from the dock. The other bridesmaids and Cat were engaged in the usual wedding chit chat but Kjersten zoned it out. Instead, her eyes and her entire attention were drawn to Galen. *Look at me.* She willed him. *See me.*

But he kept his face turned to the front of the boat, eyes fixed on the approaching shore.

So, Kjersten glanced ahead as well. The sun was bursting out ahead of them, burning away the heavy gray clouds. The entire panorama took her breath away and she was happy for Maggie and Tom. *They deserved this beautiful day. Galen looks so good. His hair curls.* Her fingers twitched with the forgotten sensation of running her fingers through it.

Kjersten glanced over at Cam. *He looks good, too,* she admitted grudgingly. Though shorter, he was broader than Galen with well-developed arms. His hips were narrow and his belly, washboard flat. But there was something too slick about how his hair was coiffed, something too polished about his veneer. He glanced up and caught her looking at him. He grinned at her, and Kjersten deliberately looked away. *Asshole.* Dismissing him from her thoughts, she glanced back at the sky and the water. She breathed the rich, fresh lake breeze then exhaled slowly. *This is so weird, being here with both of them. We pretend to be polite strangers. How odd, with everything that has happened between us, with what we've been to each other, all three of us. Oceans of history, all moving under the surface.*

It was then that Galen turned from chatting softly with one of the bridesmaids to look at Kjersten.

Her gaze locked with his and her breath caught. There was naked longing in his gaze, desire for her, and it consumed her, set her aflame. Suddenly, the two of them were locked in a moment. There was a depth to his look that pierced through her and ensnared her. There was so much in his eyes, knowledge of himself and of her, and a nearly painful yearning suddenly stirred to life and echoed in Kjersten's soul.

Found, I feel found, and I didn't know I was lost.

"Hey," Cat whispered and elbowed her, breaking the spell. "Don't be so obvious."

"What?" Kjersten asked.

"You two look like you're going to eat each other alive. The girlfriend's noticing. He does have a date, you know. You two are so not happening tonight."

Kjersten looked up and found Sarah's eyes upon her, speculation in them. Still, she couldn't resist glancing back at Galen. He was still looking right at her, seemingly oblivious to all of the people around them. His gaze seared her, nearly tangible. Every part of her ached for him. *Did I even understand that I still cared this much when I lost him? Somehow it hurts more now. Maybe we were too young before, too inexperienced to know what we had.* Awareness of each other was a live current passing through the air between them, connecting them, drawing them together, back to each other.

"Man, you two got it bad," Cat commented.

Kjersten glanced down then, breaking the connection. *He has a date, maybe a girlfriend, so why does he look at me like that? Does he still feel something for me? I can't speak to him here or at the reception, but when will I see him again?* Her eyes felt suspiciously full and she swallowed the tears rising in her throat.

"I feel sick," Cam's date announced loudly from her seat near the other end of the boat, breaking the spell. She turned and rushed down the length of the pontoon to where Kjersten and Cat were sitting. She climbed up on the bench, staring down at the water.

"What?" Cat asked.

"I think I'm going to throw up. It's either the mojitos or the water or…" Suddenly, the girl leaned over the side of the pontoon and began to vomit into the lake.

"Oh, gross," someone commented.

Both Sarah and Galen stood up and shifted away from the sick girl.

"You okay?" Kjersten asked.

Cat reached over and pulled the girl's hair back.

"Cam?" Kjersten called. "Your date needs help."

Cam took a step back under the Bimini cover, took in the scene of the miserable and ill girl, and then growled, "Can this get any worse? Paige, you're just embarrassing."

The sick girl began to sob miserably.

"Come on, Cam. Have a heart," Kjersten protested. "She's in bad shape."

"She's pathetic." Cam scowled, turning away.

"Cam, you're such an asshole," Cat exclaimed. "You need to take care of her."

"I didn't sign up to babysit. Obviously, she can't handle her booze. She can go to our room when we get to the lodge."

"Seriously Cam. You need to step up here," Kjersten insisted.

"I don't have to do a damn thing, including listening to you. You always were a bossy bitch, Kjersten."

"Don't you call her that," Galen broke in.

"Come on, Odgers. You know she's a bitch, a hot one, I'll give you that, but a bitch."

That was all it took. Galen pushed through the crowd, took a swing, and clipped Cam in the chin. Then he stood, fists raised, on the balls of his feet, ready to fight.

"Stop them!" the pontoon driver shouted.

Cam also clenched his fists, clearly ready and eager to go, but then, to Kjersten's amazement, he took a deep breath, straightened up and adjusted his jacket. "You know, Kjersten, Galen, you two deserve each other. Everyone here knows you want to fuck her and from the looks of it, she wants to jump your bones, too. You've been eye fucking each other the whole time we've been on this boat. Just go get the job done, Galen. Maybe she'll show you some of the things I taught her. I know you'll appreciate them." With that, he turned away and walked to the other end of the boat, leaving a stunned silence in his wake.

Kjersten closed her eyes. *Let me disappear right now. Don't let me be on this boat, going to this reception. Let it be over with now.* She didn't dare look at Sarah, Galen's date.

"Wow," Cat mouthed to Kjersten, once awkward conversations had started back up. "Wow, am I glad that I came."

The island and the brilliantly illuminated, glassed in gazebo where the reception was taking place finally came into view.

Cam jumped out as soon as they docked. He didn't say a word to anyone and just ditched his date. Cat and Kjersten were left to maneuver Paige over to the gang plank and then into Olson's lodge, where they handed her off to Maggie's mother. Galen and Sarah left the pontoon in a whispered but clearly heated conversation.

Charmingly decorated for the reception, the great room of the Eagle River lodge looked magnificent from the towering stone fireplace to the barrel vaulted ceilings. The woodsy décor had been given a rustic chic wedding makeover with foliage chains adorned with tiny white lights and multicolored lush cabbage roses. The rectangular head table was raised on a dais and looked out over the other round guest tables. Kjersten, who was seated at the head table, was relieved to find herself at the opposite end from Cam and Galen. Despite her best intentions, she caught herself stealing glances at Galen. *Stop it. He's here with that Sarah girl. I'm not going there.* As for Cam, he had already found another attractive female wedding guest to sit with him. Cat appeared to be having a good time with another one of Coach's former players, a big guy who had graduated a few years before Kjersten.

"They look so happy," Tami, the bridesmaid seated beside her commented.

"What?" Kjersten said. "I'm sorry. I didn't hear you."

"Tom and Maggie. He doesn't take his eyes off her and she's glowing."

Kjersten truly looked at Maggie and Tom, but for a moment another face, a beautiful one with red gold hair, filled her mind's eye. *Jessica Odgers.* Kjersten shook her head. *Why think of Mrs. Odgers? Tonight is about Maggie and Tom.* They did look brilliantly happy. Tom also appeared relaxed and content, not a demeanor that he usually wore. One of Maggie's young daughters was on her mother's lap and the other was seated between Maggie and Tom. The bride was radiant in her old fashioned, A-line lace gown. They looked like a family, like they were meant to be together. Kjersten was so very happy for them and what they had together, but she also ached with loneliness.

* * * *

This evening sucks. Why did I bother to come? Coach is too busy to talk. There's no one else here that I want to talk to at all. And with Kjersten and Cat here, could things get any worse? From his seat at the head table, he glanced over at the red head who'd been giving him the eye earlier. She smiled at him again. *She's not bad and at least I won't have to go back to the room with Paige.*

Just then, someone began to clink a fork against the glass.

"Kiss. Kiss!" someone shouted.

Smiling, Tom drew Maggie to her feet. He turned and smiled with tenderness at her.

Cam leaned a little forward in his seat, looking around the other bridal party members to get a better view of the bride and groom.

Odgers was blocking his view, since he, too, was leaning forward and looking up at the newlyweds. Cam glared at Galen, who, unfortunately, didn't look his way. Maggie said something, and both Galen and Coach turned their heads toward the bride, in Cam's direction.

Holy shit. Their profiles are the same, Cam observed. Their noses, their lips, their jaws, all of the lineaments were the same. *They could be father and son.* Cam rose to his feet, to get a better view. He studied Galen's features and Coach's, and then he glanced over to another table where Kyle Odgers and Sandra Odgers O'Brien sat. Those two siblings definitely resembled each other. On the other hand, Galen resembled his brother and sister only in coloring, the fair hair and skin. Cam glanced back at Coach and Galen, looking closely. The builds were the same, the broadness of shoulder and thickness of thigh, the large, deep socketed eyes, though Tom's were blue and Galen's were brown. Even their very smiles were the same.

Suddenly, a realization struck him like a bolt of lightning. *Why didn't I guess before? Why hasn't anyone else noticed? Odgers is Coach Murray's kid! That explains everything.*

Cam was unable to take his eyes off Coach or Galen. *How could they have kept this secret for so many years in a small town where everyone knew everyone else's business? How could no one else have guessed? No wonder Coach had treated Galen as if he was special. He was his kid and I was just one of his players. Does Odgers even know?*

Chapter Twenty-Three

Promise

~ Kjersten ~

It was time for Tom and Maggie's first dance. "Please join me at the dance floor," the DJ directed, "for Mr. and Mrs. Murray's first dance."

The music opened with fanfare and then there was only Harry Connick's voice and he was crooning "It had to be you" while Tom led Maggie out onto the dance floor and twirled her once and then drew her into his arms. The crowd pressed in close and tight around the dance floor. Kjersten became aware of a tall, hard body on her left side. She looked over. *Galen!* He smiled that devastating half grin that had her melting inside. Curiously, she looked around for his date, but Sarah was nowhere to be seen. He moved right up behind her as the crowd pressed closer. Suddenly, she became aware of the rich musky scent of his cologne, of him. She longed desperately to lean closer into him, but she resisted the urge, with so many people around.

Suddenly, she felt long, warm fingers reach down and entangle with hers. *He's holding my hand.* Electric currents shot up her arm. She couldn't breathe and felt nearly faint though there was only the most minimal of touches between them, fingers just barely intertwined. She didn't dare to look at him. *God, don't let the song end. Please let this moment last forever.* Aware that the lights had been dimmed for the First Dance, Kjersten closed her eyes and let the moment take her. Ever so gently, she squeezed his fingers back. There was magic, heat, music, and nearly excruciating awareness of the man beside her, touching her. Still, she had to ask. “Sarah?” Leaning towards him, she whispered the name so that only he could hear it.

“I told her,” he whispered back.

“What?”

“About you… About us.”

Us. For a moment, she felt as if she would swoon. *This can’t be real.*

“Come with me, now.”

“Won’t she be in your room?”

“I got her her own room. It’ll just be us. I want you. Now. Tonight.”

“Is she your girlfriend?” Kjersten looked directly up at him.

“No, just my date. A friend. I won’t say she understood. We probably aren’t friends anymore, but she knows.”

“Okay.” The word was a whispered promise, and Galen’s eyes on her became hot, hungry, and possessive.

Hope and hunger coursed through Kjersten.

The DJ broke in, “Let’s give a round of applause to Mr. and Mrs. Murray and let’s welcome the rest of the bridal party onto the dance floor.”

Suddenly, one of the groomsmen, a former teammate of Coach’s who was likely the same age as Kjersten’s father, appeared before her. “Would you care to dance?” he asked.

Kjersten glanced longingly back at Galen. “Later,” he mouthed to her. “I’ll find you. I promise.”

She nodded, and allowed the groomsman to lead her onto the dance floor.

Chapter Twenty-Four

Unexpected News

~ Galen ~

Galen stood and watched Kjersten gracefully move over the dance floor. Then, in no mood to dance, himself, he made his way over to the bar. *It's going to happen! We're going to get back together!* Aware of a twinge of guilt over Sarah, he decided he would send her an apology. *But I can't let this opportunity go. This is once-in-a-lifetime. I can't risk losing Kjersten again. I have to seize this opportunity. Sure, we're both a mess, but together, we are okay.*

He walked up to the bar where a few guests lingered. "I'd like a Windsor Sour," he said to the bartender.

"Odgers." Cam Fawst nodded at him, an odd look on his face. Cam was seated a little further down the bar. His tie was undone and his shirt was unbuttoned, revealing the thick mat of dark hair on his chest. "The drink's on me," he stated to the bartender.

"Thanks," Galen responded automatically, his mind still on Kjersten and what the evening ahead promised. He wasn't about to let Cam ruin the magic. *I won't think about the two of them together. We've all made mistakes.*

"You know," Cam's voice was deep and dark. "Coach looks happy with his little Phy Ed teacher. I don't get it. That guy played in the NFL. So why did he stay in this little pisshole of a town?"

"Maybe its home to him. Thanks for the drink." Turning away from Cam, Galen took a long swallow.

"I'll have what he's having," Cam ordered.

"Got it," the bartender agreed.

"You know, I used to pretend or maybe wish that Tom Murray was my dad," Cam commented once the bartender had moved away.

"Look, Cam, I appreciate the drink, but you and I have really nothing to say to each other. So, let's just drop the social bullshit."

"I don't know much about my real dad. Just his name really. Never had anything to do with him. Did you know that?"

"No," Galen replied, though he'd suspected as much.

"My mom dated Coach for a while. Just like a month or so when I was ten. He got me into football."

"That's great, but I'm really not interested in anything you have to say. I shouldn't have hit you on the pontoon, and I'm sorry for that, but that's it." Galen turned away.

"Oh you should be interested because I know something that concerns you. Coach didn't really date anyone seriously until Maggie came along. He and my mom just hooked up for a while. You see, Tom was mourning the loss of the love of his life."

Galen didn't react.

"It turns out the woman he loved didn't want him. At least that was Bethany's story. Bethany's my mom, though you probably know that. She lives in Waukesha now, but she knows everything and anything that has ever happened in this town. Well, I just got off the phone a few minutes ago with her. I had this idea, more of a suspicion actually, and I wanted to ask her about it. At first, she wouldn't say anything, she said it was someone else's secret. But then, she came clean. You want to know what I learned tonight?"

"No." Galen began to walk away, but Cam, moving quickly, grabbed his arm, stopping him.

"Oh, but you should. It's about a secret, an old one, and it concerns you. Actually it is about you."

Galen went cold.

"You know that woman that Coach loved. Well, she was your

mother, and she and Coach were together before your dad had that accident. But the thing is, that guy isn't even your real dad. Murray is."

"Shut up!" There was a roaring in Galen's ears. "Shut the fuck up," he repeated.

"I only figured it out tonight. I don't know how they kept the secret all these years. It's obvious now, though. Look in the mirror, Odgers. You two look so much alike. I wonder how many other people have figured out that Tom Murray is your dad."

Galen said nothing. *Tom Murray is your dad.* The words echoed through his mind. *It explained so much and yet it couldn't, shouldn't be true. Mom!* The word was a cry from his soul. *Why didn't you tell me?*

"You know, it used to bug the crap out of me that Coach paid so much attention to you. But now it makes sense. It wasn't because you were a special player or anything, but because you were his kid. Thinking about it, I wasn't his son, but he took an interest in me. Shit, looking back, I can't understand why I was ever jealous of you at all. He had to be interested in you. Me, I was the special one."

"You're fucking crazy." Galen turned away.

Cam leaned up against the bar on his elbow. He swirled his drink in his hand and then offered Galen a lopsided grin. "At least I already knew that I was a bastard. Seems like it's news to you."

Galen nearly ran out of the bar.

* * * *

Kyle eyed the deep, plunging neckline on the curvy bleached blond seated beside him. "So, you were a couple of years ahead of me in school, right? You were in my sister's class?"

"No." The woman took a sip of her wine and leaned closer, pressing her breasts together. "I am a year younger than she is. You sure you don't remember me? Cassie, Cassie Cramer?" She pressed her breasts together and leaned them up against his arm.

"Honey, I wouldn't forget someone who looks like you."

"Well, I did look different back then. I was heavier and my hair was brown. I also had braces."

Kyle studied the pert face before him. "Well, let's make up for lost time now." He leaned forward, his eyes on the full red lips.

"Kyle! Kyle!" A hand firmly gripped his shoulder. "Galen?" He turned to look at his brother. "This cute, little lady is Cassie and—"

"I need to talk to you… now."

"Slow down and say 'hi' to Cassie, here."

"Look, I don't mean to be rude, lady, but I need to talk to my brother now. He'll find you in a few minutes."

"Okay, I'll just go get a drink."

"Don't go far," Kyle called to her, letting go of her hand as she left the table.

Just then, Sandra appeared at the side of the table. She looked stunning in a green silk dress with her auburn hair piled artistically on her head. "Joe said you wanted to see me."

"What's this about?" Kyle demanded. "That girl is totally hot for me, so it better be good."

"Is Coach Murray my dad?"

Sandra and Kyle exchanged stricken glances, then Sandra pulled back a chair and collapsed back into seat.

"Is it true?" Galen demanded.

"Who told you?" Sandra asked.

"Cam did. I had to hear it from that asshole. Why didn't you tell me? What the fuck! Why didn't Mom tell me?"

Kyle groaned and ran a hand through his hair. "It's not like we knew all this time. Mom didn't tell us either."

"We just figured it out a few months ago," Sandra admitted.

"For Chrissakes!" Galen agonized, running a hand through his hair.

"We didn't really even know anything," Sandra continued. "But I found these pictures in the house. They were sexy pictures of Mom and a guy who was most definitely not Dad."

"Coach?" Galen asked.

"They were seeing each other before Dad's accident, when Mom and Dad were separated," Sandra confirmed. "I'm guessing he's the guy in the picture."

"You can't see his face."

"Nah," Kyle broke in. "Just a horny, naked guy."

"Wow," Galen muttered. "I always wondered why Dad was like he was. He never came to any of my games, never did anything with me. It's like he pretended that I didn't exist."

"He never came to any of my stuff either," Kyle snorted. "And I think I am his, unfortunately."

"He's just not there mentally," Sandra offered. "I think he may have had mental problems before that even."

"What did you want us to say?" Kyle leaned forward at the table. "There didn't seem to be any point."

"Maybe something like, 'You're a bastard and Tom Murray is your dad.' Sandra, Mom never said anything to you?"

She shook her head. "I'm sorry, Galen, but she never did. I tried to talk to Dad about it once, to see if he knew anything. But he's in another world."

"I have to talk to Coach."

"Not right now. Not on his wedding day," Sandra protested.

"You can't," Kyle argued. "Don't ruin his wedding night for him."

Galen shook his head. "I just can't get my mind around this. I need to be alone, to think."

"But I saw you with Kjersten earlier… I thought maybe something was going on with you two?" Sandra prompted.

"I can't go to her now, like this. I've already put her through so much. I just gotta get out of here. Tell her that I had to go, please. Will you do that for me, Sandra?"

"You should tell her yourself," Sandra admonished.

"You're gonna fuck it up again," Kyle muttered. "Where are you gonna go?"

"I don't know, but I can't dump this on her, too. I gotta figure things out first. "Galen headed blindly for the door.

Chapter Twenty-Five

Left Behind Again

~ Kjersten ~

After thanking Maggie's father for the dance, Kjersten headed back to the table. Cat was already sitting there, sipping at a drink.

"Where's your guy?" Kjersten asked, referring to the former player that Cat had been flirting with earlier.

"Trey will be back in a few minutes. Listen, I'm going back to his room tonight. So, you'll get the room to yourself."

Kjersten blushed and smiled. "Thanks."

"That's a good thing, right?" Cat prompted with a wink. "Odgers couldn't take his eyes off you."

"Maybe," Kjersten conceded. "He didn't want to dance. I think he went to the bar. He should be back any minute… Cat, I'm so excited, I can't stand it. It doesn't even seem possible that after all this time, we could get back together."

Cat rolled her eyes. "A case of true love. But there's my guy now, and I have a case of true lust going. So, I'll see you in the morning?" She stood up.

Kjersten nodded and watched her friend walk away. Hopefully, she peered around the room, looking for Galen. Finally, she spotted him. He was at a table with his brother and sister and they looked to be having a very animated conversation.

He looked so handsome, but distressed now.

Why? What's wrong? she wondered.

The Odgers were speaking back and forth for a few more minutes. Then, Galen stood abruptly and headed out of the ballroom.

Where is he going? When will he come back?

Sandra and Kyle had their heads together at the table and were conversing intently.

Kjersten sat, watched, and waited. Five minutes passed. Then, ten. Then, fifteen. Still, there was no sign of Galen. *Where is he?* She grew restless and impatient. She rose to her feet and made her way over to the table where the other Odgers siblings remained seated.

"Excuse me." She stood at the side of the table. "Hi Sandra, Kyle."

Kyle rose to his feet. "Kjersten."

"Hi, Kjersten," Sandra greeted her, but her expression was anxious.

"Do you know where Galen went? He was here just a few minutes ago," Kjersten paused, embarrassed to have admitted to have been watching him.

"He's gone," Kyle spoke flatly. "He left."

"When do you think he'll be back?" Kjersten asked.

"Not tonight," Kyle snorted.

"But he said," Kjersten paused.

"Kjersten, Galen left here upset," Sandra's expression was sympathetic, concerned. "I don't think he's coming back tonight. He got some news that, well, it sort of overwhelmed him."

"What kind of news? I mean is everything okay?"

"Everything's not okay, but nothing horrible has happened," Sandra explained. "It's a family thing. Galen will explain it to you."

"You mean, he left for good? For the night?" Kjersten stammered. Her heart sank. *Not again. How could he leave me again? And he didn't even say 'goodbye.'*

I'm sure he'll call you," Sandra offered. "You okay, Kjersten?"

"Yeah.... I'm fine." Kjersten recovered herself.

"I'm so sorry," Sandra muttered.

Kjersten straightened up and swallowed the lump in her throat. "I guess it just wasn't meant to be. I hope you both have a nice evening."

Heartbroken again and aware of Sandra and Kyle's eyes on her, she gathered her skirt with dignity, and turned away from the table. *I'm such an idiot. He doesn't know what he wants. I'm so done waiting for him to come to his senses. I'm not going to let him do this to me ever again.* Still, a thought nagged her as she headed out of the ballroom. *What did he find out that made him leave?*

"Shoot." Back in her hotel room, later that night, Kjersten struggled to unzip her dress. The zipper was high up between her shoulder blades. Cat, who had not returned to the room and was clearly with her hook up, had helped her to zip it up when they were getting ready for the wedding. *What a disaster.* For a moment, Kjersten quit messing with the zipper and walked over to the table. She picked up the still filled champagne flute that she had brought back to her room. With a trembling hand, she raised the flute to her lips and took a long drink of the bubbly coolness.

Just then, there was a knock at the door. "Cat? I'm coming." *I wonder what happened with her guy.*

Kjersten opened the door wide, prepared to see Cat, but, to her amazement, it was Galen who stood there. His expression was desperate, and a little dangerous. His bow tie was undone and his shirt unbuttoned uncharacteristically low.

"Galen? What's up?"

He didn't answer. Instead, without asking her permission, he stepped into the room and closed the door behind him. He took a hold of her hand, drawing her up against him while he wrapped his other arm around her waist. He groaned as he pressed his face into the warmth at the base of her neck.

For a moment, she softened into him, lost in the magic of this unexpected embrace. Then, the thought of his harried expression filled her mind's eye, so she drew back, to look at him. "What's going on? Galen?"

He leaned his forehead against her own, so that their lips nearly touched. "I don't want to talk or think or anything. I just want you. I want you now. I need you. God, I need you so much right now."

She melted inside at his words, and then leaned in to kiss him. But that wasn't enough for Galen. He reached to her sides, to push down the offending material of her dress. The corseted top resisted.

"The zipper."

"What?"

"It's stuck."

He fiddled with it for a moment, while hungrily kissing her. "Do you like this dress?"

She laughed. "No."

"Good." He gripped the two sides of the dress at the back and ripped.

Kjersten shivered in anticipation while he shoved the dress down her body, revealing her black, strapless bra with matching black garter belt and stockings that she'd put on earlier that day. She stepped out of it, reveling in the way his eyes caressed her long, lean form. She reached back and began to pull the pins from her hair, then shook out the long, flaxen waves.

"You are so beautiful." He slid his hands up to cup her breasts. "You smell delicious." He nuzzled into her neck.

"My turn," she murmured and began to unbutton his shirt, pulling it up and out of his pants. Then, she reached for the buckle. He stilled her hands and sought to pull her up. "No, I'm in charge." Brashly she pushed him back, until his legs hit a chair. Then, she pushed at his chest, forcing him down into the seat. "Tonight, you are going to do what I say."

Galen couldn't seem to speak in response. He sat in the chair, staring at her in awe. Pivoting slowly, she bent over at the waist, giving him the full view of her heart shaped ass and the black, lacey thong that bisected the curves.

"Come here, Kjersten." Galen nearly whimpered. "I can't take this."

"You will and you're going to love it." She rose slowly from her bent position, turned and kneeled down before him, reaching out and shoving his slacks down his hips so that his cock sprang free. She took the head right in her mouth as he groaned and thrust up. She slid her tongue down to the base of it, while cupping his balls gently with her hands.

He grasped her breasts.

"No!" She smacked his hand lightly with an open palm.

Galen's eyes were bright with hunger and anticipation. "All right," he agreed. "We'll do it your way." Still consuming her with his eyes, he leaned back in the chair, cupping the back of her head with one hand.

Now, Kjersten grinned with satisfaction, then leaning forward. She took one testicle in her mouth, savoring the musk of him, the salty taste. Tenderly, she pressed her tongue against it. She released it and administered the same attention to the other testicle. Then, she lifted them with one hand and ran her tongue along the raised line that extended back from his ball sack.

Galen thrust up, the tip of his cock, wet with a fluid.

Kjersten rested her hands on his thighs and stood up. "Look at me." His eyes flew open as she reached back and undid her strapless bra, allowing it to fall to the floor. Now, she reached down and shimmied out of her skimpy black silk thong,

Galen groaned. "You are so beautiful."

"Screw beautiful," she responded, stepping back in the V of his thighs. "I'm hot. Fuckable."

He chuckled and reached for her again. "I've missed you."

"No, don't touch me."

"Not yet?" he questioned.

"It'll be worth it, I promise." She stood poised over him, then hesitated. "Do you have … I mean, I didn't plan."

"I did," Galen dug around in his pocket and pulled forth a condom.

Kjersten took it from him. "Here, let me." She tore it open, and sheathed him. His cock was big, thick and ready for her. Then, she straddled his hips, and rubbed her vaginal lips over the head of his penis. With her fingers, she opened herself, then rubbed his cock from her clitoris, down her passage, to her vagina, moistening herself. She teased herself and him until he was wild eyed, nearly coming apart, but still he stayed seated.

Her voice throaty, she asked, "I hope you brought more than just one."

Now he grasped her hips and pulled her down, burying his cock in her deeply. His eyes met hers as he bit into his lips and thrust up into her again. "Oh yeah. I plan on fucking you all night long. Ride me. Do it now!"

He licked and suckled each breast as she began to move on him. He met her thrusts, and sought to rub his thumb against her clit so that the two of them grew more frantic, more frenzied together. Desperately she ground against him. Galen grabbed her hips and began to thrust hard up into her. As her motions grew more frantic, her orgasm close, he demanded, "Look at me! Look at me as you come!"

She screamed as she came apart, his hoarse groan followed a moment later as he thrust powerfully into her then held her hips to receive him.

For a moment, they remained still, sweaty and spent. Then, he kissed her. "I needed that. You."

Her mind was still slow, and post-orgasm sluggish, so she didn't respond. So, all she said was, "I'm thirsty."

"Is there anything left in that champagne bottle?" he asked, eyeing the black bottle on the nightstand.

"Um hmm." She stood up, and turned, naked, and unselfconscious to get it.

He pulled the condom off his cock and disposed of it. Then, he watched in appreciation as she took a healthy swig of the champagne. "Save some for me."

She nodded in agreement and then handed him the bottle.

He drank as well and then rose and took her hand. "Let's go take a shower. I want to eat you out in the shower."

She shivered in anticipation and followed him eagerly. There was nothing more to say. In fact, there wasn't really any time for talking at all that night. They fucked and slept and then fucked some more. They burned insatiable, desperate, and hot for each other.

Early in the morning, before she was truly awake, she heard him making a phone call. "Yeah, I'm okay... Not now. I'll be home soon. Yeah, just as long as it takes me to drive there." He set the phone back in the receiver. He was quiet for a moment, then, she heard him sigh. He got to his feet and moved about the hotel room quietly dressing. Kjersten waited for him to say something, anything, but he didn't say a word. She was aware when he stood over the bed looking down at her. Still, she pretended to be asleep. *Do something! Say something to show me that this wasn't just a one-night deal for you.*

But he said nothing, just left the room quietly, closing the door after him. As he left, Kjersten smothered her feelings of dismay and disappointment. *Why am I such an idiot? All I am to him is an easy one-night fling. Or, he would have said something before he left. I am so done beating myself up over him. Last night was what it was, but it's over. I'm a big girl and I can handle my own choices and their consequences.*

Chapter Twenty-Six

Focus

~ Galen ~

It was a beautiful November day, perfect weather for a football practice, but Galen was having a tough time staying focused. While he waited for the whistle signaling the beginning of play, his thoughts were miles away. All he could think about was Kjersten. *She must think I'm a jerk because of how I left that morning. I didn't know what to say to her. With me and my family, it's always drama. I didn't want to dump those problems on her, tell her that I'm Coach Murray's bastard and that everyone lied to me all these years. I didn't want to ruin things after that incredible night. Where do we go from here? But leaving the way I did, that just made things worse.* Around and around, his mind spun.

Suddenly, a whistle blew, indicating the start of the drill, instantly tearing Galen from the quagmire of his thoughts. He stepped back, caught the snap, and looked for a receiver. *Marvin's wide open.* He threw the ball short. *Shoot.*

Marvin jogged back. "What was that, Galen? Didn't you even see me?"

"Sorry," Galen muttered, shaking his head. "I wasn't thinking."

"No. You weren't. Damn, pay attention. Don't waste my time. Get focused, man. You've been in another world since last weekend."

"I hear you. I was just thinking about…"

"That girl. Man, you gotta get your head straight. Think about her after practice."

"I know. I know."

Marvin smacked him on the back.

"Get back in formation," Coach Felder directed. "Now!"

Galen took his position behind the center. He called the same play again. Marvin was in motion. He drew his arm back. *I should have called Kjersten right after the wedding. I should have explained why I left that night.* He didn't see the hit coming. He wasn't watching for it. He had an awareness of impact, then the world went red and black.

* * * *

Tom headed down the long hospital corridor. *I knew this day was coming. This conversation is long overdue.* Galen had called him and asked him to come down to Chicago the night before. There had been something in his voice that clued Tom in that the time had come, and even though he had rehearsed for it so many times, usually by Jessie's grave, he felt so unready for it.

He knocked on the hospital room door.

"Come in," a deep, unfamiliar voice called out.

Tom opened the door. "Hello?"

There were several young men in the room. Ben Happe was seated in a chair by Galen's side. Tom recognized the Bearcat running back, Marvin Richardson, and the enormous lineman, Moe, who were both seated on his other side. Galen was lying on the bed, looking pale but composed. His arm was in a sling.

"Coach."

"Hi Galen. Boys," Tom nodded his head in greeting. "Ben, good to see you." He held out his hand to Ben and then to the two other young men in turn.

"Hi, Coach Murray," Ben said, shaking it.

"We should be heading out." Moe rose to his feet.

"Yeah, we'll see you tomorrow, Galen." Marvin agreed. "We'll bring you a burger."

"Sounds good." Galen smiled. "Thank you guys for stopping by.

Just laying here kind of sucks."

"You'll be on your feet in no time," Moe commented. "The doctors said you won't miss more than a couple of games."

"I just hate being out, just laying here." Galen smacked his hand down on the coverlet. "See you guys."

The two football players headed out of the hospital room.

Wanting to delay this long awaited moment of confrontation with his son, Tom turned to Ben. "Ben, what are you doing down here in Chicago?"

"I was just coming down to spend the weekend with Galen. I got here Thursday night and I'm heading back to Milwaukee tomorrow."

"He's been hanging out here at the hospital with me since yesterday afternoon. So much for a fun weekend together."

"It wasn't that bad," Ben countered. "I'm gonna head back to your apartment. I have some homework to do." He and Galen exchanged a glance. "G-man, I'll come and see you tomorrow before I leave."

"Sounds good," Galen answered.

"See ya, Ben." Tom rose to his feet. *I feel warm. My heart is pounding. He knows! Somehow he knows!*

Then, once the door shut behind Ben, it was just Tom and Galen alone in the hospital room.

"How was your honeymoon?" Galen asked. "Mexico, right? You still look tan."

"It was great. We, Maggie and me, took her girls with us. We went to a family resort in Cancun. It was a blast."

"Great." Galen looked away.

A heavy silence fell in the room.

"So how did this happen?" Tom waved his arm at Galen in the hospital bed.

"Just a hit in practice. A helmet to the chin and collarbone. Marvin said it was a spear. I was knocked out. Don't remember it. Now the collarbone hurts like hell and I have a headache, but I'm okay. They want me to take it easy for a couple of days." Galen glanced away from Tom and out the window. "It was my own fault. I wasn't paying attention. I was thinking about … other stuff."

Tom waited. *I gotta get the discussion going. I'm the mature adult here.* "I'm glad you called me, Galen, but you obviously have something on your mind. What is it?"

Galen's jaw flexed. He didn't say anything. He just stared out the window. Finally, he turned his head and met Tom's glance. There was such naked pain on his face that Tom nearly cringed. "You knew my mom, right?"

The thought 'in the Biblical sense' popped into Tom's head. *Crazy.* He swallowed. "Yes, I knew Jessica."

Galen skewered him with his eyes. "Well?"

"Well, what?"

"Be man enough to tell me. Don't make me drag it out of you."

Tom sighed. Then, he looked directly into the eyes of the young man that he had lied to for nineteen years.

"Yes, I am your father." It felt rough and awkward to say the words and he didn't experience the euphoria he'd always anticipated of the acknowledgement. "How did you find out?"

"Cam Fawst told me at your wedding. You couldn't even tell me yourself. I had to find out from him." Galen spit the words out like bullets.

"I didn't want you to find out that way." *How did Cam even know? Who else knows?*

"Why didn't either of you tell me? Why the big secret? Were you embarrassed of me?"

"No. Never. I stayed in Eagle River because of you, because I wanted to be around you."

"Why did you and Mom break up?"

Tom exhaled. "We got together when your mom and Jim were split up. They were going to get divorced. All of that had happened before I met your mother. But then Jim had that car accident. He was in the hospital for months and then…" Tom tipped his head down.

"What?"

"Well, then your mom ended things between us. She felt that she had to be responsible. He wasn't able to take care of himself and he was Sandra's and Kyle's dad. And, to be fair, I wasn't the best bet back then.

I wasn't exactly prime dad material, but when I found out that Jessica was pregnant with you, I wanted to be around to watch you grow up, to be a part of your life."

"I deserved to know that you're my dad. I had a right to know that." Galen nearly growled the words.

"You did. You did. And this is going to sound weak, but the opportunity never presented itself. Then, your mom got sick. It didn't seem like the right time."

"All of those years, you could have told me sometime."

"I know. I know, but things were good between us. I didn't want to mess that up. It was all that I had with you."

"Coward."

"That's fair." Tom shrugged his shoulders and hung his head. "You're absolutely right. I didn't know how to be a dad."

"Well, you better figure it out quick. I don't even know what to say to you. God, how could you just lie to me all of these years? The whole thing has been a fucking lie! How could you and Mom do this to me?"

"I deserve this, Galen. I know I do. I've had it coming. You should be angry. I know this doesn't excuse anything, but remember your mother and I both loved you and we both did our best to be there for you no matter what. You don't have to forgive me or understand what happened or why we didn't tell you. Your mom didn't want me to tell you, and so I didn't. Then, when she got sick, it didn't feel like the right time."

"I guess it never was the right time," Galen snarled.

"I'm not trying to excuse anything, but we both loved you more than anything and you have a family. You have Kyle and Sandra and her kids."

Galen said nothing. The corner of his jaw twitched. "You and Mom messed up so many things… Like father like son, I guess. Did you love her?"

Tom looked away. He found his eyes filling with tears and he swallowed the lump in his throat. "More than anything. I loved her more than anything. Then, you came along and you changed my life. It may sound corny, but you saved my life... Because of you, Eagle River became my home. I have friends. I belong. I coach. It all happened because of you and Jessica. Then, when your Mom died, I didn't think you needed anything more on your plate. So was I a coward? I was afraid to fuck up the relationship that we had. I didn't know how to be a dad."

"Well, you're kind of a dad now, to Maggie's girls. Their dad is out of the picture, right?"

"Yeah, I am. I feel like I've been given a second chance with Maggie and the girls. Galen, I'm sorry that we kept this secret. I knew it was wrong then and I know it now. I'm sorry you had to find out the way you did. You are the best thing that ever happened to me."

Tom hesitated for a moment, then went to his son and awkwardly embraced him, careful not to touch his injured collarbone

Galen remained stiff for a moment, but then softened and accepted his father's attempt to comfort him.

Chapter Twenty-Seven

Predictions

~ Ben ~

"This is Ben Happe of WKBJ, the voice of Great Lakes University. As everyone knows, Saturday is the big game. The Great Lakes University Coyotes versus the Illinois University Bearcats and WKBJ seeks to provide a balanced view of the news and of sports. So today we have two Bearcats with us. Welcome Marvin Richardson and Galen Odgers."

"Thank you for inviting us," Marvin countered smoothly. "We appreciate the opportunity to promote the great sport of football."

"Marvin, the Wolverines have had another fine year. Your record is currently nine and one, an improvement from last year's eight and three. What do you foresee happening in the near future?"

"Us winning big."

"Galen?" Ben questioned.

"I'm not going to be making any predictions about the game. I don't want to tempt fate this close to a big game," Galen replied stiffly.

Marvin rolled his eyes at his friend. "Listen here, Ben. I'm gonna call this one, just like Namath did his Super Bowl. This game's in the bag. The Bearcats are going to roll over the Coyotes."

"Wow. Those are bold words, but not completely out of hand with the way the Bearcats continue to show improvement. For all of those listeners out there who have just joined us, you just heard those bold words from Marvin Richardson, running back for the Illinois Bearcats."

"Well, it could happen. But we gotta stay focused. It won't be easy, but we have a solid team. The Coyotes aren't going to just give it to us." Galen swallowed nervously.

"You're right about that," Ben commented, nodding at Galen. *Calm down, dude. You're doing fine.*

Still, Galen appeared awkward and uncomfortable seated behind the microphone. The table was low and there wasn't much room under it to accommodate his long legs, so he kept shifting them around, banging the table with his knees. Ben knew that any interview was way out of Galen's comfort zone but he'd agreed to this one as a favor to Ben.

"Galen, how does it feel to be considered one of the premier up and coming young quarterbacks?"

"I just want to do my best for the team."

Deciding to give Galen a break, Ben shifted his attention to the tangibly more comfortable Richardson. "Folks, the Bearcats have a great throwing game, a good defensive line, and also a good running game. This combination is what makes them one of the most potent teams in the Midwest today. Marvin, you're considered to be one of the best running backs playing the college game today. What do you consider your greatest contribution to your team?"

"Ben." Marvin's amused baritone was warm caramel over the air waves. "I've got happy legs. I'm fast and I'm tough. Yeah, those would be my greatest strengths."

"We've certainly seen evidence of that this season."

"I think you're wrong there, Marvin," Galen interrupted.

"What?" Marvin was a little affronted.

Ben paused, too, surprised that Galen had opened his mouth unprompted.

"Yeah. Marvin's super-fast, like track star fast. And I've seen you stand up from some huge hits and then get back into the game and run twenty or thirty yards. But what Marvin does that is so great is he makes other guys on the team feel like they can do it, too. Marvin pumps his team up."

"It ain't hard being pumped up when you got the best QB on the field," Marvin countered smoothly, smiling at his friend.

"It's easy to see why this Bearcats team has been so successful this season with such camaraderie between the players. We have a caller."

"Hi, this is Tania Fred."

"Just Tania will do," Ben broke in.

"Okay. I just want to tell Galen Odgers," the high female voice broke into hysterical giggles, "that he has the cutest butt I've ever seen and I want to give him my number."

"Thank you, Tania," Ben hastily interrupted once more. "We have another caller on line three. Do things like that happen to you guys a lot?"

Galen blushed and Marvin just shook his head.

"Hello… Hello?" A deep and familiar voice broke in. "You guys know who this is?"

"Sal? Sal, is that you?" Galen queried incredulously.

"Sure is. Hi, kid. Kyle told me that you two boys were gonna be on the radio down there, so I got the number. Galen just about grew up in my bar." Sal boomed. "Are you kidding? I'm practically a blood relation. Hey there, boys."

"Hi Sal," Galen leaned in to his microphone.

"Galen, am I on the air?"

"Yeah, Sal."

"Your brother told me you were gonna be doing this show. Hear that everyone, I'm live," Sal shouted out to his bar.

"Gale Odgers is the pride of Eagle River, Wisconsin, and I'm sure that folks in Marvin Richardson's home town feel the same way about him. Only problem with either of those boys is that neither of them play for the Wisconsin Badgers, don't ya know. Wait," Sal spoke away from the receiver again. "I'll ask them. You coming home to Eagle River any time soon, Galen?"

"I hope to,"

"Thanks for the call, Sal," Ben said. "Boys, we have another caller."

"Bye, Sal," Galen stated.

"Okay, caller, we gotcha. You're on the air."

"I'd like to know how you guys think the Bearcats will do against the huge Coyotes offensive line? They steamrolled over you last year, and Cam Fawst is playing well."

"Not as well as Galen here. Our team is primed and ready to rock and roll," Marvin responded definitively. "We're gonna be picking Coyotes out of our cleats."

Galen leaned close to his microphone. His eyes were narrowed and his expression, fierce. "Cam Fawst and the Coyotes are going down tomorrow."

"Well, there you have it," Ben stated. "Bold prediction from these two Bearcats. We are all looking forward to the big game tomorrow."

* * * *

It was a bitterly cold afternoon and from where he stood at the front of his team, Cam glared at the gray and green hoard filling the stadium. The game was a sellout, and Owen Arena fairly thrummed with excitement. He could feel it in the racing of his own pulse, in the adrenalin coursing through him. *It all comes down to today, to this game. I will face Galen Odgers in a football game and I will win. I'll win in front of all of them. In front of Kjersten, in front of all of Eagle River.*

He looked up in the stands at that area of the student section where Kjersten used to sit with her friends. She hadn't come to a home game since they'd broken up two years before, since she'd cut him out of her life. But now, he glimpsed her distinctive silvery pony tail. *She wasn't wearing Coyote or Bearcat colors. She was dressed all in black, but I'll bet she came for Odgers. Always Odgers!* Cam nearly ground his teeth with frustration. This time, he'd show them all. *I am going to kick Odger's ass one way or another. Fuck them all!*

For a while, the game went well for Cam and the Coyotes. They advanced the ball through a combination of runs and short passes and then Wrenshall, the kicker, made a field goal. In contrast, in the first quarter, Galen and his Bearcats appeared out of sync. He got sacked a couple of times and failed to make a first down in several critical possessions of the ball. Cam was just beginning to relax enough to smile and enjoy the moment when the unthinkable happened. Odgers lofted a giant arching pass that somehow ended up in the hands of a Bearcat wide receiver who made it nearly to the end zone before he was taken down by Coyote defenders.

As the Coyote defense set up, Cam shouted out, "Watch Richardson!" Still, the Bearcat running back took the hand-off from Odgers and then cut through the Coyotes defensive line like a knife through butter. *Touchdown!*

The crowd roared and Cam's hopes sunk. *There's still time, plenty of time.* But the tide had turned and the Bearcats were on fire. Seemingly, Odgers had entered that heightened state that only the best of athletes achieve. He could do no wrong. Richardson was also playing brilliantly. Cam and the Coyotes were having a decent game, but luck and fate were definitely not in their corner. The final score was twenty-one to ten, with the Bearcats triumphant.

After the game, a devastated Cam lingered in the locker room. Not sure how it had all gone wrong again, when he'd held it in his hands. He stared down at those same hands that had betrayed him now.

"What's up, Cam?" one of the offensive linemen asked. "The press is out there to talk to you."

"I'm not up for it today." Cam shook his head. He wasn't up for it at all. *I feel sick, sick about losing in front of everyone, losing to that bastard Odgers.* So, he slowly iced his shoulder, showered, and then dressed, not wanting to see or talk with anyone really. The other guys on his team were aware of his mood and left him alone.

Finally, he emerged from the locker room and began to head down the corridor. He heard familiar, throaty, feminine laughter but before he could place it, he'd turned the corner and stood facing Kjersten, Ben Happe, and Galen Odgers.

"Fuck," he muttered under his breath. *Why them? Now?*

Upon seeing him, the group of three broke apart and stared at him.

Ben spoke first. "We came down to see Galen after the game."

"No shit," Cam responded. "That's just what I need, an Eagle River reunion right in my own stadium. The perfect ending to a crappy day." He shifted his bag on his shoulder and glared first at Kjersten and then at Galen. "So you're back with him, huh?" He gestured with an elbow.

"What the fuck, Kjersten? I don't get it. I don't get it at all, any of it." He dropped his bag to the ground and moved in towards Galen. He was a little shorter than Galen now, but thicker and royally pissed.

Ben and Kjersten automatically stepped back as an enraged Cam confronted Galen. "Goddammit! What is it about you? First Tom, and he's your dad." Cam ignored Kjersten's gasp. "Then Kjersten, and she keeps coming back even when you dump her. Why is it always your turn? Why are you the golden one? I'm so fucking tired of you being in my life, getting everything that I want, that I deserve. You're always there like a shadow, a fricking nightmare. Why not me? Ever?" Cam had snapped. He reached out and grabbed the front of Galen's shirt.

"Fawst, I've never liked you, but I don't have any problem with you tonight. It was a good game. It's over now." Galen offered, holding his hands up.

"Shut the fuck up," Cam interrupted. "I don't give a shit what you think. I've spent my whole life looking over my shoulder at you. You bug the crap out of me. I'm fucking done with it and with you." Then, shaking off Ben, who grabbed him by the shoulders, Cam swung at Galen, striking a glancing blow to his chin.

Galen fell back against the wall, rubbing his chin. "I don't want to fight you, Cam. You're not worth it. You've always had a problem with me. I've never understood why, but I'm done with it."

"No, you and your slut girlfriend aren't worth my time... But the truth is you seriously piss me off." He raised his fists again and moved in on Galen.

"Leave him alone," Kjersten interjected, jumping between her two former lovers.

"Stay out of this, Kjersten," Galen shouted.

"Do you suck his cock the way you did mine, Kjersten?" Cam taunted. "She can make your eyes roll back in your head, can't she, Odgers. I taught her that."

"Please, Cam," Kjersten broke in again.

"Stay the fuck out of this." He brushed her to the side more roughly than he'd intended. He felt a moment's remorse when, out of balance, she fell and struck the wall with her shoulder. For a moment, he paused, turned to help her, but then Odgers was on him.

The two were well matched. Galen had a longer reach, but Cam was thicker and more seasoned. Both were enraged with a lifetime of anger and hate. Cam assaulted Galen with a combination of punches to his head and his chest. Galen ducked and dodged and bided his time. Then, launched and landed a heavy blow to Cam's side and followed it with another.

Cam fell back, and Galen followed up with a few more landed blows.

"Stop them, Ben," Kjersten pleaded.

"Let them go, Kjersten," Ben directed, leaning casually against the wall. "This has been a long time coming."

"I don't want Galen to get hurt."

"He can handle himself," Ben commented dryly, pulling her down the corridor, away from the fighters.

The blows flew, and within a few minutes, several other Bearcat and Coyote players having stepped out of their respective locker rooms, gathered around to watch the fight and cheer on their quarterbacks.

The free for all continued, neither man getting the upper hand until several security guards burst upon the scene. Seeing the security guards, their respective teammates pulled Cam and Galen apart.

Bleeding and panting heavily, held back by their teammates, both men glared at each other.

"This isn't over, Galen," Cam promised.

But Galen shook his head. "It's okay, guys." His teammates released him and when Kjersten returned, he pulled her to his side. "You were the one who made up this contest between us. I'm done, Cam. I'm through with you and all of this bullshit," he waved his hand. "I'm done letting you mess up what matters to me."

"Boys, is this finished, or do I need to call the police?" One thick set security guard asked.

"You're gonna get them out of here?" the other guard asked of the assembled players.

"No more trouble," Ben inserted. "You get your guy out of here," he spoke to the Coyote players. "We got ours."

"Get 'em out of here," the other security guard agreed.

So Galen and Cam were escorted out of the building and to their team buses.

"Where's Kjersten?" Galen demanded once outside. "Where did she go?"

"Man, don't worry about that." Marvin stepped forward by the bus, took in the situation at a glance, and directed Galen up the steps. "Let's get you out of here before you get into any more trouble."

"But I have to speak with Kjersten. Now."

"You want to end up in jail tonight? Get in the bus, Galen."

Looking over his shoulder, he stepped up into the bus. As he did, he glimpsed a tall, thin blond figure standing alone by the main gate. He was leaving her yet again. *This time, I'm gonna make things right between us, somehow. Things aren't over between us, Kjersten. They're just beginning.*

Chapter Twenty-Eight

Fishing

~ Ben ~

"I promised my mom that we'd be back before eight," Ben said as he reeled his fishing line in. "My feet are freezing anyway."

"Come on, Ben. It's only seven," Galen protested. "I want just one more walleye."

"We've been out here forever and I haven't caught shit. You're at your limit anyway. Let's just be done."

"What's wrong with you, Ben?" a perplexed Galen asked. "You used to love to fish."

"I still do. It's just that we've been here for hours and nothing is happening. Besides," Ben blushed and looked away, his voice went soft in embarrassment. "Cat said that she might call tonight."

Galen shook his head. "We'll be back in plenty of time."

"I want to take a shower and—"

"It's a phone call, Ben. She can't see you."

"We've been out here long enough."

Galen reflected for a moment and then nodded his head. "All right. One more cast." He drew his rod back and cast it high out over the lake. "Besides, I wouldn't want to risk you missing out on a phone call even to go fishing with your old bud, even though that friend almost never gets a chance to come home much less go fishing."

"Come on, Galen. It's not like that. Don't be like that. I really like Cat and we've already caught plenty of fish. I'm hungry and my neck feels sunburned."

"You're whipped," Galen chuckled.

"Maybe." Ben put the lid on the worms and set his rod in its holder. "She's thinking about coming up and visiting."

"Why didn't you have her come up for this weekend?"

"Nah, you and I have spent Memorial Day together for so many years. It's good, and I want to prepare Mom for Cat. It's getting kind of serious between us, so I have to sort of break it gently to my mom."

"Yeah, I get it." Galen began to systematically jerk the line with his wrist.

"I mean, Mom knows that I am seeing someone." Ben rolled his eyes. "Mom's been hell on wheels since I got home… I just hope that she's not too tough on Cat. You know how Cat is."

"Unconventional," Galen offered.

"Yes, and no girl is good enough for my mom. I just don't want her to mess things up with Cat."

"You guys pretty serious?"

"Oh, I don't know," Ben tried to sound cool. Then, he added, "I've never dated anyone like her."

Galen knew his friend well and recognized that Ben was obviously head over heels for his first real girlfriend. He jigged his pole a little then leaned back and rested his sandaled feet on the side of the boat.

"We got set up," Ben hedged.

"Who set you up?"

"Kjersten did," Ben finally admitted. "They're friends."

"I knew that." Galen acknowledged with a nod. "I met Cat at Tom's wedding."

"Oh," Ben responded.

"You two talk much?"

"Cat and I? Almost every night."

"No, I mean you and Kjersten."

"Not lately. I think that she is supposed to get back from her semester in Italy soon."

"Yeah, I know."

"You do?" Ben asked.

"Yeah. We talked a couple of times before she left for Italy."

"Oh?" Ben glanced over at his friend.

Galen didn't elaborate. Instead, he leaned back in his seat. "It's so beautiful right now. Let's just sit here for a few minutes more. I don't think that I've been so still in forever. It's peaceful here. We'll head on in a few minutes."

"Thanks, Galen."

Not a minute passed before Ben shifted anxiously in his seat.

"This feels wonderful." Galen closed his eyes and slid his baseball cap forward.

"Come on, Galen," his friend protested anxiously.

Galen burst out laughing. "You are so gone." He started the boat's engine. It gurgled and then turned over. "Don't make it easy on a girl. They get bored that way. You gotta be a challenge."

"Oh yeah, and I'm supposed to take your advice seriously. Since when did you become a lady-killer?"

"Girls go for the strong, silent type, like me."

"Give me a break."

"I'm serious. I do the me, Tarzan, you, Jane routine, and I have them swooning at my feet," Galen teased.

Ben just rolled his eyes. "Yeah, that really worked for you and Kjersten."

"I wrote her a couple of letters," Galen offered. "She wrote me back. That's something."

"Yes, it is," Ben agreed.

Galen lapsed into silence.

"Come on, Galen. Let's get going now," Ben anxiously prompted.

Galen nodded and then steered the boat slowly around and headed back in the direction of the Happe cabin. "It's too bad your parents didn't have this cabin when we were kids. It's awesome."

"It took them twenty-four years of saving to get it. They've been coming up every weekend since they bought it. I'm glad you could get away for the weekend... Besides, when we were kids we had the

Solheims' cabin."

"We used to sleep in that pop up camper."

"Good times," Galen agreed with a faraway look in his eyes. "This weekend was exactly what I needed. It feels good to get away from campus." He turned the rudder and they proceeded into an area where the lake narrowed into a channel that was shaded by trees. Both young men's eyes were drawn to the large, glass fronted cabin further down on the opposite shore. Here the trees receded from a shoreline that boasted a sugar sand beach. A T-shaped dock extended out into the water where a pontoon boat and two jet skis rocked gently in the current.

"The Lund's out," Ben commented. *The Solheims are here.* He swallowed.

"Yup," Galen commented laconically. He appeared unruffled.

Silently, they glanced up at the familiar lake house, for it was far larger than a cabin. It remained still and quiet. They motored on, past still closed up summer cabins. The lake was unusually quiet with the restless peace of still cool, late spring. The sun was just beginning its descent and splashes of bright fuchsia pink and a soft purple glow adorned the darkening sky. They cruised slowly past a small island on which Ben and Galen had often played as kids. Both young men remained lost in memories of long past summer days. The only sounds were the gentle purr of the engine and the soft lapping of the water against the small boat's hull. Around another bend and Galen slowed the engine, so as not to frighten the fish, for two other fishermen were anchored in boat off to his left.

A tall, lanky, tow headed teen turned in the boat, peered at them, and then waved to them. "Hi, Ben. Hi Galen," the boy called out.

Galen stared blankly at the kid not recognizing him, but there was something very familiar about the chiseled lines of his features.

"Hi, Soren," Ben echoed, smiling with genuine warmth as he greeted Kjersten's little brother. "You and your parents here for the weekend?"

It was then that the other fisherman turned and Ben recognized Kjersten's delicate features below the brim of a Twins baseball cap. He hadn't recognized her because of the bulky life jacket and the baseball cap she was wearing, under which her pony tail was tucked.

"Ben, Galen," she acknowledged. "Hi. You two up for the weekend?"

"Yes," Ben answered, glancing nervously between his two oldest friends. "We came up last night." He looked over at Galen, expecting him to say something, anything, but Galen was frozen, staring at Kjersten. "When did you get back from Italy?

"Just last week, and we came up to the cabin yesterday." Kjersten proceeded smoothly enough. "We're doing the family thing this weekend. The whole gang's here."

"How are your folks?" One quick glance at Galen made it clear to Ben that he would be responsible for observing the social niceties in this situation. *Say something, Galen. Anything!*

"Everyone's good," Kjersten responded.

"How was Italy?" Galen finally managed.

"Wonderful." Kjersten's eyes lit up. "The whole semester was incredible. A once-in-a-lifetime."

"Are you going to be around tonight?" Soren asked eagerly. "Because if you're going to be around, you could come over. I know Mom and Dad wouldn't mind."

Kjersten was glaring at her brother like he had sprouted horns.

"We could play some video games," Soren continued. "Also, I wanted to talk to Galen."

"About?" Galen asked abruptly.

"Football, you know, and playing in college."

"Sure. I can do that. I'll be heading back to Chicago tomorrow morning. So, if you want to, we could talk some football tonight," Galen agreed.

Ben nearly groaned aloud. He kicked at Galen's shin. *Shut up. Not tonight.* "It's good to see you, Kjersten and Soren, but we've gotta be getting back," Ben said. "Mom said that she was going to start throwing things on the grill around seven and it's already seven thirty."

"We had some luck earlier," Galen offered. "Ben had a good sized northern and I had a small mouthed bass. How did you do?"

"Krissy got two decent sized walleyes and I caught a couple, too,"

Soren answered.

"One was huge," Kjersten gestured with her arms. "A monster."

"This must be a good spot. I'll have to remember it," Ben bantered.

"Solheims are superior fisher people." Kjersten smiled mischievously and one dimple was charmingly accentuated in her left cheek. "It's our Swedish heritage."

"Then what's wrong with Galen here? He's Scandahoovian, too." Ben countered.

"Not as much as I once was," Galen grumbled.

"What?" Ben asked.

"Nothing."

"Come on, Galen. Let's go," Ben whispered under his breath.

Dutifully, Galen gave the engine a little gas and they eased past the other boat. "I'll call you later tonight if it works."

Soren waved.

Kjersten merely nodded silently as Galen and Ben glided around another bend, and then they were gone.

"I remember that kid when he was little. He always had snot on his face," Galen commented.

"Soren's a good kid. I like him… You're not really going over there tonight, are you?"

Galen grinned at him. "You bet your ass I am. This opportunity is golden."

"Just don't screw this one up."

"I don't intend to."

They travelled in silence for a few minutes, then Happe's little lodge came into view. The cabin was recessed back from the lake, lost in a forest of blue spruce. Two giant weeping willows shielded a rustic and aging pier. Smoke rose from the grill set in the clearing behind the house Mrs. Happe was already frantically waving from the shore.

"We're late," Ben groaned. "She's going to be upset. You'll have to charm her out of her mood."

"I'll have to charm her?" Galen snorted. "She's your mother."

"Exactly. She can see through my bullshit right away."

Galen and Ben pulled up to the Happe dock, tied the boat down and headed up to the picnic table by the cabin.There, Mrs. Happe had dinner ready and waiting for them on plates wrapped in aluminum foil while a fire crackled cheerily in the fire pit. Mr. and Mrs. Happe were very pleased to see them, and so it was a pleasant meal and conversation flowed. But all through the hamburgers and then the angel food cake with blueberries, Galen couldn't stop thinking about Kjersten, about what he wanted to say to her. Finally, the seemingly endless meal was over.

"Mom, thanks for dinner," Ben said, pushing his chair back. "Do you need any help with cleaning up?"

"There's not much to do," Mrs. Happe responded with a happy smile. "Just throw your paper plates in the fire and I'll put away the angel food cake. Are you sure that you have had enough? Galen? Ben?"

Galen patted his stomach. "No, thanks Mrs. Happe. I'm done. It was delicious. Thank you."

"Mom." Ben rose to his feet. "You mind if I disappear for a while?"

"Are you going to call your girlfriend?" Mr. Happe teased.

Ben blushed red.

Mrs. Happe swatted her husband in the arm. "Behave yourself, Gus. Leave the boy alone. I think it's sweet he wants to call Cat."

"You sure you don't need any help?" Galen asked his hostess.

"No, I'm just fine, Galen. It feels good to be cooking for you boys again. We've missed you."

"Well, then, I think I'll go for a little walk, burn off some of this delicious dinner."

"Don't go far," Mrs. Happe advised, shaking a finger. "There could be bears out there."

"Bring a flashlight in case it gets dark," Mr. Happe advised.

"Yes sir. Thank you both." Galen headed back to the house where he picked up a windbreaker and the suggested flashlight which he tucked into his pocket. Then, with determination, he headed out the gravel driveway toward the road.

Though it was nearly eight o'clock at night, it wasn't dark. As he walked the well-remembered trail, occasionally he glimpsed the flash of early-in-the-season fireflies. The only sounds to be heard were his own footsteps on pine needles, the croaking of frogs, and the chirping of crickets. The air smelled fresh and rich in the way that only a breeze coming off a lake does. He moved quickly and definitively. *I have to see her. I have to talk to her tonight. This is it.*

After about a fifteen-minute walk, he arrived at Solheim lake home. He headed straight up to the front door and knocked.

A dog barked, then the door swung open.

"Hi, Galen." Soren stood there, a grin, lighting his face. "Come in. Where's Ben?"

"Hi, Soren. Thanks. Ben isn't here and it's just me... Look, I do want to talk about football with you, but tonight I really need to speak with your sister. Is that okay?"

Soren looked serious for a moment, reflective. "You aren't going to get her upset, right. I mean, you are… well, Kjersten is my sister and I don't want her hurt. Okay?"

"I want to make things right this time."

Soren pondered this for a moment. "Okay."

"Would you tell her that I'm here?"

"She went back down by the dock. Just walk around back. You'll run right into her."

"I'm sorry. I don't mean to be a jerk."

"Go ahead." Soren waved around at the back of the house. "My parents and I are playing cribbage. Kjersten doesn't like card games so she's outside. Probably on the swing."

"Thanks."

"Sure," the boy countered. "No big deal. Just don't hurt her. Okay? Then I'll have to kick your ass and I'm not sure that I can, but she's cried enough over you."

Galen nodded in agreement. "I don't want to hurt her."

"Okay. Well, I'll see you later.

"Thanks." *Nice kid.* But Galen's heart was beginning to pound as he took the oh-so-familiar path to the back of the house. Nothing and everything had changed since he'd last been here. The grass gave way to sand where Adirondack chairs encircled a fire pit. Just off to one side was a big swing where Kjersten sat, gazing out over the water and rocking back and forth, the swing creaking in time to the gentle lapping of the water.

"Kjersten?" he called.

Immediately, the creaking stopped and she looked up.

"Galen? Is that you?"

"Yeah." He walked over to the swing.

Kjersten straightened up and adjusted the loose sweatshirt that she was wearing. "I think Soren's in the house."

"I know. I told him that I wanted to talk to you. I need to talk to you."

"Okay." Her face shone palely in the moonlight. "Okay. I'm listening. Do you want to sit down?"

She's so beautiful it hurts. "Sure." Galen sat down beside her and the ancient wooden swing creaked under his weight. He chuckled softly.

"What?"

"We've done this before so many times. And now, here we are again. I didn't know back then how much I would miss moments like this, moments that I just took for granted."

Nervously, Kjersten shifted her body away from him. "This fit better when we were little," she affirmed.

"Oh, I don't know," Galen commented. "It feels pretty good to me right now." He was very aware of the warmth of her thigh through her jeans. He breathed in the fresh breeze off the lake. Now, there was an underlying note of vanilla, of her. It was so familiar and yet exotic. He glanced over at her, but she wouldn't meet his gaze. He studied her profile. "I want to explain to you what happened the night of Coach Murray's wedding, why I left."

She glanced over at him. Her eyes were bright with emotion. "Don't worry about it. There's nothing to say really. It's just what you do, leave, when you can't handle things." Her tone was flat and brutal.

Fair. "I know," he agreed and she appeared surprised by his candor.

"Just let it go then. Please don't bring it up and embarrass us both."

"But I don't want it to be over. I don't think I ever did. I was just messed up after Mom died." He reached out took her right hand in his. Hers was cool to the touch.

But she pulled her hand away. "No. Not again. I can't go through this again, Galen. You've broken my heart too many times. It's a pattern with us and it's not a healthy one." The pain was there, etched into her lovely features. "You make a habit of pulling away just when we get close."

"I want to talk about it. All of it. Mom dying. Us breaking up. Cam." He spat the name out.

She stared down at her tennis shoes, her long curtain of hair sliding forward to hide her face. "Yeah." She tucked her hair back behind her ear. "Cam and I happened. And I don't regret it. We had some good times and I learned from it. It helped me to understand that I need to be okay with myself before I can be in a relationship. I can't be in a relationship with someone who can just turn off his feelings. She was quiet for a moment. "It's not like you haven't dated other people since we broke up," she muttered in a small voice.

"I know. It's just that, Cam? I don't get it. He's such an asshole and you knew that."

"I never claimed to be perfect." Kjersten shrugged. "Maybe dating him, at least at first, had something to do with wanting to get your attention. Just let it go."

He studied her features intently. "Well, it pissed me off, still does. But I know I was a total wreck. I was hurting. I didn't know how to deal with things." He shrugged. "I fucked up. Then, you were with Cam, and that about killed me. I mean, just thinking of him with you makes me want to throw up."

"Okay, we're done here," Kjersten rose to her feet. "I'm done. I'm not going to listen to jealous bullshit. You dumped me, remember. You wouldn't take my calls. You ignored my letters. You checked out. We both saw other people. You're the one with the Cam hang up. Not me."

"I know. I'm sorry. Please, just sit back down. I don't want to talk about any of that either. It's all done… This is hard, but I gotta say it. I just want to know if you feel anything for me at all? Do we have chance?" The words burst out of his mouth in a staccato rhythm.

Kjersten sighed heavily and sat down. "Of course I care about you, Galen, but you are always running away, shutting yourself off from me, and I'm done chasing you. I know now that just because you want something, it doesn't necessarily happen. I loved you, Galen, part of me always will, but I can't do this thing that we do anymore. So I'd like you to leave now."

"It wasn't always like that. We were good together. Remember? That night of the wedding, I found something out, something enormous, and I wanted to tell you, but I couldn't handle it yet."

"That's always been the problem, Galen. When two people are together, you handle things together. You've never gotten that. I don't know what you found out at the wedding, but it doesn't matter now. You cut me out again… It's too late, just too late for us." Her words were soft and pain filled. She stood up and began to walk away. Every line of her body was sorrowful and yet determined.

Galen stood up and went after her. He put his hands on her shoulders and pulled her up against his body. He gripped her upper arms gently, feeling the strength in them. Closing his eyes, he pressed his nose into the silkiness of her hair. He inhaled deeply of her and she groaned softly in response. *She hasn't forgotten how it can be between us.* Her slender curves fit into the hollows of his firm muscular one. "Please… please," he whispered the word into her hair. For the first time in forever, he felt right, like he was home.

And for a long moment, the spell held. She leaned back into him. He could feel her heart racing against him. All of his senses were on instant alert. He was growing hard and hungry. He nuzzled the tender skin of her neck. *It can't end now. It can't be over, not when we both feel this way.*

"Stop." The word was weak and soft. "Stop." The word was louder and clearer. Then, she pulled away from him.

I can't hold onto her. I have to let her go. He gripped his hands in frustration to keep from reaching out for her.

"No, Galen." She pulled away and turned to look at him. Her eyes were wild and bright with tears. "I can't. I won't risk you hurting me again."

No words came to him. Instead, he reached out once more and rested his hands on her denim covered hips, he drew her back to him. She didn't resist. Instead, she leaned back into him and her eyes closed and then she was kissing him, deeply, passionately, desperately. They couldn't get close enough to each other. Her hands gripped his shoulders and then her nails dug into his back. Galen ground his erection against her, straining ever closer. Then, releasing her hip, he drew his hand up and between them and gripped her breast. He felt her nearly growl at the sensation.

Suddenly, the lights came on on the Solheim deck. Galen and Kjersten broke apart, both breathing hard.

Mr. Solheim stepped out on the porch and then headed for the boat house. He didn't appear to notice them.

Kjersten stared at Galen, her eyes raw and bright with emotion and tears. She touched her lips with her fingertips, the motion nearly breaking his heart. Then, she turned and ran to the house.

Galen was left standing alone in the moonlight. *She hadn't said there was a chance for them, but she hadn't denied it either.* The kiss that she'd initiated had given him a very different message. *She still cares. There's still a chance for us, despite what she says.*

He headed back to the Happe cabin with a new lightness to his step.

Chapter Twenty-Nine

Changes

~ Galen ~

Galen had thanked the Happe's, said 'goodbye' to Ben, and then began the hour long ride home. The whole way home, his mind was spinning. When he turned onto the gravel lane into the farm, he was wide awake and not tired at all. There was too much to think about. *Kjersten kissed me back.*

Surprisingly, the lights were on in the clapboard house. Most nights, Jim Odgers didn't bother to turn the lights on. Galen parked the car and made his way to the screen door. Swinging it wide, he stepped into a brightly lit kitchen.

"Hey there, little brother," Kyle grinned at him from his chair.

"Hey Kyle. Sandra? What's up?" Galen asked taking in his two older siblings.

Kyle grinned. "We've been waiting for you, Galen. We have news for you. Big news."

"Sit down," Sandra directed, looking calm but pleased.

"You know that Sweet Clover Dairy consortium? They've bought a couple of farms out in Pleasant Valley," Kyle commented.

"Yeah, I think so. The Happes said something about the Wilkins selling out. The farm has been in that family for generations." Galen sat down on a chair.

None of the kids wanted to work it," Kyle continued. "They've all moved away and Jerry's getting too old to do it by himself."

"Kyle, you're one of a dying breed," Sandra commented, patting his hand.

"Not anymore. Galen, the family dairy farm is a thing of the past. The deal is Green Clover has offered me a job managing three or four dairy farms for them."

"What?" Galen echoed, totally taken off guard. He glanced between Sandra and Kyle.

"The farm has been just barely scraping by for years. You know that," Kyle stated.

"Well, I knew things were tight."

"Tight," Kyle snorted. "I've been worried that we were going to go bankrupt every year for the past four. Somehow, we've scraped by, but we've been hurting big time for a while now."

"You never told me."

"You had things going on. You needed to concentrate on school and football. There wasn't a thing that you could do anyway. So, I started working at a couple of the Green Clover farms part time. I liked the way things were run at those farms. I also like that the full time guys who work there get time off and benefits. So when Green Clover needed another manager, I applied. The personnel manager there thought that I would be a good fit because I'm young and I know the industry inside and out. All the dairy farmers around here know and like me and I have some college. I finished my Associate's Degree at the tech last fall."

"You graduated?" Galen asked dumbfounded.

"It wasn't like I was going to some big, fancy school like you. Besides, until the very end, I wasn't sure that I would finish. Not many people take five years to finish an Associate's Degree," Kyle derided himself.

"I wish that you'd told me about it sooner. I mean, I knew that you were taking classes. Did you walk and everything?"

"Nah, I just had them mail the diploma to me. I don't need all that crap. Listen, Galen, I took the job. I'll be the Assistant Manager of Production at Green Clover, Pleasant Valley. The head guy is an old friend of Tom Murray's. Tom's the one who told me to apply for the job."

"Congratulations." Galen reached for his brother and hugged him tightly.

Kyle pounded his younger brother enthusiastically on the back. "I finally feel free of all this," he said and waved an arm about the room. "I haven't felt this good since before Mom got sick. I feel good, there are no two ways about it. Life would be perfect if I had a stogie."

"Galen, we're thinking of selling the farm," Sandra cut straight to the point.

"What? Are you serious?"

"It's too small to run as a business," Sandra explained. "We can get a good price for the land now. We'll move Pop into town, to an assisted living facility. It's no good him being out here all day on his own."

"What about you, Kyle? Where are you gonna live?"

"I was thinking about renting a place over on Half Penny Lake. There's a small cabin that would be great for me. The owners are some retired people who don't hunt anymore, so they're renting it out. It's right on the lake, so I can fish whenever I want."

"But we have to get moving on all this," Sandra stated. "It's what's best, Galen. The farm will go under if we don't sell while we can.

"We prefer selling out to being foreclosed upon," Kyle explained.

"A bid came through on the land Wednesday and just tonight Kyle was offered that job. All of this is sudden for us, too. We didn't keep anything from you, except how bad the farm's financial situation is," Sandra said.

"But both of you guys kept sending me money."

"You never told me that you were sending him money." Sandra pointedly stared at Kyle.

Kyle was embarrassed. "I just sent him a couple of fives or a ten when I had them handy. Couldn't stand thinking about the kid having no money down there, but don't want to get off the subject. If we sell the farm now, we'd get out from under our debts and make some money, too."

Galen thrust his hand through his hair. "It's weird thinking about you not being here," he commented, looking at his brother.

"This is my chance, Galen. I want to do other things, too. Maybe travel a little. I've worked this farm every day all day since I graduated from high school, pretty much by myself. I'm fighting a losing battle out here."

"I understand. You've had this whole place on your shoulders since you were eighteen. It sucks. I get it. Does Pop know what's happening?"

Kyle snorted.

"Galen," Sandra broke in. "We've all known for years that something's not right with Pop. Dr. Walker, he's the new general practitioner in town, had us take Pop to a neurologist at the Mayo Clinic in Rochester; his name is Dr. Brady. He told us that Pop has pretty significant mental deterioration at this point, dementia. Pop needs full time care. It's the right time now."

"You mean he needs a keeper."

"He sure does," Kyle inserted. "He just wanders off, and then I have to drop everything and go look for him. He's gonna hurt himself sometime, but there's no telling him. It just doesn't sink in. I've been trying to take care of this place and him, but there's no way. You know what one of those places cost? The money from the land will sure come in handy taking care of Pop. We'll all be starting off free and clear."

Galen recognized the entreaty in Kyle's voice. "I had no idea that things were that bad."

"We've been treading water around here for years, just keeping our heads above water, and putting off making decisions. We're taking control now. It's the best for everyone, including Pop," Sandra concluded.

"Okay." Galen agreed with a deep breath. "Have you told him?"

Kyle and Sandra both nodded.

"We did tonight," Kyle said.

"It didn't go well," Sandra commented.

"That's putting it mildly," Kyle shook his head.

Galen considered for a moment. Then, he exhaled slowly. "This has been a lot to swallow in one night, but I'm with you guys all the way on this. Change is good." He nodded his head. "Hopefully there will be a lot of changes."

"Good," Kyle commented clapping his brother on the shoulder.

Sandra smiled. "Wow, I'm glad that's over. Let's celebrate." She rose to her feet. "I don't have champagne, but I brought some Leinies." She pulled three bottles of beer out of the refrigerator and handed one to each brother.

"Summer Shandy," Kyle groaned, "a girly drink. Let's pull out the Jack Daniel's and really celebrate."

The siblings sat around the table chatting and planning, unaware that someone else was listening in on their conversation.

Chapter Thirty

Confessions

~ Cam Fawst ~

Cam watched Tom make his way through The Nasty Habit. The bar was quiet, but that was to be expected as it was a Wednesday night and eight at night, way too early in the evening and in the week for the hard partying crowd. Tom was squinting through the darkness, obviously trying to locate him. Cam raised his hand and waved and as he watched, a perky, petite waitress intercepted Tom. There was a brief discussion and then she led Tom over to where Cam sat at a round table.

"Cam, good to see you." Tom held out his hand.

Cam rose and shook it firmly. His smile was wary but genuine. *Had Coach heard about his fight with Galen? Would he be pissed with him?* "Good to see you, too, Tom."

"I was glad you called. Maggie and her girls are at her sister's. I needed to get out and I'm always glad to see one of my players."

Inside, Cam cringed. *One of your players. It shouldn't bug me, but it does.*

"So what brings you to Eagle River, Cam?" Tom smiled as he took a seat.

"My mom had to have a procedure, and the trainers said my ribs needed a break so coach gave me two days."

"Your mother all right?"

"She should be fine now. She was having some woman problems."

Tom nodded, clearly not wanting to pursue the subject. "I'm glad she's going to be okay. I thought that Bethany had moved to Milwaukee."

"She did for a while, but then she moved back. Eagle River is home to her."

"Can I bring you anything to drink?" The pert, pony tailed waitress interrupted.

"What you got there, Cam?"

He twisted the bottle in his hand. "Spotted Cow."

"I'll have one, too."

The mini-skirted waitress who was gazing at Cam in blissful adoration smiled, nodded, and backed away to the bar.

"You've certainly impressed her." Tom chuckled.

"She wants to be impressed. That's her number." Cam gestured at the small, folded napkin in the middle of the table. "Watch her when she walks by again. She'll check to see if I've picked it up yet."

Tom scowled disapprovingly.

"Relax, Coach," Cam smiled a sardonic half smile against his tanned skin. He picked up his napkin and tucked it into his pocket. "I'm working at that knight in shining honor stuff. You're right, a lot of girls go for that."

"You could try a little sincerity."

"Oh, cut the crap, Coach. We both know that you're no different than me. You forget, I knew you when you were a player, back when you dated my mom. You knew all the angles, just like me. That's the thing that burns you, isn't it? You were just like me. Now you're all married and reformed. But back in the day, you were just like me." *And not like Galen Odgers.*

"Point taken," Tom acknowledged. "It's because we are alike that I'm trying to prevent you from making the same mistakes that I've made in my life."

"I'm a big boy now, Coach, and I've been handling my own business for years.

"That's true," Tom acknowledged. "You're looking well, Cam. You're playing well, too. You're doing a good job on the football part of the deal, you just gotta work on the personal side. Remember, it's a package deal." Just then, the waitress arrived with their drinks.

Cam reflected on how Coach had changed. The gray haired, content, slightly thickened at the waist man sitting in front of him was a far cry from the magnetic football hero of Cam's youth. In the past few years, Coach had definitely lost the hungry, haunted look that had characterized him as a younger man. He remained a rugged, good looking, older man, but his edge was gone. He was wholly domesticated. Deliberately, Cam dismissed his critical thoughts. Coach had let things go a little, but he was still one of the few who could understand, who could appreciate Cam's efforts.

"With the NFL draft coming up, the scouts and the reporters are digging through everything. I talk to a chick and I wonder if she has been hired by someone. This dude offered me some hash last night. He's a friend of mine. I almost killed him because there were people around who might be from some team. It's enough to make a guy seriously paranoid."

"You're eating it up, Cam. Don't bullshit me. I know you too well, just like you know me."

Cam grinned. "Everyone likes to be appreciated. It's nice to get some attention."

"You put in a solid season. You'll end up playing professional football somewhere."

"Somewhere," Cam echoed. He toyed with his drink. His expression had undergone a dramatic change, from pleasant and relaxed to brooding. "I read an article in *Sports Illustrated* about how this year's draft class is kind of weak, but how there are some superstars coming out next year."

"I saw it, too. They mentioned Galen Odgers," Tom commented. "The article said he was one of the most talented young quarterbacks coming up."

"What the hell? Give me a break." Cam scowled. "All it is is spin with Odgers. Smoke and mirrors. He's got nothin'."

"Galen is a ball player, plain and simple. He has all the gifts."

"If you're going to waste my time talking about Odgers, let's just call it a night." Cam rose abruptly to his feet.

For a moment, Tom studied his former player. "You know, don't you, Cam?"

"That Galen is your son? Yeah, I figured it out. I am surprised no one else has. When you look at the two of you it is pretty obvious."

"It's true. I'm proud of that boy. But you were always special to me, Cam. I may not have told you ever, but I'm proud of you, too. You may not be my own flesh and blood, but I couldn't be prouder of you if you were."

Cam swallowed hard and took a deep breath. It took him a moment to compose himself. Then, he stared at Coach. These were the words that he had always longed to hear and had never expected. He hesitated.

Tom toyed with the candle in the jug in the middle of the table. "I never knew how to raise a son, but I could coach and that's what I did with you boys. I like to imagine that I made a difference in the lives of the young men I've coached. I know I sound corny, but Maggie tells me I have to speak from the heart. But that means I gotta tell you what I think. Cam, you've got a big chip on your shoulder. You always have. It's weighing you down. Forget about how everyone else is doing and worry about yourself. You have some good skills. Work at making them better. You're not the biggest or strongest, so be more accurate than the others."

"I've worked hard. I've earned what I've got. I deserve to play ball in the pros."

"Who you trying to convince?" Tom observed wryly. "The scouts are talking about you going in the third or fourth round of the draft. It's all going to work out just fine."

Cam visibly tensed. "I just hope that I get picked." He drew absentmindedly with his fork on his woven place mat. "They're saying that I don't have the power or size to make it as a quarterback in the NFL, that I might end up playing Canadian football."

"There's nothing wrong with the CFL, Cam. Lots of good ball players play in that league."

"Beautiful. I'll be playing in the Klondike. Ice ball."

"You do a good job up there, and you would have more credibility to the NFL. There are a lot of decent places where you could play.

Montreal and Vancouver are both great towns."

"Yeah. I guess. Well, as long as I get to play and can make some money."

"You're lucky you're good enough to go pro. Think about all the poor bastards who aren't. Most of them don't even get a degree out of their college years… Will you earn your degree in May?"

"I gotta couple of credits left, but I can finish them whenever."

"Make a point of doing it. You gotta have a degree for the real world, when you're done playing ball. Save money while you're playing. Invest it. Then, when you're done, you can do what you want with your life. You'll have money, a name, and a degree. You'll be able to get on with your life."

"I'll be careful. One day, I'm gonna be rolling in the green stuff. Now that the season is over, I've been talking to some agents about endorsement opportunities."

"I should have known better than to worry about your business sense," Tom snorted.

"You got that right. I'm gonna be rich. Besides, I have responsibilities. I have a daughter now."

Tom Murray coughed, choked, and then blew his soda out his nose. As he wiped at his face with a napkin, Cam simply waited with his eyes twinkling in amusement. This time, he'd gotten his former coach's attention.

"When did this happen?"

"Mackie's about six months old."

"Who is the mother?"

"Her name is Sarah. We dated for a little while and the girl was pretty cool. Then, she kinda lost it, wanted to be around me all of the time, and started whining about marriage and commitment. So I told her to get out. I didn't hear from her for a couple of months, then her lawyer contacted me. We did the DNA test. Sure enough, the kid is mine. So, now I'm hooked into paying child support for the next twenty years. But I gotta tell you," Cam leaned forward, his face, lit up and enthusiastic, "I don't mind. That little girl, aw man, she's a doll. Mackie. Her name's Mackenzie, she even looks like me. I get a kick out of holding her. I like being a dad. I've been thinking that I might want her around more of the time. You know, shared custody. You want to see her picture?"

It was Tom's turn to sit back and watch in bemusement as Cam pulled a photo of a cherubic dark-haired baby girl out of his wallet. Two enormous bright blue eyes dominated the chubby little face. Tom took the picture.

"Don't blow it, Cam." Tom's voice was serious, all traces of banter gone. "I can't tell you how lucky I am to be getting this second chance with Maggie. Being alone is tough... You've gotta keep your nose clean and your head on straight. You gotta take care of that little girl. I envy you the chance to have a relationship with your own child."

"I plan to. Mackie's my daughter. I'm going to take care of my girl. I am going to be a good father." Cam finally dropped his searing stare from Tom's face. He exhaled slowly, allowing the tension to drain from him. When he raised his face, the venom was gone, the smooth, handsome mask was back in place. "Son of a bitch, Coach, you're probably the only man who still tries to tell me how to run my life."

Tom raised his bottle. "Well, here's to football and to kids. The two best things in life." He paused for a moment, his face contemplative. Cam could see the wheels spinning.

It was then that both of them became aware of the scream of fire engines rushing by. Sal appeared, rushing his massive bulk towards the door.

"What's up?" Tom called out.

"There's a fire at the Odger place! The old barn is going down, maybe the house."

"Is anyone at home?"

"Galen and the old man, for sure," Sal shouted back.

"I'm coming, too." Tom was already on his feet. He glanced back at Cam.

Cam merely waved his hand. "Get going, coach. He's your boy. I get it."

Chapter Thirty-One

Conflagration

~ Galen ~

Galen never knew what woke him up that night. *Is it morning yet?* He rolled over in bed and lifted up the shade. There was a red, bright glow behind his shade. *Blood red moon tonight. Weird.*

Having to take a piss, he kicked his legs over the bed. He heard roaring outside. *Windy.* Padding his way to the bathroom, he wiped at his forehead. *It's warm in here. Hot. Why did Pa turn up the heat?*

It was then that he heard the sirens. Perplexed, he padded down the hallway towards the kitchen. There was a flicking light coming from under the door. "Pop, you in there?" He reached for the doorknob. "Shit!" It burned his hand.

He leaped back. *Fire!* There was a fire in the front rooms of the house. He rushed back into his room and grabbed a t-shirt. He wrapped it around his hand, hurried back through the hall and, grasping the doorknob, he pulled it wide.

A blast of heat and red orange light hit him and he fell back. He threw the door shut. *Smoke detectors, why weren't they working.* He glanced at the one over his bedroom door. It hung open and there was no battery to be seen. There was no way that he was going to make it to the front door through the kitchen. So, he ran towards the back hall. *Maybe I can make it through the back door*. He ran to the door to the mudroom.

He could see the flames outside the windows. They were huge and terrifying. One entire side of the house was burning.

The screen porch. Galen could see the flames dancing there as well. He was truly trapped. All three doors to the outside of the house, the front door, through the mudroom, and out through the screen porch were blocked with flames. *The windows.* Suddenly, over the roar of the flames, he heard the crash of glass. Covering his head with his arms against the flames now leaping out at him from the walls, he ran blindly back to the sound, down the hall, towards his bedroom. It was getting harder to see and nearly impossible to breath.

Suddenly, there was another crash, and an axe thrust through the remains of his bedroom window.

Galen, coughing, stepped back.

"Galen? That you?" a firefighter demanded in that automated robot voice of the respirator.

"Gene?" Galen questioned, recognizing the cafe owner who also served as a volunteer firefighter in Eagle River.

Barely aware of the glass cutting into his feet, Galen climbed out of the frame of his first floor window. Once outside, he saw a small group of firefighters were gathered there.

Suddenly, a body slammed into his bod.

"Slow down, Kjersten," Gene directed. "He's bleeding. His feet. We need to get him checked out. He breathed in a lot of smoke."

Sobbing, she held onto him. "I thought you were dead. Thank God you're okay!"

In shock, struggling to breathe, with burnt hands and cut feet, he held onto her. "What's happening, Gene?"

"The barn caught on fire first. Then, the house. We didn't know how to get you out. Kjersten, here, brought us around to your room."

"I was driving by and I saw the fire," Kjersten broke in.

"Is there anyone else inside?" Gene demanded.

"Pop! He must still be inside."

"No," Kjersten broke in. Her features were tinged crimson by the rising flames. "He's not."

"Where is he?" Galen demanded.

Kjersten shook her head.

"Gene? Where's Pop?"

But Gene and the other firefighters were already hurrying around to the front of the house, leaving Galen and Kjersten to follow along behind.

As they rounded the corner of the house, Galen could feel the heat from the fire on his face. The entire front facade was burning, but the old barn was a flame unto itself. The entire structure was in flames. The wind whipped the flames which roared. As he watched, the barn door collapsed, revealing the inside, the loft and the stalls. Galen made out a dark figure standing up in the hay loft.

"My God," Kjersten whispered.

"Pop?"

"He wouldn't come down. They tried to get him to come down. But he wouldn't."

Galen stared in horror and dismay at the darkened figure of the man whom he'd once thought was his father. He was standing absolutely still and upright, like a black statue against the flames. There was a rumble and a growl. Then, the roof of the barn collapsed and the flames reached hungrily for the sky.

"No!" Galen yelled, rushing forward, but he was tackled from behind. He fought and scrambled, trying to get free. "I have to get to him! I have to save him. Pop!" He fought with near superhuman strength, but the firefighters held him until he collapsed, sobbing.

* * * *

Hours later, Kyle waited in the chair by the side of the hospital bed. Groaning, he shifted. "You think that we're ever going to get out of here?" he muttered.

"What?" Galen asked from where he lay still in his hospital dress. He rested his bandaged hand beside him on the bed,

"I said, do you think that we're ever going to get out of here? You know, it gets old seeing you in hospitals."

"For me, too. I'm ready to go," Galen commented morosely. "Where are we going?"

"Good point," Kyle conceded, leaning his head back against the chair. "You'll stay with me tonight."

"I still can't believe that Pop did it? I mean why now?"

"He knew we were going to sell off the land. Let's face it, he may have been off his rocker, but he wasn't stupid. I don't claim to understand why he did what he did, but maybe he didn't see any alternatives. Maybe he was just done."

"I think he was done a long time ago."

"I just hope," Galen paused.

"What?"

"That maybe he's finally at peace."

Kyle nodded. "That was a hell of a way to go. You think he meant to kill himself?"

"Who knows?"

Both men were silent for a moment.

"So what now?" Kyle asked.

"I guess we plan a funeral and then get on with things."

"Things," Kyle repeated. "When the hell are we going to get out of here? You can walk, can't you?"

"Yeah," Galen agreed. "And my lungs feel okay."

"But your feet are wrecked and your arms don't look great either. What were you doin' trying to run into that fire?"

Galen glanced down to where the aforementioned appendages were wrapped in gauze. "I don't know. I'm not sure I was thinking. I guess I wanted to save him."

Kyle patted his shoulder. "Gene said there was no way anyone could survive after the roof collapsed." Kyle was silent. "All of us tried to save him for years, and we all failed. I guess you gotta want to be saved. Finally, he shook his head. "I'm gonna go get a Coke," he said as he rose to his feet, opened the door into the hospital corridor, and wandered down the hallway, peering into the darkened corners, seeking out a pop machine. He wandered up to a nurse's station.

"Can I help you?" an efficient-looking, middle-aged woman asked him.

"I'm just looking for a pop machine."

"Just out there, in the waiting area."

Kyle headed through the doors. He saw the concession machines and the pop machines. There, he dug in his pocket and pushed a quarter into the machine.

"Kyle?"

Kyle startled and then turned. "Yeah?" He turned and saw Kjersten Solheim standing there, her arms wrapped around herself. Her eyes were red rimmed, as if she had been crying.

"How's Galen?" she asked.

"He's gonna be fine. He's a tough little shit."

"Oh, good." She hesitated a moment. "They wouldn't tell me anything because I'm not family."

"Well, his feet are a little crispy, but he'll be fine."

"That's good news." She chewed on her lip nervously. "Would you tell him that I was here?"

"Yeah, sure."

Still not moving, she stared at him. "Well, I guess I'll just go home now." She turned slowly, and rubbing her arms walked towards the glass exit doors.

Kyle watched her go, shoved another quarter into the pop machine, and then pressed the button for a Mountain Dew. It dropped down, he grabbed it, popped the top, and took a long swig, savoring the cold lemon-lime burn down his throat. He headed back to Galen's room, opened the door and plopped down in the chair. "Well, that was weird."

Galen glanced over at his brother. "What?"

"You won. Kjersten Solheim was in the waiting room this whole time. It's been hours."

"Go get her." Galen sat up straighter in the bed.

"She just left."

"Go after her."

"No, I saw her go out the door."

"Shit, Kyle. Why didn't you bring her in here? You think she's still in the parking lot?"

"I don't know. I'll go check."

Kyle was only gone a moment. "No. She's gone."

"Shoot, Kyle. Why didn't you stop her? Bring her in here?"

"Look, it's like two in the morning. Pa just set our house on fire and killed himself. I'm not thinking straight. If she's waited this long, she still cares about you. She's not done with you."

"You think so?"

Kyle reached down and grabbed a pillow that had fallen off the bed and to the ground. He threw it at his little brother. "Don't be a dumb ass. Of course, she wouldn't have stayed if she didn't care. She still loves you. Just don't fuck it up this time."

Chapter Thirty-Two

An Unexpected Gift

~ Kjersten ~

Kjersten set her book spine up on the blanket, rolled over, and closed her eyes. On her skin, the subtle yet warm caress of the late afternoon sun alternated with the gentle sweep of a cool breeze.

"There you are!"

Kjersten glanced up to see Lauren and Cat bearing down on her.

"What's up?" she asked, sitting up.

Cat and Amy plopped down on the blanket next to her. Cat held out a thin package that looked like it could hold a book. "Something came for you in the mail."

"Oh." Kjersten pulled her hands out from where they were tucked deep inside the sleeves of her thick, cream colored Irish knit sweater.

"Well, open it," Lauren urged.

"Why are you two so interested in this?" Kjersten asked suspiciously.

"The deliveryman was kind of hot," Cat offered with a wink.

"You're such a freak," Lauren teased.

"Who are you kidding," Cat countered. "You thought so, too."

Seeing that it was marked fragile, Kjersten carefully peeled open the tape on the package. The object, which was wrapped in bubble wrap, was hard and flat. Setting it on her lap, she got to work on the bubble wrap.

She pulled the paper back and revealed a picture of a boy and a girl of middle school age. They wore t-shirts and shorts and their limbs were long and summer tan. The girl was tow headed with a long pony tail, while the boy's hair was sun kissed and a little overgrown. He held a fishing rod, and the girl, a hooked largemouth bass. The girl, obviously proud of her catch, was gazing right at the camera. The boy, on the other hand, was gazing at the girl. Kjersten drew a deep breath, taking it all in. Then, with shaking hands, she set the picture down on her lap.

"Is that you?" Cat prodded.

"Yes, that's Kjersten," Lauren agreed.

"It's me," Kjersten confirmed. "And Galen. That's it? There's no letter?" She reached for the package and held it upside down. A card fell out. She opened it. There was a single line scrawled on the note card. She read it softly to herself. "You had me hooked from the beginning—Galen."

"Come on," Amy demanded. "Please read it to us."

"It says: You had me hooked from the beginning. And it's from Galen."

Amy clapped her hands together. "That is so sweet!"

"Well, what are you going to do?" the ever practical Cat demanded. "I know what I would do if Ben sent me a picture of us."

"I'm going to call him," Kjersten responded, rising to her feet, picture in hand.

"The delivery guy is still here," Cat responded with a sly smile.

"So?" Kjersten questioned in confusion, gathering her things.

"There's no postage on that package," Cat said. "Look."

Lauren waved the package in the air and Kjersten grabbed it.

"You mean, he's here? Galen's here?"

Both women nodded and grinned.

Just then, Galen stepped out from behind the interlocking branches of several pine trees that stood not far from the girls. He'd been concealed in the shadows behind the heavy, sweeping branches. Awkwardly, he stuffed his hands into his snug fitting, faded Wranglers. He was wearing a red flannel shirt that emphasized the broadness of his shoulders.

He looks bigger, thicker, and more mature. Now, he was a solidly muscular man, no longer a tall, gangly boy. His hair was longer and darker than she ever remembered having seen it and it gently curled around his collar. *Galen's a man now, and we're not kids playing at love anymore.*

Completely unprepared for this encounter, Kjersten stood frozen as Galen moved toward her. Her heart pounded.

"Come on," Cat directed, rising to her feet.

"What?" Lauren asked.

"Let's go," she directed. "Leave the lovebirds alone." Cat dragged a reluctant Lauren away.

"Kjersten." Galen walked towards her. "I don't want to let you go, to have 'us' be over. It's never really been over for me."

She moved closer to him, drinking him in with her eyes.

"I didn't know you were at the hospital the night of the fire until after you'd left. That's when Kyle told me."

Not believing that he was here, that he had come for her, she walked right up to Galen, and into his arms.

"I've done so much wrong, made so many mistakes," he began.

She inhaled his scent and the feel of him. *Like coming home.* "Shut up," she murmured into the warm skin of his neck.

"What?"

"Shut up."

"Okay." He chuckled and held her tight, closer still, lost in this longed for embrace. Finally, Galen drew back. "I miss you, Kjersten. I want you back. We were meant to be together, but we just got lost for a while. Maybe we both needed to grow up some. But now's our chance." He reached out and tucked one long blond strand behind her ear. "I'm not giving up. You're the one for me. You always have been. I know that now. When things were hard for me, I pulled away from you. That won't ever happen again. No matter what, I want to be with you. Is there any chance that we can try again?"

She opened her mouth and then shut it. *Words. I want to say something wonderful, something grand, to tell him how I feel.* But she couldn't think of anything except, "You have me hooked, too." It was all that she could manage in this overwhelming moment, all that she needed to say, because words suddenly became very unnecessary as lips met and hearts merged.

Epilogue

~ Tom ~

It was Jessica's birthday again, and Tom was back visiting her grave. There was a steady breeze blowing with a hint of rain to come. With one hand, he popped his collar up and adjusted his baseball cap. He held a bouquet of lilacs in the other hand.

"I can't stay long, Jessica. Maggie's in the car. I just wanted to drop by and wish you a happy birthday." Tom paused and glanced at the tombstone. "I wish you could see Cole, Galen and Kjersten's little boy. He's your spitting image. Galen's going to have his hands full. He's a fire cracker. They live in San Antonio, but get back to Eagle River pretty often. The football career is going well for Galen and Kjersten joined a veterinary practice down there. I'm so proud of our boy.

"Maggie and me, we're doing well. The girls are getting big, one's in high school and one is in middle school. They are busy with soccer and volleyball. We rarely have a quiet night at home, but I'm loving every minute of the craziness. You know how quickly it goes.

"And Cam, he may not be my son, but I think of him as one and I've talked to you about him often enough. Well, he's retired from the CFL, and he's a businessman now, a successful one. Cam's on wife number three, they keep getting younger and blonder, but he's a devoted dad. He has three or four little girls now." Tom chuckled.

"Jessica, that's all I have for today. I just want you to know that I still think about you. I feel you around me, like you're watching out for me. I never did a thing to deserve all of this. I've been so blessed with you, my life here, coaching, all my players, and then Galen and his family, and Maggie and the girls. You've been my guardian angel… I love you and I always will." With that, Tom placed the lilacs on the grave. He straightened, turned, adjusted his cap once more, and headed back to his car. The breeze carried the scent of lilacs after him, a benediction.

About the Author

Isabelle Kane believes that romance and love are among the most delightful aspects of the human experience. She seeks to provide her readers with rich tapestries of stories in which love is just one element of the forces that intertwine the lives of her protagonists. She believes every dreamer deserves the adventures and escape offered by an exciting novel. The greatest sources of joy and inspiration in Isabelle's life are her husband and their three children.

For updates on Isabelle's writing, please visit her at
http://www.kaneandtremaine.com/,
on Facebook
https://www.facebook.com/isabellekaneromance/
on Twitter @KaneIsabelle.

She loves to hear from readers. You can email her at
kane.tremaine@gmail.com

Other Works by the Author with Melange Books, LLC Satin Romance Imprint

Calypso's Secret

44423356R00146

Made in the USA
San Bernardino, CA
15 January 2017